THE TRAP

ALEX ROSE

PART 1

ONE

When his wife died in his arms after a long battle with ischaemic heart disease, the world's number one killer, the man cursed God for not giving them more time. Time, thereafter, became all-important, and he ran his life by it. Every morning he'd wake at five, take fifteen minutes to fully rouse himself, then rub cream into his eczema. That was allocated five minutes exactly, even if he hadn't completed the job.

Dressing for his jog was allowed exactly sixty seconds. He'd feed and fuss the dog for dead-on two minutes, then head out the door. The drive from his end of the village to the imaginatively named Village Café, at the other end, was allocated two minutes, which sometimes involved running a red light. He'd lay up his car in the car park and walk down the lane to the gate into Yenders field, which always took him one minute.

The final four minutes were given over to stretching. At 5.30 exactly, he'd enter the field and run. At 5.45, he'd head back and have a cup of tea and a bacon sandwich at the café, finishing at exactly 6am, right around the time that the late August sun woke up.

The route along the track that encircled hedge-bordered field took him a neat fifteen minutes exactly the first time, so he stuck to that time frame. His wife had died eight months ago and since then he'd lost two stone, so his speed was up. Four months ago he'd managed two revolutions in the allotted quarter of an hour. Yesterday he'd been three hundred metres from a full third circuit when his time ran out. Today he was determined to complete that trio of laps.

As the jogger passed the gate to complete his second lap, his gaze was drawn to a woman on the other side. She was about thirty, slim, pretty, wearing a pink baseball cap and matching pink T-shirt and shorts. Ingram was a small village, population ninety-two, so he immediately knew she wasn't a local. She waved and he returned it.

A hundred metres into lap two, he looked back and saw the woman clamber over the gate and begin jogging after him. He had no ideals about ever dating such a pretty young thing, but they could flirt. He wanted to slow down and let her catch up, but he couldn't spare the time. He figured he'd widen the distance and eventually come at her from behind.

That didn't happen. She was younger and fitter and was soon bouncing right behind him.

'I didn't know others jogged here,' she called out.

'Just me, I think. Every morning. You're not local.'

'Visiting,' she said, now coming up on his right side. 'I always try to find a good spot.'

'There's none better. But surely you didn't come all the way here for a jog.'

'Visiting my mother,' she said.

They completed his second lap of the field while making small talk. She told him she worked as an assistant manager at a café in another Northumberland village. He told her what he did for a living and that he, too, was a second-in-command. On the third revolution, he checked his watch. He was on course for completing his task. That was when the small talk changed into something else. 'I bet the wife loves your stamina.'

The jogger glanced to his right, to read her face. The words had had the hint of a *come on*, and now her expression said the same. He tried not to stare at her bouncing breasts. 'I'm a widow.'

'Sorry to hear that. No girlfriend?'

They hit a corner and turned. The summer heat had made the dirt track solid, yet still the corners could be slippery. The woman faltered with a yelp and fell back. The man continued ahead. She soon caught him again. 'No girlfriend,' he said. 'Why do you ask?'

'Because my bastard husband cheated on me just last night. And I want revenge.'

Of course he knew what she meant, but he wasn't so forward and feigned naivety. He gulped. 'Revenge how?'

She pointed ahead. 'Shall we go in there?'

Her finger indicated a kissing gate in the hedge, beyond which he knew was a gully between fields. The high hedges made it a very private place. He knew this because he and his wife had once walked alongside the stream at the bottom of the gully and stopped for sex.

Still the naivety. 'Why? It's no good for running.'

'I know. But no one will see us.'

Shocked, he watched her yank down the front of her shorts far enough to expose pubic hair. Just for a second, but enough. The message was clear. His mission was about to be delayed by twenty minutes or so. His pace slowed because his heart had a new reason to thump fast.

'Okay,' he said.

She sliced across his path, towards the gate, and he followed. Once they were through, he trailed her down the steep side of the gully. She leaped across the thin stream and turned to face him. Her smile had gone.

'What's–' he said, the rest of the sentence lost as he felt a mighty thud in his back. He was propelled forward. The sloping land fell away beneath him and he landed hard in the stream. Awkward footing on a rock made him collapse into the water.

'No sex for you,' a voice said. Soaked, the jogger rose to his feet and saw two men. One was much bigger than his crony, but otherwise they resembled each other: jeans, matching black jackets – and balaclavas. The jogger's heart began an overtime shift.

He looked at the woman, expecting her to wear the same terrified expression as his own. It wasn't there, and nor was surprise. The innocence sluiced right off her, and he knew right then she was part of this. He had been tricked.

He was reminded of his fortieth birthday, when he'd promised his wife he would join a gym and get fit. 'Someone thinks he can pull a young lass,' she'd said.

But he hadn't, which now made him such a fool for ever thinking this young lass fancied him enough for a dirty liaison in a gully.

He knew what she did want from him. 'I can give you money,' he said to her, thinking she was the ringleader.

The bigger of the two men responded. 'Not why we're here, old fart. You were at school with a girl. You were both five years old. You hit her in the face with a snowball. Remember?'

Fifty odd years ago? Of course not, and he said so.

'Ruined her life, and you don't even remember. That was my mum.'

The jogger looked around, seeking an escape route. But the gate was the only exit from this long strait of hedge-lined land, and the two men blocked it. He couldn't outrun them, he knew. 'I don't know your mum. I don't know you.'

'My mum made me promise to make you sorry one day. Guess which day it is? Grab him.'

The jogger had no time to react. All three of his assailants latched hands onto his clothing. He was pushed down into the water for a second time. Fearing he might be drowned, he screamed for help. But he knew no ears would hear the cry. Too early, too remote. The only place within three hundred metres was the café, and that would be noisy with the commotion of cooking. He suddenly hated them for it.

The two men forced him onto his back on the embankment, his ass by the edge of the water. The smaller man, who hadn't yet said a word, held his torso down while the bigger brute, standing in the water, stretched out the jogger's legs like a bridge across the stream.

The animal then sat astride the jogger's legs, facing him. He put his whole weight on the jogger's knees, which blasted the old man with pain.

'Please don't,' he moaned, knowing full well why he was in such a position. 'I'm sorry about your mother.'

'I made that shit up, dude. Can't believe you fell for it.'

If that was a lie, maybe these people didn't know him. This might be a robbery after all, which promised a sliver of hope. 'I have thousands of pounds in cash. I can get it for you. Please.'

The thug bounced a little on the jogger's knees, sending waves of agony through his legs. 'That's my girl, there. I'm highly offended you wanted to fuck her.'

'I didn't. I wouldn't. Please, get off me. I can get the money.'

'You do have something we want, that's for sure, but it ain't money. Are you ready to help?'

'Yes, anything!'

'Good boy,' the thug said. 'Here's what we need you to do...'

TWO

THE DAY BEFORE

Emma Catalano's usual morning routine started with the bathroom mirror. She examined herself from head to toe. The black hair she'd inherited from her mother had yet to show any signs of greying. She was forty-three but those glossy locks could pass her off as mid-thirties on a good day.

Good or bad, the days didn't prevent wrinkles around her eyes or a slight yellowing of the teeth. Her husband was four years older and happy with his ageing. He'd said a switch would flick when she hit forty-five and she wouldn't care about appearances any more. She'd said that might be a male thing.

Her eyes went down to the reflection of her naked torso. The scar on her chest was only eight weeks old and still neon-bright. If a day would come when she didn't care about it, that was a long way away. An ever tingling arm was a reminder during the hours she was dressed.

That routine completed, she turned to the next: homework. She wasn't one to ever clock off and could always squeeze in emails or reports during free time. She donned a dressing gown and sat at her bedroom computer.

Half an hour in, she heard a grunt behind her. Freshly

woken, Joel sat up in bed. They swapped hellos and he got up to kiss the back of her neck. 'Birthday girl up?'

'Haven't checked,' Emma replied. 'It's still early, so let's give her another half hour.'

He laughed. 'You mean, let's give *you* another half hour.'

'You rumbled me. I'll be quick.'

He rubbed her shoulders and headed into the bathroom to pee. She could tell he wasn't impressed. She checked the time on the monitor and saw it was a little later than she'd expected. It was her weekend off, her child's birthday, and they had a trip planned. Work could be put aside just this once.

She tore herself away from the computer and trekked to their daughter's room. She knocked but walked straight in. Minny was sitting up in bed but fast asleep, her laptop on her legs and fingers on the keys. It looked quite cute, although Emma hated it when Minny cruised the internet late into the night.

Emma couldn't help herself. She touched the screen to wake the computer. YouTube as always. She leaned over to type in LOUD ALARM, pressed play on a video, and scarpered from the room as a wailing noise filled the air.

It was worth a giggle as she heard the nineteen-year-old stir and moan, and then shout, 'Dad! Kill you.'

From the bathroom, Joel yelled, 'What's that? What's she blaming me for now?'

And why had she blamed Joel? Because he was the fun parent, of course. Her strict and proper and boring mother couldn't play jokes, could she? A little upset by this thought, Emma returned to her bedroom to dress. When Joel was also ready, they got what they needed and entered Minny's room.

She was now awake and playing on her phone. When she saw them, she rolled her eyes, lay back on her bed and covered her head with a pillow. Her father held a small birthday cake with a single candle burning. Emma carried two wrapped gifts.

'Don't do what I think you're about to,' Minny said.

Both parents launched into 'Happy Birthday'. Minny remained under the pillow until the song was over. She took the cake, blew out the candle, and reached out both hands for the presents.

Joel had bought his daughter perfume and a wireless charging station for her mobile, that vitally important extra limb to a teenager. She hugged him for it. Emma had gotten her a smartwatch. Minny was less than ecstatic and unable, or unwilling, to hide the emotion.

Emma ignored it. 'Just like my watch,' she said, showing off the device on her wrist. 'We can connect them. Here, let's put each other's numbers in so we can call each other from them.'

'We've got phones, Mum.'

'Sure. But this is cooler. Futuristic.'

Emma worked the watches while Minny pretended to be intrigued. Afterwards, she tested the setup by calling Minny's watch from her own. Minny let it ring and didn't answer.

Emma hung up the call. 'Now we're connected. Phones can be put down and lost. But if we wear these all the time, we're always connected.'

Minny wasn't impressed. 'Manacled together, you mean.'

An hour later all three of them were downstairs. While Joel loaded their bags into the car and Minny ate breakfast to YouTube, Emma turned off everything that burned electricity on standby. When she returned to the kitchen, she noted that Minny wasn't wearing her watch. Emma headed upstairs and found it on Minny's bed.

'My internet is slow,' Minny said when Emma returned to the kitchen. 'Did you turn the Wi-Fi off?'

'Sure did. We won't be here, will we?'

'We're still here now. Are you going to turn the fridge off as well?'

'Very funny.'

Thirty minutes later, they were ready to go. Emma closed all the windows, locked up the house, and then handed Minny her smartwatch. Huffing, Minny put it in her suitcase.

When she got in the car, Joel, ever paranoid, suddenly decided he'd forgotten something. Emma knew he hadn't. He was a bank manager and was obsessed with security. She knew he'd be double-checking her work.

While they waited, Minny, in the rear of the car, jabbed a finger at something on the seat beside her. 'Why are you bringing this and why are you treating it like a precious child?'

The item, which was held steady by three cushions and even wore a seatbelt, was Emma's MoYu 21x21x21 Rubik's cube. It was the largest cube commercially available, had 2,709 pieces, and had cost her £840. She loved puzzles and this was the ultimate test. The world record was about an hour and a half. Emma had been tackling hers for three weeks and it was only three-quarters complete. It was her pride and joy.

'It keeps me calm,' she said.

'Waste of time.'

Unlike social media gossip, apparently.

The women sat in silence thereafter. When Joel returned, he was all smiles and missed the air of tension. 'Contain your fun, ladies. We'll be there soon.'

Their home was in Ingram, in rural Northumberland, so usually they liked to holiday in big cities like London or New York or Paris. But last week one of Joel's employees had mentioned that her daughter's husband had just acquired a cottage in the woods outside nearby Whittingham. Good for a weekend break. Joel had managed to secure it free of charge, although he expected the staff member to figure on his overlooking a little bit of shoddy timekeeping here and there. They had it for this Saturday and Sunday night.

They could drive the five miles home come Monday morning and both easily make it to their jobs. Unfortunately, Joel had to pop into work right now, which meant driving past their ultimate destination and another five miles east, to the village of Alnwick.

Emma parked a hundred metres up Main Street from his bank. It was 8.32 in the morning and the street was almost dead, with only a newsagent's open and a handful of other stores preparing for a day's business.

Only when the car stopped did Minny tear her eyes off her phone and realise they weren't where they were supposed to be. 'Hey, this is Dad's work. What's going on?'

'I told you,' Emma said. 'He's got to open the vault.'

She tutted. 'So he has to come back tonight as well?'

She knew that two keys were needed to unlock the bank vault, and they cycled between Joel and his assistant manager and two other qualified keyholders. Joel had wrangled this weekend off at short notice and there was nobody else to carry key number one, so he'd been forced to make this detour now, and again at closing time.

'It's no big deal,' Joel said. 'I'll come back alone tonight. Anyway, now you get to see my spy skills in action. Watch this.'

Joel exited the car and made a pantomime of ducking into shop doorways as he made his way towards the bank. Halfway, he approached a car and a man got out. The assistant manager, Emma knew. She was aware of this security routine but had never witnessed it unfold live. It was quite fascinating.

'He looks like a man casing the bank,' Emma said. Minny didn't laugh.

Joel returned to their car as the assistant manager

approached the bank. 'Get ready to drive away fast, and knock down any men in balaclavas.'

Minny dumped her phone, now for once interested in her parents' lives. 'What if there actually are robbers inside the bank?'

'Peter will hit the alarm for the police. And we'll see bullets fly.'

'Awesome. What if the robbers make him call you and say the coast is clear?'

'He'll call me and say just that.'

Minny's brow creased. 'But you'll walk into a trap.'

'Nope. That's our code for a trap.'

'Your code for a trap is to say all is clear?'

Joel laughed. 'Robbers will expect a trick. So my assistant can hardly say something like, "The stars are pinholes in the blanket of night". That sounds like a code. So, if all is clear, he'll say something insulting.'

Minny grinned. 'Ah. So "the coast is clear" means it isn't. And "Come on by, you ugly bastard" means all is clear?'

Joel gave a thumbs up.

Two minutes later, his phone rang. He put it on speaker and they all heard the assistant manager say, 'Get your infected cock down here.'

Joel seemed embarrassed, but Minny laughed. 'All clear, I guess.' Joel gave another thumbs up. 'But what if there's robbers anyway and the assistant manager is in on it?'

Joel for once didn't have a sarcastic reply. 'Then today crime will pay.'

Joel headed into the bank to unlock the vault. The two women waited in silence. When he returned, they finally set off on their mini holiday.

None of them was aware of the motorbike that pulled out from behind a parked van and followed the car.

THREE

Like a lot of adolescents, Minny had turned sour against the dominant parent, Emma, around the age of fourteen. By seventeen she'd mellowed a little, but there remained an aura of hostility around mother and daughter.

Emma was puzzled as to why she was burdened with Minny's disdain and Joel remained immune. She thought it had to do with his role as a father, but he had a different opinion.

'I just laugh and joke everything off,' he'd once said. 'It disarms people. It helped me get promotions at work, too. Minny just can't stay angry at me. Try it.'

She had, without success. He'd always had a quick wit, while she found it hard to adopt a comical attitude. At work she was known as a micro-manager and none too popular with the lower-tier, and her rigidity had filtered into her home life. Joel was more carefree.

He was the one who'd allowed Minny to try to develop a career as a YouTuber, while Emma had hounded their daughter to find a standard, salaried job. Minny had had four boyfriends and Joel had liked them all, but they'd walked away because, at least in Minny's words, her mother had been 'too in their face'.

Perhaps, though, time was the problem. The hours Emma worked meant she didn't see Minny as often as she liked, and even when at home she was always wrapped up in dealing with something that could easily wait until she next clocked-in. This holiday was a chance for some fun and bonding. Although the former wasn't something she often engaged in – unless she was solving puzzles – and the latter might be out of reach.

Peach Cottage was in the strangely named Peach Woods, which lay at the end of a dirt lane – guess its name – a half mile from Whittingham. Bare countryside enveloped the property. As Joel drove them down Peach Lane, with the woods visible ahead, Emma turned in her seat and spoke to Minny. The teenager wore headphones and didn't hear, so Emma waved a hand between Minny's eyes and the phone.

Her daughter tutted and looked up. 'What?'

'How about you and me take a stroll to see what's in the woods?'

'No, I want to check the internet signal here. Some other time.'

So much for that.

As Joel made the turn off Peach Lane and onto a smaller dirt track that bored through the woods, the car almost collided with a woman in pink jogging gear. She had to leap aside. That put her by Emma's window, so she buzzed it down.

'I'm sorry about that. We didn't expect anyone out here.'

Jogging on the spot, the young blonde woman waved it off and straightened her pink ball cap. 'Then it's understandable. Don't worry about it. I pass by the cottage every day on my run. You renting the place?'

'Yes. For the weekend. Are you–'

'Have a good stay,' the woman said. 'Gotta run. Literally.'

She ran out onto the lane and vanished. Joel called her a twat with a death wish and continued along the track, which delved fifty metres into the woods and abruptly ended ten feet from a postcard-like cottage.

It sat in a circular piece of clear land delineated by ornate border stones with a single break wide enough for their car to pass through. The cottage was constructed over two floors and had natural pale stone cladding, although this timeworn appearance was ruined by modern slate roofing and red house bricks bordering all four windows. Because the woods cast eternal gloom even in summer, a Victorian-style lamppost featured by each corner of the property and two more lurked outside the front door. It had an exterior boiler in a nearby enclosure painted to blend in with the forest undergrowth.

'Gorgeous,' Emma said.

'Cool,' Joel offered.

'Can't sunbathe,' was Minny's review.

Emma asked Joel to take the bags indoors. He hung back to collect them while Emma unlocked the front door and checked out the property. Minny went straight for the back bedroom, which was hers. Emma looked around the living room first, then the kitchen, which she found stocked with all the necessary appliances and implements, but of course no food. Alcohol was no issue, though. Three shelves in the living room and two in kitchen held old, expensive-looking gin. There was a pantry in the kitchen, but it contained only household supplies and some tools. They would have to go shopping.

Joel lumbered in with everyone's suitcases, dumped them, and headed for the back door. Emma followed him out onto the back deck, where there was a hot tub and a dartboard dangerously close together. 'No darts,' he said. 'We need a shop. We should have sent that jogger for us.'

'Too late now. We'll never see her again.'

At that moment, the female jogger reached the end of the lane, which fed into a main road running around Wittingham. Directly across the road was a pub called Black Boar, in whose car park sat a 2002 yellow van. Behind the vehicle was a road-legal Kurtz RT1 dirt bike. She hauled the van's sliding side door open.

In the cargo bay were her two colleagues, sitting in the glow of a nightlight in the shape of a cartoon cat. For this mission they had adopted the names Jekyll and Hyde. Hyde was playing on his phone, while Jekyll, as always, had his eyes closed and was listening to a podcast via earphones.

Hyde, the bigger man, was thirty-eight and inked across most of his upper body. A pair of lightning bolts zagged up the side of his neck, behind his ears, and their tips met on the top of his completely bald head. He'd had them done at the age of twenty while whacked out on drugs, but he didn't rue the decision. In his line of work, such an appearance had benefits, and he wasn't one for thinking too far ahead.

Just like in the famous novel bearing his name, Jekyll was a sharp contrast to his comrade. He was nineteen and baby-faced. They looked like the last two people who'd ever be best friends.

When Denise climbed into the van, she and Hyde shared a sloppy kiss.

'What did you see, baby?' Hyde asked her when they unglued themselves. He sat back and yanked her onto his lap. She put her head on his solid muscle shoulder.

'They came,' she said. 'Nearly killed me with that car. All three of them. We're good to go. So can we go eat?'

'Soon. We need to carry on watching, baby, cos the guy has to go back to the bank to lock all the till money and shit in the vault.'

'Oh yeah. But that's not for a while yet. Let's go eat. He can watch.'

She meant Jekyll, who said nothing. But he'd heard because he opened his eyes. He gave only a nod when Hyde said, 'I'm going to have to take the van. So wait in the bushes or something. That okay?'

Jekyll obeyed the next command and exited the van. There were some bushes over by the entrance to the pub, but he didn't go hide there. Instead, he sat in a bus shelter on the main road because it also gave him a good line of sight down the track that led to the cottage.

Hyde drove the van out of the car park and beeped the horn as he blew by the bus stop. Jekyll watched it vanish around the bend then returned his eyes to the track.

The buses along here were once every two hours, but one drew up just a few minutes later. The driver opened the door but held up a hand. Over his podcast, Jekyll heard him say something about the stop being a timing point and he was taking no passengers yet. Jekyll responded with a thumbs up.

With time to kill before he moved on, the driver put his feet up and read a newspaper. Jekyll's view of the track was blocked so he had to shift to the other end of the shelter.

Ten minutes later, the driver put down his feet, put away his paper, and opened the bus's doors. He said Jekyll could now get on, but the young man gave a thumbs down. The bus moved on.

Half an hour later, Jekyll saw activity on the track. A car. The Catalano car, in fact, coming his way. He pretended to study the bus timetable, but he watched the vehicle enter the main road and zip away.

He was supposed to call Hyde if he saw this, but he left his mobile phone alone. The happy family had just arrived and the cottage was probably empty of food. They were going shopping and sightseeing, that was all. No big deal. They'd be back and sound asleep in their beds when it was time to rock their world.

FOUR

Joel didn't find darts, but Emma got two bags of food for the cupboards and the freezer. Afterwards, the family headed out for a stroll. They took in Whittingham's parish church and a Roman road called the Devil's Causeway. Minny saw some of it, but mostly her eyes soaked up YouTube videos and social media gossip.

There were hiking trails, quaint pubs, and a fairground, where Joel tried to win Minny a teddy by hanging from a bar for two minutes. He achieved thirteen seconds. The sun stayed visible the whole afternoon and all three of them returned to the cottage content with the day's events.

Joel wasn't entirely happy, though. Just minutes after arriving back at their holiday home, he had to leave again to go to work. He took the car. As it exited Peach Lane and drove past the pub, he had no idea he was being watched. Or that, seconds later, a man on a Kurtz motorbike followed his vehicle.

When he returned, darkness was descending. Minny decided she wanted to shoot a new YouTube video. She hadn't even unpacked yet. Her bedroom was too small for her green screen so she opted for the living room, where she could sit at a large oak dining table.

Joel and Emma decided to give her space and use the hot tub.

Emma undressed in their bedroom, where there was a full-sized mirror hanging off the bathroom door. She stripped and checked her reflection. Joel walked in and also started to undress. 'Upset?' he said.

'There's no hot water for the shower. I can't find a key for the padlock on the boiler enclosure.'

'I'll text the owner. But that wasn't what I meant when I asked if you were upset.'

She knew exactly what he meant. She traced her chest scar with a finger. 'Are you?'

Joel dragged on his swimming trunks and hugged her from behind. He, too, traced her scar. 'I'm only upset about this thing if you are. It doesn't bother me. Like you always said, you can't hate evidence of what saved your life.'

It was indeed her outlook, but sometimes it was hard to find the strength to believe it.

She had gone to her local GP with an inverted nipple, but the diagnosis had been a collapsed milk duct. She believed that until a few months later, when the nipple gave off a gross discharge. She returned to the doctor, who ordered a biopsy. Ten days later, the results were in. Stage 2b breast cancer, which had spread to her armpit lymph nodes. It required a mastectomy.

She swore never to have reconstructive surgery. She would not play a role, wouldn't wear camouflage. Immediately after the procedure, she was told to wait a few days before inspecting her new appearance, but she waved that off. She was now physically changed forever and would not pretend it wasn't so.

It hadn't been easy to view the scar and her flat right chest, but that initial exposure had been the worst of it and acceptance became easier as the days passed. The scar, as she had later told Joel, was a big neon sign proclaiming she was now cancer free and would live.

Because she was still weakened and her right arm tingled a lot, there had been good days and bad, and the latter had pushed her to seek counselling. Rather than use professionals, she had found an organisation called Flat Friends, which was dedicated to helping women just like her.

A few days a week she entered their closed Facebook group to chat to new friends, and last week had met a trio of ladies for a day out in Newcastle. Talking to similar women had boosted her confidence a lot. These days she could openly discuss her ordeal with anyone who asked, and that included some brash fools she dealt with at work.

'Emma?'

She snapped back to the moment, having been lost to thoughts. 'Sorry. What?'

'I said do you believe me when I say it doesn't bother me?'

She smiled at him. 'I do.' She wasn't fully certain she'd told the truth.

Joel threw her swimsuit at her, which she caught and stepped into. Then they hit the hot tub. Joel drank beer and Emma enjoyed wine. They forgot all about work and other troubles, and discussed their plans for the next day. At one point Emma pulled down her swimsuit to scratch at her breast scar, which often itched when she was warm. She exposed herself because Joel was the only one who could see.

Or so she thought.

'Jesus, the boss was right, she's missing a tit,' Hyde said. He was a hundred metres away, crouched in the woods and using binoculars to watch the Catalano couple on the illuminated deck. 'I'm not fucking her now.'

Hyde continued to watch. A few minutes later, he elbowed his younger friend's flank. 'Hey, there's yours.'

By 'yours' he meant the daughter, Minny, who had appeared on the deck. She didn't wear a swimsuit. She seemed annoyed about something and was gone seconds later. Jekyll didn't even look.

'Two tits,' Hyde said. 'I might swap you. We could do them, you know. Both those women. Take turns with each.'

Jekyll said nothing and still hadn't glanced at the cottage. He lay back against a tree, eyes in the canopy as he listened to a bizarre mysteries podcast via earphones.

Hyde raised the binoculars to his eyes again. 'Worried about the boss? I doubt he'd give a flying shit if we fucked those women. Besides, how would he find out? Not off these three arseholes, that's for sure. They won't be able to tell anyone anything when this is all over.'

FIVE

Emma woke and threw her eyes around the room. The only illumination came from the window, whose curtains glowed with low morning light. She checked her smartwatch and saw it was 6.15am. All was silent, but it hadn't been seconds before. She knew a noise had woken her, not a long sleep. But what kind of noise, she had no clue. The fact that early morning daylight smothered this part of the world prevented panic, but there was a definite ball of concern in her gut.

She got up, threw on her dressing gown, and went to the window. All was serene and normal outside. Had the noise been beyond the woods or–

'Dad! Come here!'

Minny. She sounded like she was still downstairs, where they'd left her alone to make videos after they'd retired to bed. Emma opened the bedroom door and moved to the top of the stairs.

'Minny?'

'Come here. Please.'

Please. If Emma had doubted the worry in her daughter's voice, that word made it unmistakable. Had Minny heard the noise, too? Emma rushed to their bed and shook Joel awake, and grabbed her mobile in case it was needed. 'Something's wrong downstairs. Come on.'

Her obvious worry snapped him wide awake in a flash. Without seeking another word of explanation, and wearing just boxer shorts, he rushed down the stairs and she was hot on his tail. Joel bashed open the living room door without stopping, but he froze the next moment.

Behind him, Emma couldn't see what he saw. But she knew it was real bad when he cursed. She pushed past him. Into hell.

The living room light was on, curtains still shut. With a throw over her legs, Minny was sitting on the sofa, where she must have fallen asleep. Behind her was a masked man.

Holding a machete to her neck.

A second, bigger man stood nearby, also wielding a gruesome blade. 'Chuck the phone away,' this man said. He pointed at the carpet with his blade, indicating where he wanted the mobile. When Emma's device thumped to the carpet, he pointed his weapon at her. 'Shut the door behind you and sit down. Do it right now or you'll need to wash this carpet.'

'Who the hell are you people?' Joel said, his fists clenched. He was two decades removed from his time in the Royal Air Force, but it had given him a sturdy soul. 'Take what you want and get out of my house, you bastards.'

The big man spoke to his comrade. 'Cut one of her ears off.'

'No,' Emma yelled. She dropped to her knees and pulled Joel down with her. He was reluctant, but also wise. When they were both sitting, the big thug said, 'Nice. You just saved your kid. I guess that makes you good parents. To respond to the first question, I'm Hyde and my mate here is Jekyll. He's no doctor, but it remains to be seen if I'm a monster.'

Minny wasn't crying, but there was terror in her wide eyes. The man holding a blade at her neck was rock-solid, like a mannequin. It was obvious to Emma that he wasn't the one running the show. She focused on the big man. 'What do you want? You can take whatever you want. If you just go, we won't even call the police.'

'Just take what's in the damn house and go,' Joel said. 'We have credit cards and there's cash and jewellery. My watch is on the fireplace there. It's worth two grand.'

Hyde looked at the fireplace, and the other guy was watching Minny, so that gave Joel a couple of seconds unobserved. He used them to glance at Emma and mouth the words MY BANK WILL PANIC.

She understood. If a typical business employee didn't turn up for work, the bosses might make a phone call or even pop round to make sure everything was okay. Not so if a bank manager with a vault key failed to appear. The police would be the ones making the visit, in case of kidnap. An hour from now Joel was due at his bank. In two, armed officers would kick in the front door of the cottage.

But that wasn't good news, Emma realised. If these home invaders were trapped here and unwilling to surrender, all hell could break loose. With her family in the eye of the storm.

The big brute approached the fireplace and lifted Joel's watch. Emma waited to see if the offered booty would be enough for these thieves. With luck, they'd take the watch and leave.

Not so. Hyde said, 'Nice and all, but we're not here for bits and bobs that people bring on holiday.'

Joel got to his knees. Emma grabbed his arm, unsure if he had shifted position for comfort or because he planned something dangerous. 'You know who we are, don't you?' Joel said. 'This wasn't random.'

Hyde folded his arms, which put his blade vertical and just

a half inch from his masked face. 'Sounds like you think you know what we're all about. Let's hear it.'

'I know exactly why you're here. And you're wasting your time. I can't get you into my bank vault.'

Emma had had this very suspicion deep in her gut. A thief had once tried to tackle Joel outside the bank, and one time he'd been followed halfway home before alerting police. He had told her many tales of banks or their workers being targeted. And he'd told her that most of these instances never reached the public ear.

It had always felt like a matter of time before Joel became the star of one such story, to be spread around the banking community to keep everybody security conscious. This very moment was one she'd worried about for years.

'Is that right?' Hyde said. 'That would be a shame, given all my planning. I guess we're going to have ourselves some international true crime breaking news.'

'It takes two keys,' Joel said. 'You can have mine. But I can't get the other key. And the cameras in the bank have facial recognition. They'll set off the alarm if you go in.'

'Not the plan at all. Listen to me carefully, or two of you will live to regret it. No more lies. You don't know what we know.' He held up Joel's watch. 'If this is worth two grand like you say, that will do me. I'll be out of here. So how much is it worth?'

Emma couldn't stop herself. She didn't know what Joel was going to say, so she got there first. 'Seventy-five pounds.'

The brute's mask creased as he grinned. 'Good. Your missus here seems to be the smart one. Let's cut to the chase. I know about the bank keys and the cameras and all that shit. So what? I won't be going anywhere near your bank. But you will. You have to, to open the vault for a day's fucking people out of their money.'

'How do you know that?' Joel said, a fraction more scared, but also a little angry.

'You have to walk into that vault to get some of that lovely cash out. And today you'll be wearing clothing that's nice and baggy so you can make an unauthorised withdrawal.'

Joel made no reply, so Emma chose to seize the opportunity. But she could think of nothing to say. They both just stared at the armed thug.

'No lies, good,' he said. 'So now you know what we want. It's dead simple. Your man there goes about his business as usual. You and your kid stay right here. He walks into that vault, and he walks back out about a stone heavier. He comes back here, hands over the dosh, and we all go our merry way. But if the cops show up, some people will be losing weight instead.'

SIX

Joel was escorted upstairs by the dickhead calling himself Hyde, who blocked the bedroom door and watched him dress. Joel put on his suit, and it felt very bizarre. He didn't speak throughout the process, and he was asked no questions.

When Joel was ready, the brute jerked his head as a way of saying *let's go*. Joel walked past him, their shoulders just inches apart. At no time did the man hold up his knife or keep his distance. He knew what Joel knew: that any kind of attack would cause bloody feedback downstairs.

Back in the living room, Joel sat with his wife on the floor again. Emma seemed deflated, and her eyes were on the floor. The other criminal, Jekyll, seemingly hadn't moved an inch and still stood statue-like with his blade against Minny's throat. At least his daughter seemed less terrified now. It was probably shock.

The big bozo checked the time on Joel's watch. 'Just after seven. You go at half past.'

He might as well have said two months from now, for that was how long those thirty minutes seemed to take to pass. Nobody spoke. Hyde sat in an armchair and put the TV on, and skimmed through a channel of music videos. If the scene hadn't felt so scary, it would have been surreal.

There was a clock on the TV screen. When it struck half past, the big brute turned off the device and stood. 'Time to go.'

The half-hour wait had given Joel opportunity to think. The last thing he wanted was to leave his wife and daughter in the company of this pair of freaks. He had managed to construct no adequate lie to explain why he needed them with him, so he didn't bother with one. 'I want all of us to go,' Joel said. 'I don't want to leave my family here alone.'

'They're not alone. Me and my man are here. Don't worry, we'll protect them if anyone breaks in.' Hyde seemed to find his own joke funny.

Joel said, 'I don't know if this will work. The assistant manager and I always search each other after we leave the vault.'

Another laugh from the beefy bozo. 'What, don't you trust each other?'

'It's policy. I'll be searched and he'll find the money.'

The man turned serious. 'Don't you worry about your second-in-command. All you need to be concerned about is the mess in here that the cops will find if you fuck this up. Look at your daughter. Have a look. See that blade half an inch from her jugular? Do you?'

He seemed intent on an answer, so Joel gave it. Yes, he did see.

'If at any point you think a SWAT team can get through that door and across this living room before Jek slices her head off, then go right ahead and call the cops. Pick what's more important to you. Your kid being over five-feet tall, or getting a pat on the back from your bank for saving their cash.'

That was no choice at all, was it? Joel stood up. He walked over to his daughter.

'Careful,' he was warned.

Joel leaned in to kiss Minny on the cheek. He said, 'Everything will be okay. I promise.'

A tear fell from her eye as she nodded. Joel then knelt before Emma and repeated his pledge. She wished him luck.

'He doesn't need luck,' Hyde said. 'Just common sense and love for his family.'

Joel was escorted to the front door by Hyde, and shoved out. The robber lobbed Joel's mobile phone at his feet. Joel wasn't sure how the bastard had gotten hold of it. But they knew he needed it. They had certainly done their research.

Both men stared at each other. Joel's brain appeared to have fogged-up.

'Now what?' he said.

'Have a good day at work, darling,' Hyde said, and shut the door.

The morning wind seemed to knock some sense into Joel, and for the first time he truly accepted that what was happening was real. Not a wild dream. The open land gave him a sense of relief that he was safe, and he had the urge to run, and not stop until he crashed into the nearest police station.

But he looked around and realised that the bozo calling himself Hyde was right. The clearing in which the cottage sat was at least fifteen metres from the surrounding trees, and nobody could cross that bare ring of land without being spotted. Absolutely he could engineer the capture of the two bastards inside, but he'd also guarantee that they went down for double murder.

Until this moment he'd had no idea what he was going to do. He'd just wanted to get free so he could assess his options for saving his family. But now he knew he faced just one forward path. He would do what had been ordered.

He was going to rob his own bank.

SEVEN

Twenty-seven minutes after Joel left, a phone rang. Emma didn't realise it was hers until Hyde pulled it from his pocket. She hadn't seen him take it from the floor.

'Answer it,' he said, lobbing it onto an armchair. 'And remember you'll lose your security deposit on this place if your kid's blood ruins the carpet.'

Emma scuttled to the chair and snatched the phone. The name is the screen was SLAVEPIT, a joke title for her workplace. 'It's my work,' she said. 'Do you want–'

'Answer it. Everything needs to look fine and dandy at Casa Catalano.'

She took the call, her eyes never leaving her daughter's. After listening for a few moments, she told the caller to wait, covered the microphone, and spoke to Hyde. 'The duty manager can't make it in and they want me to go in and–'

'Say yes.'

She paused. 'To work? All day? But–'

Again he interrupted. 'Just say yes and hang up.'

Puzzled, Emma did as ordered. When the call was over, she

tried to put the phone in her pocket. Hyde saw this and demanded it. She slid it across the carpet towards him.

'I can't leave my daughter here alone,' Emma said. 'I can't go into work.'

Hyde picked up her phone. 'You can and will. Everything has to appear normal.'

'But this isn't like my husband's bank. I'm not necessary. They can just call for a duty–'

Her words died as Hyde launched her phone against a wall. He hit a mirror over the fireplace and it burst into a rain of shiny shards.

He pointed his machete at her face. 'You will go to work because we're not having someone come here looking for you. You will go in and act as if everything is normal, and then come home, and that will be the last time you question me. Or you'll fucking regret doing so. Understand.'

Emma nodded.

'Good girl. Do you need to get changed?'

It took Emma a few moments to gather her thoughts. She desperately didn't want to abandon Minny, but knew there was little she could do to avoid it. 'No, my suit is in my office. Look, I can easily call back and pretend I've had an accident. Please. I...'

She could see only his eyes beyond the ski mask, but they told her everything. Which was that she should shut up, and instantly. She looked away and turned mute.

'Look at it this way,' Hyde said, taking a seat next to Minny on the sofa. The teenager shifted a little to widen the gap between them, even though it caused her throat to brush against the flat side of the machete blade held by his partner. 'By the time you get home, we'll be gone. It'll be like normal with your man and your kid here alone, happy to see you. Just another day's work done. Unless you tell someone something you shouldn't, in which case you'll get back here to find two bodies in a burning house.'

EIGHT

When Joel approached his assistant manager's car, which was parked up the street from the bank, he held out a McDonald's bag. Luckily, he'd found enough money for two meals in the door pockets of his car. 'Bought you breakfast.'

Peter buzzed his window fully down and eyed the bag as if it contained horse manure. 'You know I don't touch that foul shitness.'

Joel shrugged. 'More for me.'

None for him, actually. He didn't touch the food as Peter headed into the bank to make sure baddies weren't hiding in nooks and crannies. The call came a few minutes later.

'Get that vibrator out your arse and help me open up.'

Once inside the bank, Joel headed to his office, where he looked through his bookcase for novels and non-fiction he'd never read, and dumped them in the plastic swing bin by his desk. He put both McDonald's bags of food on the desk and laid his phone next to them.

Peter poked his head in. 'Ready?'

Joel nodded and both men left the office. Staff had begun to arrive for their shifts, so both men talked by the shuttered front entrance, buzzing it up and down every time someone arrived.

After some small talk and jolliness with the crew, Joel and Peter walked to the vault. It had a lock on either side of the door, which required the turning of both keys at the same time. It was a rather mundane security feature because few serious bank robberies were committed by a single individual.

Door unlocked, the two men entered the vault and began making up till trays for the five cashier positions. Each tray was also allocated what the staff called a boom: a wad of fakes notes with a dye pack inside. If a masked man shoved a gun in a cashier's face, he'd get that little bonus gift amongst his booty. It had never happened yet.

Peter counted out cash for the trays while Joel loaded them with booms removed from a separate safe. As he did so, he carefully watched his assistant manager for those moments when his eyes were averted. A camera recorded them working, but nobody would replay the footage until it was too late.

Tills prepared and on the trolley, the two men left the vault and locked it. 'Okay, done,' Peter said. 'Back to the holiday, then?'

'Yeah, I... shit.' He patted a pocket. 'I might have dropped my phone in the vault.'

'No, I saw it on your desk.'

'Right. Cheers.'

While Peter delivered the tills to the cashier positions, Joel returned to his office for his phone and then bid everyone goodbye. He waved to Peter as he headed for the exit.

'Stop right there, you thieving bastard.'

With a hand on the button for the shutter, Joel turned. Peter approached and told him to hold out his arms. The two managers, having had access to the cash stores, had to pat each other down before one could leave the building. It was an unflappable routine.

'I trust you,' Joel said.

Peter laughed. 'But you've got an expensive daughter.'

Joel's face remained impassive. 'You handled the money, Peter. I only touched the booms.'

'Scared I'll touch your dick again? You know you liked that.'

Joel laughed. 'It's a bit silly, don't you think? I mean, we don't do this search right after leaving the vault. Either one of us could have hidden cash somewhere else to collect another day.'

Peter lost his grin. 'I agree, but rules are rules.'

'Give it a miss this time. I have to rush home.' He pressed the button to raise the exterior shutter. It opened an inch before a hand suddenly grabbed his arm, freeing the button and halting the shutter's rise.

Peter's humour had been swapped for concern now he knew Joel wasn't kidding. 'Cameras are on us. The big cheeses might be watching. I know it's boring but... come on, dude. Arms out.'

'What if I don't?'

That line froze Peter for a second. It was the last thing he'd expected from his manager. He made an audible gulp. 'What's going on, Joel?'

'Just let me walk out of here, Peter, no search. I need the money. I'm being blackmailed.'

Because Joel had taken the only car, Hyde told her she'd be driven to work in a van, and then he made a call. The crunch of woodland debris announced the van's arrival a few minutes later.

'Go get dressed,' he ordered her. He followed her upstairs. He stood in the bedroom doorway as she dressed. She kept her dressing gown in place and her back turned as she dragged on jeans and a long-sleeved T-shirt.

As she fed her left arm into the T-shirt, she felt it catch on her wrist. Her smartwatch. The kidnappers hadn't taken it. It gave her a little hope, for perhaps she might get a chance to call... someone, to do... something.

Clothing in place, she cast off the dressing gown. 'Very nice for an older mare,' Hyde said. 'Let's go.'

He didn't vacate the doorway and she had to squeeze past him, which made her shiver with disgust. He followed her downstairs and stopped in the hallway. Hyde opened the front door and she walked out. The grimy yellow van was parked facing the house, which gave her a clear view through the windscreen. Her breath caught. Behind the wheel was a face she knew. The female jogger from yesterday. She knew then that these people had carefully planned this. She wished Joel's car had sent the bitch sailing.

Hyde grabbed her arm and led her to the side of the van. He hauled open a sliding door and ordered her in. She didn't object or even delay, yet he gave her an impatient shove before she had both feet inside. She stumbled into the far wall and slipped over. There was a wall between the cab and the rear, making the cargo area dark and box-like when he shut the door.

She heard him speaking to the jogger. They were quiet, so she distinguished no individual words, but from their tone she guessed they were boyfriend and girlfriend. Soon, the door shut and the engine started.

'Stay quiet back there,' the jogger yelled. Emma didn't hear Hyde again, and that set her heart racing. It appeared that the two men would be staying with Minny. If they touched her, she would skin them alive.

The van started moving. Emma spent the whole journey in the dark, thinking of what to say to the woman. Was there a chance the jogger could be swayed from this mission, somehow convinced to free her and help rescue Minny? But she worried for so long over how to broach the subject that it was all of a sudden too late.

The van stopped. A near-invisible hatch in the cabin bulkhead opened, and a face filled it. 'We're here,' the jogger said. 'We need you to do everything you normally do on a day at work. We know that you always stop at a café across the road. So that's what you'll do. Right?'

A dozen questions were in Emma's head, but what tumbled from her mouth was: 'Yes.'

She heard the woman exit the van. The sliding door rasped open. The jogger stood there with a small knife. 'That's not needed,' Emma said. 'I won't try anything.'

'I almost wish you would,' the jogger said, but she seemed a little nervous. Her threat was probably bravado. Still, Emma hadn't lied. 'Out you come.'

Emma found herself in a familiar car park. It was the one behind the row of shops on Cloudburst Street, which was home to the café the jogger had mentioned. Where, as stated, Emma would savour a cup of coffee every day before heading in to work. The people who'd kidnapped her must have been watching her movements previously to know this. It was a scary thought. Did they also know where she lived? Her home was five minutes away.

Her eyes shifted away from the woman. Above the terraced row of shops, and far in the distance, she could see the very top of a tall brick chimney. Cheviot Prison. A place containing almost five hundred convicts, many of them far worse animals than the two who held her daughter captive.

Five hundred dangerous men bowed to the will of Governor Catalano, yet right now she felt powerless.

TEN

Peter's eyes widened, but he seemed unable to find words.

And then Joel laughed. He slapped his friend's shoulder. 'You should see your bloody face.'

Peter looked puzzled, then gave a big sigh of relief. 'Was that a joke?' When Joel put out his arms, Peter called him a twat and began the search. He found no contraband or money, as always. Joel then checked Peter's clothing and, after a few more jibes, the two men parted ways. Joel returned to his car, but he didn't start the engine.

It was just after 8.30. At 8.45 everything would be ready for the bank's 9am opening. The duty manager would always call a Team Five meeting in Joel's office to spout motivational crap. After that, Peter would work through emails.

Joel waited until 9.30, then walked to the bank. He slipped down an alley alongside, to access the rear yard. The bank had a large, wheeled bin for general waste, which was locked in a cage to foil thieves expecting either old banknotes or private customer information. Joel had a key.

Inside that bin, he found the black bag from in his office. Good old anally-retentive Peter.

He rushed back to his car with the heavy bag and drove to a nearby supermarket, where he tore open the bin liner on his back seat. Inside were the books he'd discarded, all covered in sauce and salad and grease from two McDonald's meals. He imagined Peter's face as the man saw the full bin and the nasty mess inside. He would have cursed Joel as he tied up the heavy, stinking bag and took it to the backyard.

Joel delved to the bottom and wrapped his fingers around a wad of paper. When he'd pulled out all three booms, he tied up the bag again and put it in his boot. Each boom contained £10,000 in counterfeit £20 notes held tightly together by a currency strap. Only the top and bottom £2,000 were composed of intact notes, with the middle section hollowed out for a dye pack. He was lucky because some banks hid their explosive presents between just a couple of notes, but that ran the risk of a robber flicking through and realising he'd been duped.

When Joel opened one of the wads, he saw that the taggant had, of course, already fired. Some packs were designed to fire when opened, so that a thief would be coated in dye. These were different. The packs remained neutral in the tills, but once they passed a certain distance from a magnetic plate at the bank entrance, a sixty-second countdown initiated. He'd heard the dye packs activate while he drove – just a little click instead of a boom.

Some banks used bright red dye to instantly ruin the notes and packs were known to generate intense heat or even release tear gas. Again, these were different. They employed SmartWater ink, which was invisible and undetectable except under ultraviolet light. Far better for tracking the cash.

But he'd gotten what he wanted. Three hundred intact fake notes for a total of £6,000. Six grand for the bastards who'd kidnapped his wife and daughter. Hopefully they would be long gone by the time they realised their loot was bogus. And, even better, they'd start spreading the chemical around and its unique code would link them to the bank robbery. If SmartWater was used as evidence in court, scumbags went down every single time.

Unfortunately, the ink was now on Joel's fingers, where it would stay for weeks no matter how hard he scrubbed. So, a month off sick was in order.

He might just get the rest of his life off when the powers that be learned of his role in the robbery.

ELEVEN

There was a man holding a giant knife to her throat, yet it was the other thug, Hyde, that Minny couldn't take her eyes off. He was bigger and meaner, clearly the one in control. She didn't trust him a millimetre. Throughout the time her mum and dad had been here, he hadn't paid her much attention. But that changed when he returned after kicking her mum out the door.

He came in and snatched the throw off her, exposing her naked legs and knickers. He turned the armchair so he could sit facing her, and he covered his own legs with the throw. He just stared deep into her. His machete was laid across his lap and a finger stroked it. Was that to scare her? It damn well worked.

He stared for so long that her frustration overwhelmed fear, and she had to say something. 'Why do you keep looking at me?'

'Because you look so different to your photos.'

'What photos?'

'I checked you out on Instagram. You like to pose. There's thousands of photos, in hundreds of folders. It seems you can't do anything without stopping to pout for the camera.'

She was still annoyed. 'So what? I like to show my face. You hide yours.'

'Yeah?' He yanked off his balaclava, exposing a bald head and a lightning bolt tattoo coursing up each side of his head. Even without them he would have looked mean and nasty. He appeared to be about her dad's age.

Her fleeting boldness was gone. 'Why have you taken your mask off?'

He laughed. 'Have a guess. Go for it.'

'I don't know.'

'But it scares you. You've seen films where bad guys rip off their masks. I bet you think it means we're not scared of being recognised because you ain't gonna live to describe us.'

Minny needed a second to compose herself. 'Please don't kill us. You don't need to.'

'If your dad waltzes through that door with a bag of cash, no problem. You get to live. But you won't tell anyone what we look like–'

'We won't, I promise.'

'–because I'll know about it. And then we'll be back one day. I know where you live, where your mum and dad work, where you and your mates like to hang out. It will be bloody. And if I'm in a real bad mood, I'll do that thumbs-down thing on one of your YouTube videos.'

'You've been watching us?'

'Hell yes. Preparation. We know everything about you. I know you're a nano-influencer. What does that mean? A YouTube thing?'

Minny glanced back at 'Jek', who was still masked, still mute, still immobile. He was either zoned in to his role or there was something loose in his head. 'It means I don't have a lot of subscribers. And yes, YouTube. I do cosmetics reviews.'

'Explains why every photo has you plastered up like a barbie doll. Can you even answer the door without wearing all that shit? How many package deliveries do you miss because you're hunting around for lipstick?'

Minny offered no answer, but not because of fear or frustration. Sometimes, if her skin was playing up, no, she would not answer a knock at the door without at least foundation applied.

'Jek prefers the girl-next-door look. How you look now. So that makes him happy because you're his. I get your mum. More my age. She looks good for it. That Italian blood. How come she kept the name Catalano instead of Sharpe when she got married?'

It worried her that these people knew so much. She took a deep breath to try to relax. 'I don't know. She just did.'

'And you got the worst of it. You're Wilhelmina Catalano-Sharpe. Do your mum and dad want you to sound posh?'

Actually, her mother had wanted her to have an uncommon name, but Minny held no desire to answer this bastard. She simply shrugged.

Hyde raised his machete, but only so he could use the tip to carefully scratch his boxer's nose. 'The girl-next-door look is quite good, actually. The pictures don't do you justice. I might swap with my man there.'

'No,' Jek said from behind her. It was the first time he'd spoken. His voice croaked the word, probably from lack of use. His next words came out fine. 'We agreed she's mine. And I want her right now.'

She stiffened. Hyde laughed. 'Then go for it, pal. Get her upstairs.'

The blade of Jek's weapon touched her neck. His free hand grabbed her hair, tightly but not painfully. She was forced to stand, to walk. As they left the living room and mounted the stairs, her brain fought for a ploy, a solution, an escape plan. It was still buzzing without success when Jek led her into her own bedroom. She was unable to speak.

When he kicked the door shut behind him and released her, she leaped away and onto the bed. She had planned to create distance between them, but realised with horror that she'd manoeuvred herself right where he wanted her.

'Please don't do this.'

He took off his mask and dropped it. She was surprised at how youthful and sweet he looked, and how clean his blond hair was. He looked like a college kid who wouldn't dare even break the speed limit. She had to glance at the machete he wielded to remind herself that beneath the pleasant shell was a monstrous mind.

Seeing her look at his weapon, he dropped it onto the carpet. She continued to stare, this time in assessment of her chances of grabbing it. He must have realised this because he kicked the machete under the bed.

'Relax, miss. Please. I'm not going to touch you.'

She didn't relax, even when he sat on the floor with his back to the door. Could she leap off the bed and get to him before he reacted? If she was fast, precise, she might manage to knock him out with a kick to the face. But how would she then get out of the house with the bigger animal downstairs?

'You can't escape,' Jek said, as if having read her mind. 'Look, I brought you upstairs only because my... Hyde was starting to eye you up. I did it because otherwise he would have brought you up here instead. If he thinks we had sex, he won't touch you.'

'And you won't touch me?'

'No.'

'But what about my mum? Your friend wants to rape her.'

He seemed genuinely disgusted at the prospect. 'I'll do what I can to prevent that. I promise. This isn't what we came for.'

'So you won't kill us? If you get the money? That's all you want, isn't it? Money?'

'Yes,' he said, but after a long pause. The kind that gave her a sinking feeling.

TWELVE

The coffee shop waitress knew Emma by sight, for she was a veteran customer. As soon as she walked in, the lady, who seemed to work seven days a week, gave a wave and made a gesture that meant *the usual?*

Emma nodded and took her favourite table, in the middle of the full-length window.

Three other patrons were present: a couple and a handsome middle-aged man in a suit. Ingram was a small village and she recognised the married couple. The man was a new face. She wondered if he was a lawyer for one of her prisoners.

She looked out the window, watching the traffic. So many people were around this early, going about their day, none of them in abject fear for their lives and those of their family. She saw many smiles, and she wondered if she would ever find such contentment and fun again. Even if they escaped this mess without harm, what would it do to her psyche? Would she–

Her thoughts were interrupted when the man in the suit walked by her table. He stopped, turned, and did it again. Then he paused next to her.

'I don't believe in love at first sight, which is why I gave you a second look at me.'

Was that a chat-up line? She just glared at him, unsure. He said, 'It's okay, just a joke.'

She gave a weak smile. 'Sorry. I'm just tired.'

'Must be all that running through my mind all day.'

'Nice. I've got no time to chat, unfortunately. I'm just waiting to order.'

He didn't get the hint. 'I know what's on the menu. Me 'n' U.'

'I reckon I should keep my lips shut about now.'

'They look lonely. They should meet mine.'

On another day she might have smiled at that one. Instead, she showed him her wedding ring. 'You've got to practise your chat-up lines some more, so the next girl will surely fall for your charm. Now, if you don't mind, please leave me alone. I'm having the day from hell and I don't need a man trying to hit on me.'

He didn't leave her alone. In fact, he pulled out a chair and sat at her table. Before she could object, he said, 'I feel for you. It's always a pain in the neck when you try to have a nice weekend away and a pair of vicious bastards kidnap your husband and daughter.'

THIRTEEN

Joel shook his head almost all the way back to Peach Cottage. It was disbelief that he was returning to the scene of the crime, to hand himself over to men who might subsequently kill him and his family. But he had no choice, did he?

Actually, he did have one, and he worked on it as he entered Whittingham. By the time he reached Peach Lane, he figured it could work. It was risky, but it was all he had. Heading back into the cottage was a bad idea. He would not be able to stop the kidnappers from killing all three of them and making their escape.

Just short of the turn for the track in the woods, he parked and searched his boot, where he knew there was a clear plastic A4 wallet with documents inside. Then he turned the car so it was at the mouth of the track but facing back towards Wittingham. A quick getaway would be required.

He honked the horn for five seconds then got out with the £6,000 in twenty-pound notes inside the A4 wallet. He'd swirled them about inside so they filled it, to make sure Jekyll and Hyde could see their loot. He held it up and watched the house.

The front door opened and a man appeared. The lampposts either side of the porch illuminated Hyde, now minus his mask. Even from a distance he could see that Hyde was a bald, ugly bastard, which seemed appropriate.

The bald bastard laughed when he saw Joel at the end of the track. 'I was wondering what I've-got-control-now shit you'd pull,' he yelled. 'Go on, let's hear it. We don't get the money until I let your family walk out free? Then you drop the money as you're driving away? Spot on, right?'

Exactly that. Joel felt his heart sink. Then rise again. Just because Hyde had figured out the trick, that didn't guarantee failure. 'This is what you want, so do that,' he shouted back. 'Otherwise it means you plan to hurt us. Spot on, right?'

'And what are you going to tell the missus? Sorry I let our girl die, but look, we have money?'

Joel took a breath and willed himself to keep the terror out of his voice. 'This is what you came here for. If killing us meant more, you would have already done it. Look at all this planning you went through. Don't blow it now. Send my family out and this is yours.'

'Keep it. Use it to buy Minny a coffin.'

Upon those words, Hyde vanished back into the house. He left the door open, which was a sign. A great big one telling Joel that he had better act real quick and real smart, before he had regrets forever. So Joel ran down the track and thundered through the door. 'Okay, stop, you fucker, here's your bloody money. Leave my family alone.'

Hyde was halfway up the stairs, carrying his machete. He might truly have been en route to do lethal damage. Now, he plodded down the stairs, pointing at the living room with his blade. 'In there. Face down on the carpet.'

Joel entered the room and immediately noticed it was empty. 'Where the hell are my wife and daughter? If you–'

The remainder of that sentence was swapped for a grunt of pain as Hyde struck him from behind. The blow was powerful enough to knock him to his knees. Joel slapped a hand to the injured spot on the back of his head and was thankful to find no blood. Perhaps Hyde had used the handle of the weapon or even a fist.

'Face down, I said.'

Joel remained on his knees. It was to give himself a fighting chance, but he knew he was being wildly optimistic. His head was woozy from Hyde's strike. 'Where are they?'

'In a grave out back if I have to repeat myself.'

Joel lay on his stomach. Hyde sat on Joel's back and held the blade against his neck. The brute's free hand snatched the A4 wallet. 'How much is this? Looks like four grand.'

'Six. It was all I could get. It's a lot.'

'Fair enough. It was all a bonus anyway.'

'What do you mean? Where are my family?'

'Kid's upstairs. Wife is off to work, as planned.'

Perhaps the blow had addled Joel's brain more than he realised. Nothing made sense. Emma had gone to work? 'What do you mean?'

'I mean the boss didn't send us here for you and your bank vault. You had to go in to work so everything seemed normal, but the cash part was just a little side mission I thought up all by myself. We came for your missus.'

'For my wife? I don't understand. You said you wanted money.'

'A little porky-pie, that. Your missus is going to get us what we really want.'

PART 2

FOURTEEN

'Are you part of this?'

The man sitting across the café table from Emma nodded. 'You've done well so far, Emma. Continue to do so and your people will be safe. You have my word.'

Emma's stomach turned. This was bigger than a couple of men invading a home for money. How many were involved? How big was the operation? And, as she now suspected, did it have something to do with her prison?

'My husband and daughter are kidnapped. Your men broke into my place with giant knives. Forgive me if I don't think your word means much.'

'Play hero and the man you married and the child you birthed will end up dead. You have my word on that, too. Do you believe me on that?'

The waitress came over. Emma rubbed her left eye as the man ordered tea, so the lady wouldn't see something wrong with her regular customer's expression.

When the waitress was gone, he said, 'That was good. You could have asked her for help. You could have brought the police in earlier. These are good moves. Just a few more like that and you'll be home and dry.'

Oh, the temptation to scream for aid had been there, but she'd dampened it down. Rashness was dangerous. She needed to think of another solution. But she couldn't until she knew exactly what these people wanted. 'And what are those moves?'

'The first is to go into your prison as normal. You have Listeners, right?'

Where was this going? The Listener scheme provided emotional support for prisoners who were struggling to cope with life inside. The scheme was the work of the charity Samaritans: their response to a spike in prison suicides in the 1980s. Emma knew it was needed: the UK has roughly 97,000 prisoners, and Samaritans volunteers answer over 400,000 calls for help from them every year.

'Yes,' she said. 'But I don't understand.'

'You have a prisoner who wants to be a Listener.'

She had plenty, but read between the lines and knew this man had a specific inmate in mind. 'Who?'

'We'll get to that. You'll hear about it. And the moment you do, you're going to put the word out to all your staff that a Samaritans representative is coming down at ten to begin that inmate's training. Make sure you're there to personally meet the rep.'

'At ten? That's just an hour and a half from now. We can't–'

'If this is where you talk about policy and official channels and visit booking time frames and all that crap, don't. You're the governor. The ruler. Top dog. But today I'm your boss. Don't argue again. At ten, that Samaritans rep walks into the prison.'

Everything suddenly seemed clearer. 'That representative being you?'

'Being me. Make sure I'm not searched–'

'We always search visitors, without question. Are you planning to bring something inside?'

The man ignored the question. 'And we, the bad guys, always stick to our word. Do you remember the word I gave you earlier?'

She did. Her family would be killed if she didn't play ball. But this bastard was imposing impossible rules on the game. 'Look, it's a prison, not Alton Towers. I can't get you inside without being scanned. Or showing ID.'

'ID isn't a problem. I have a fake. As for the other bit, don't assume I don't know a few things. I'll be there as an official visitor, and they aren't subject to the same kind of search.'

He elaborated. Social visitors – prisoners' families and friends – were given what Cheviot called an A-level search, which was a full rubdown to check for contraband. Following that, they were scanned by handheld metal detectors. Official visitors got a B-level search, meaning a basic pat down. It was more about making sure someone didn't unwittingly enter the prison with a prohibited article.

He knew his stuff... but not entirely. 'But we still do the handheld scan for most people,' Emma said. 'VIPs might avoid the shame of a pat down, but you won't, Listener or not. And you're forgetting about the metal detector portals. They're at all entrances, even the delivery bays. Physically unavoidable, so everybody goes through. I go through. Even King Charles would have to go through if he visited.'

The man sat back, glaring at her. 'Well, you'd better find a way for me to avoid it.' He stood. 'Have a good day. See you at ten. You can drink the tea that's coming.'

Before he could take a step, Emma said, 'An unfortunate accident.'

He paused. 'Say again?'

'That's what I was told. My deputy governor was out

jogging just a couple of hours ago. He fell in a stream and broke both legs. But it was no accident, was it?'

'That's what he said? I guess that's because he couldn't admit the truth. Which is that he was hoping to fuck a pretty girl in the grass. He agreed to help us, albeit before we told him it involved a nasty injury. My people were nice enough to call an ambulance. We couldn't have him dying out in the middle of nowhere.'

'So he was injured to keep him off work. To make sure I had to go in.'

'And it's about time you did that.'

And with that he walked out. Emma buried her face in her hands and prayed this was all a bad dream.

FIFTEEN

When the young man calling himself Jek returned to Minny's bedroom, she said, 'What's happening? Did my dad get the money? Is he okay?'

She was worried because she had heard shouting from her father and the man called Hyde. Then there had been silence. She had no idea if that meant her dad had been knocked out or dragged away. Jek had bound one of her wrists to the horizontal bar on the headboard with a zip tie before heading downstairs, or she would have followed him to learn more.

Jek said, 'It's okay. He's not hurt. I know that ruckus sounded bad. Yes, he got the money.'

'So you're going to leave now?'

'Not yet.'

He didn't, or wouldn't, look at her. It was a bad sign. 'Why? You got what you came for. Please leave now. Please leave us alone.'

He didn't leave. Instead, he again sat with his back to the door. 'There's more to this. I'm sorry. We can't leave yet.'

'Why? Is it not money you want? What else do we have?'

There was a shout from downstairs. It sounded like Hyde ordering her father to *sit the fuck down.*

'My dad,' she said. 'What's happening? Is he being hurt now?'

'I'll go check. Please don't try to escape.'

'I won't. Please don't let that man hurt my dad.'

She'd been eyeing up the window because Jek hadn't locked it when he left her alone the first time. Now he corrected that oversight and pocketed the key before exiting the bedroom. Bang went her plan to leap out and run to the police.

She tugged at her bonds. The headboard bar was thick and solid, impossible to break by yanking on it. The zip tie cinched around her wrists was also strong. It would slice off her hands before it snapped by brute force. But the strip of hard plastic was loose enough that she might manage to get a grip with her back teeth and possibly gnaw through it.

But not just yet. Not until she had a plan. It would do no good to break free now because she had no idea where the two men were. If she released herself and was caught, they'd only bind her more tightly next time and keep her always in sight. Besides, she couldn't flee and leave her dad, for they'd abuse him out of anger. She wondered if he was also bound. If so, her chances of escaping with him were zero.

Was he even still alive? She hadn't heard his voice in a few minutes. For all she knew he'd been taken into the woods and killed now that he'd served his purpose.

Panic started to rise in her gut like acid reflux, but she dampened it. No, her dad was not dead. They would not harm him. But did she believe that? And where was her mother? Was she right now calling the police? Or was she at work and acting normal, as ordered?

But her mother was weak, selfish, and Minny feared a third

alternative. There was every chance her mum was so terrified that she had run away and abandoned her family.

SIXTEEN

Jek found Hyde in the kitchen with the dad, who he'd just finished zip-tying to a wooden chair. Joel's ankles were bound to the chair's legs and his elbows to the slatted backrest, and there was a red slap-like mark on his face. Hyde sat across the kitchen table from the prisoner, sipping from a bottle of gin he must have found in the cottage. Hopefully it had already been half empty.

The six grand stolen by Joel was on the table in two piles, one by each man. Hyde had dealt them both a hand of cards. 'Work this guy's cards for him, Jek. Can't free his arms cos he'd smash me over the head with this bottle.'

Jek said, 'I heard him yell out.'

'He hit me for nothing,' Joel said.

And he fielded another strike. Hyde leaned across the table to deliver the slap. He did it slowly, so the prisoner had time to react. Fingers barely grazed Joel's cheek. Unhappy with this, Hyde leaned a bit closer to land a more precise second blow.

'That's for acting like you're going to get me in trouble saying that shit. Who's the boss here, Jek?'

Jek looked at Joel, who seemed to be pleading for help, eyes glossy from the blows. 'Hyde's the boss. I'm just the hired help. Best do as he says.'

Hyde started dealing the cards. 'Poker. We're playing until one guy's got all the cash. Five hundred a hand.'

'He gets to keep the money if he wins?'

'Nay. We're playing for blood. His. If he wins, he gets to keep it in his body. I win, it's going all over the floor.'

Jek could see that Joel believed every syllable of this. Jek also wasn't certain Hyde was just messing with his captive. 'Seems unfair. His blood's already in his body. He doesn't really win anything by keeping it.'

Hyde gave this thought. 'Okay, freedom. He wins, we let them go.'

Joel perked up a little, but Jek didn't. This one he knew was a wind-up. 'Can I play for him?'

'I already said to do his cards for him.'

'No, I mean actually play. Me V you.'

Hyde grinned at him. 'Since when did you play cards?'

'I don't. But I know a few tricks. So if you want a real bet, here's one. I win and we don't fuck the guy over. I'm dealing with his kid up there and she'll get mardy if he gets hurt, especially if she hears it.'

'Is Minny all right?' Joel asked.

'I told you not to ask,' Hyde said, and again he stood up to strike Joel. But he pulled his arm back and kept it there, laughing at the way the target scrunched his eyes shut in fearful anticipation.

Jek sat in a spare chair. 'Let's play.'

Hyde sat. 'Okay. You win, I don't mess this guy's face up. I win, and we're both going to smash him.'

'With pleasure. I'll help you kick him around this room all day if you want.'

'Okay. Poker. Grab his cards.'

The two comrades began playing. Between them, Joel watched with an expression that bounced between relief and horror, depending on who won each hand. The first went to Hyde and increased his loot from £3,000 to £3,500. Then Jek dealt and won, to even the score again. The game took fifteen minutes. In the end, Hyde gave up his final £500 when his three kings lost to a hearts flush.

Hyde wasn't happy to see the departure of the last of his cash. He grabbed the cards and threw them in Joel's face, hard. 'No blood, look.' He grabbed his bottle of gin and stomped into the living room.

Joel squinted against the pain in his face. 'Russian Roulette next?'

Jek didn't know if the man was being sarcastic. 'Don't play games with that guy. He likes wind-ups.'

'You both seem to.'

'You saw what I just did, right?'

'But you said you've not played cards before.'

'I also said I know a few tricks. You would never have won freedom. The best you could have hoped for was what we got. A status quo. I didn't want to see your kid upset.'

'How is she? Can I see her?'

'Fine and not yet. Don't push it with Hyde. Don't talk back, don't ask for anything. In fact, don't even agree with what he says, because he'll just be leading you somewhere you won't like. Keep your mouth shut. Be invisible around him. He's looking for the slightest provocation. He told you why we're here? About your wife?'

Joel nodded. 'It seems very risky. What happens if it doesn't work?'

Jek stood up. He pretended to rub his empty hands together. But when he opened them, the ace of spades lay in a palm. 'Then no magic tricks will save you.'

SEVENTEEN

Just north of Ingram was a road called Cheviot Run. It led west out of the village, following the River Beamish through countryside for a quarter of a mile, where both water and tarmac veered north for the final 300 metre journey to HMP Cheviot. While the river passed by the massive prison on its western flank, the road terminated at its main entrance gate on the eastern side.

After HMP Dartmoor, Cheviot was Britain's most remote prison. Built in the late 1800s, it sat within tall brick walls high up in wild moorland, as if the builders had wanted to make sure it could be seen from miles around. The nearest railway was seven miles distant and finding Ingram by car could be awkward for visitors. At least HMP Dartmoor wasn't half a mile from its nearest populated area.

That said, Cheviot wasn't entirely removed from civilisation: the western corner of the squared perimeter wall was at the edge of the river, for in its early days prisoners were sometimes delivered by barge. New inmates would step off the barge and enter the grounds through a cylindrical tower, which, though unused and blocked off, still existed to this day. Canal boats often cruised by and put their occupants within throwing distance of the prison, but barbed wire at the edge of the water prevented access.

On the other side of the river was a large car breaker's yard. From a Google Earth aerial view the two properties resembled a pair of almost-touching diamonds. Given that it was the only other establishment out there, and a prime target for escaping prisoners, the breaker's yard had hardcore, fortified fencing along its two riverside edges.

The prison had been modernised in the 1970s, part of this being the sectioning of larger rooms into two or three smaller ones, and in the early 2000s it had been allocated modern amenities like a new library and fresh gardens. Prisoners liked the wide galleries and long landings, where they could mingle and watch others, and the high windows that offered ample natural light.

Those suffering the dark, maze-like hell of prisons built in the 60s and 70s often applied for transfer, officers included. As a local, Emma had begun her career there fifteen years ago and three summers previously had made governor. Her boss was always fielding calls from other governors who wanted her posting. But she was very good at her job and, more importantly, highly respected by superiors at HM Prison Service, so she had fought off all comers.

Yet Cheviot was no holiday camp. It was a category A prison, which meant the highest security. Its inmates posed the most dangerous threat to the public. And one of them was possibly involved in the kidnap of her family.

She used her watch's phone capability to order a taxi from the café to the prison. The driver was a man she vaguely knew from myriad journeys there with prisoners' visitors, and he agreed to waive his fare until next time. He bought her story that her car had been stolen.

'Let's hope the sod ends up in your prison,' he said. 'You can get some nice revenge.'

'Reduced TV time,' she said, and thankfully that was the entirety of their conversation.

The taxi dropped her at the main gate and she buzzed for entrance. While she waited, her mind ran wild and she had to again stifle bad thoughts about what Joel and Minny might be going through right now.

Once through the gate, she walked across the staff car park, towards the staff entrance of the main complex, which sat in the middle of the grounds. One problem with the facelift given to the prison was the route she had to take once inside. She was forced to trek through the staff changing room and it was bloated because of the 9am shift change. She was in no mood for company but had to engage in talk with at least eight people, half of whom had a gripe to air. She blamed a bellyache to those who spotted something off about her demeanour.

As she was about to leave the changing room, someone shouted, 'Guv, can you help with this?' Emma still found it strange that her staff used that old term, since it was also employed by inmates for other officers.

The caller was a woman of about twenty who was at her open locker. Not very pretty, no sense of humour, and very inexperienced, but she worked hard. Lucy Smith had only been at this prison, and indeed Northumberland, for three months, and Emma had barely spoken to her. She had no will to now, but she didn't want officers requesting her time later, when she might be up to her neck in trouble. So she walked over.

'What's up, Officer Smith?'

Nobody was close enough to overhear. Smith, looking perturbed, said, 'I've been told to come clean now. I'm involved in the thing that's happening with your family.'

Emma's legs turned to jelly. One of her staff had been

turned. Actually, that was the wrong word. Since Smith was new, she was probably a plant. But that would mean this lark had been planned for... three months.

'You piece of shit,' Emma said before she could stop herself.

Smith couldn't look at her. 'I know. I didn't want to do this. They made me. I owe them my life.'

'They're forcing you?'

'Not quite. I mean, yes, they're forcing me to come clean. To be part of this. So now my job here is probably over. This can't end well for me.'

Nor me, Emma thought. She had been so worked up, so panicked and scared, that she hadn't had time to consider the future. Now she did, and the outlook was bleak. Even if she gave the kidnappers what they wanted and managed to save her family, for sure there was no rosy ending ahead. This might be her last day as governor. Her last alive, even.

'Did they put you in here to watch me?' she said.

Smith shook her head. 'No. Watch a prisoner. Be helpful to him. Can't say who. But they told me to tell you I'm in on it, so I can now help you. What do you need me to do?'

Emma wanted to say something like 'commit suicide', but that wouldn't help solve the serious problem drowning her. And having one of the kidnappers' team on the inside was beneficial, for she could use this officer if necessary. 'Get me a pen.'

Smith had one in her locker, as well as a paperback novel inside of which Emma wrote something. Then she took the PAVA spray from the holster on Smith's belt and put it in the locker. 'Where are you working today?'

'C-wing,' Smith said.

'Phone whoever is paying your dirty money. Do it now. There's a man coming here who thinks his jokes are funny. I want word passed to him to bring a packet of cigarettes.'

'Cigarettes? I heard you quit years ago.'

'Well, thanks to your people, I might just start a new hundred a day habit. Make the call.' With that, Emma left the changing room.

There was a portal metal detector at the main entrance, but also another between the changing room and the security door that led into the prison proper. After passing through these, Emma made her way to the Hub, a central, circular hall with a security office in the middle.

The four prison wings ran from the Hub like spokes on a wheel. In three of the walls between these gated wing entrances were doorways and hallways that connected to various other buildings, and to external pathways that led to all remaining areas of the prison grounds. In the fourth wall was the stairwell and lift for the admin suite, where Emma had her office on the top floor.

If there was a major design flaw at Cheviot, it was here. For fire safety, each wing had a rear entrance/exit, but some areas of the prison, like the woodworking shop, could only be accessed from the Hub, and that meant escorting prisoners through it. That put them dangerously close to the main security office and the Admin Suite doors. If a riot broke out and the inmates claimed the Hub, they had the whole prison, and they had the governor.

The suite lift and stairwell doors required codes for entry, so she tapped in four digits of Minny's birthday and rode the lift up to floor three. On the two below were rooms that, a century ago, had been a lampman's chamber, mortuary, blacksmith's shop, and engineer's store, but were now used for uniforms and files and general surplus storage.

On the top floor, she entered a waiting room whose door required another code. Beyond was a corridor that passed a bathroom, small kitchen, secretary's office, and terminated at the heavy oaken door of her own office. She relaxed only when that door was shut behind her. She was boss of this world and it helped to have familiar surroundings. It didn't alter the extreme danger encircling her and those she loved, though.

The first thing any new manager liked to do was remove traces of the prior ruler, so Emma had stripped out the office and made it her own. It had a red carpet and stripey wallpaper. Since she sometimes worked long hours, there was a kitchenette and a sofa, and a wall-mounted TV with a beanbag before it. Her main desk was a large oak affair that had been resident for twenty years, although she'd revarnished it.

In another corner, and turned into a cubicle by a freestanding partition, was her security station: desk, three monitors for the prison's four dozen CCTV cameras, and intercom system. And the riot phone, which, when picked up, patched her right through to the national tactical response group. In seconds she could have a team of tough guys winging their way to Cheviot to stamp out insurrection. She'd never had to make such a call.

She went to the large window behind her main desk and used a Top Gleam glass spray and kitchen roll to clean it, then sat in her chair to enjoy the fine view. The window faced north, away from Ingram, giving her a rolling green scenery. She had her chair at a height that made the windowsill block out the barbed wire-topped, towered perimeter wall, thus allowing her to clear her mind.

It usually worked, but not today. When she undressed to climb into her suit, which hung from a hook on the wall, she glanced at her name badge. It said GOVERNOR, but right now she was a prisoner.

EIGHTEEN

Mornings were usually busy times as Emma opened emails, read over the previous night's incident logs, and dealt with prisoner requests. Today she obviously couldn't find the will. She had a raging storm overhead that threatened to strike her down with lightning, and it consumed her every thought.

However, there were tasks she couldn't ignore, in part because strange behaviour might flag with her colleagues. It was unlikely she'd be declared unfit to discharge her duties, especially in just a single day, but she couldn't have her movements being scrutinised. So, normal activity was the order of the day. Callous as it seemed, she would have to segregate her husband and daughter from her tasks as best she could. Minny always complained that her mother got lost in her work, and Emma needed a prime level of such compartmentalisation now.

So, she took a deep breath and got to the day's tasks. A-wing had a prisoner called Shaun Allersby, who was slated to be given access to a smart phone this evening, so he could watch the birth of his baby son. Bizarrely, on the very same day that he learned his wife was pregnant, he got a three-year sentence for selling class A drugs.

Her deputy had been dealing with the matter, but, of course, some violent thugs had given him time off for the foreseeable future. In another prison, Allersby had once taken a fellow inmate hostage, and again as a newbie here, which earned him thirty extra days on his sentence. But in the last seven months, since learning of his wife's pregnancy, he had been a model prisoner. So if he hadn't kicked up a stink by midday, she would authorise the video call.

Next up, three months ago a prisoner with just two more days to serve had started a fire in his cell. All prisoners had had to be evacuated from the wings. The firebug had walked out of the gate a free man, but right into the arms of police officers who arrested him for arson. As the duty governor that day, her deputy had to write a victim impact statement about the disruption to the prison caused by the cell fire. The statement was due by this evening, so Emma would be forced to author it.

A rapist who'd been bullied had told his mother and she'd complained to the prison. Her deputy had pencilled the mother in for a phone call to discuss the matter at 10am. Emma cursed, for that was the exact time she was supposed to meet with the suited bastard from the café.

At nine fifteen, a supervising officer called her from Base Zero: the solitary confinement wing. Located beneath B-wing, Zero was composed of ten cells for prisoners under punishment for serious infractions. The Zeroes, as they were nicknamed, were always escorted here and there by four officers, and always in handcuffs, but only one guard was allocated to oversee the block on a rolling rota. Comically, whoever had the shift was known as the acting block supervisor – yet had no one to supervise.

Today's pretend supervisor, a man Emma didn't get on with, said, 'I've got a prisoner request. It's from Samson. Yeah, I know.'

He probably expected her to laugh. Some requests couldn't be ignored, like a prison account balance, but the Zeroes were unlikely to get a yay for something a governor could legally refuse. Especially someone like Samson.

He was a high-level gang leader who'd been convicted of double murder two years ago and handed a life sentence with a minimum of thirty-eight years. He was suspected of many more killings, including that of a nineteen-year-old female who went missing just four weeks before he was arrested. Once banged up, he had continued to abuse and intimidate people.

Somehow, two months ago this fine human specimen had wrangled a transfer to Cheviot, and he'd been a royal pain in the ass from the get-go. His violent and intimidating nature hadn't waned, but nailing him for offences was tough given that nobody was willing to put their neck on the chopping block.

He did slip up finally, though, and commit assault on CCTV. Emma had seen the video, which had shown Samson and another inmate playing cards. Suspecting trickery from his opponent, Samson had said, 'If I catch you cheating twice more, I'll break your right thumb.'

Twice more? A strange thing to say, of course, and it had prompted the inmate to cheat again soon afterwards, believing he had a free go. So Samson had broken the man's left thumb and said, 'That's once. Remember, one more and I'll break your right thumb.'

And for that he earned his lengthy stay in Base Zero.

'What does he want?' Emma asked. The man liked music, so he probably sought access to more CDs.

'He's after getting put forward for training as a Listener.'

Emma almost dropped the phone. Samson. A powerful gang leader, and the most dangerous and volatile inmate at Cheviot. *He* was the engineer of all her distress. Her fear spiked. She had a terrible feeling she knew exactly what he wanted from her.

NINETEEN

The Base Zero supervisor found Samson's request funny, but he was alone in this.

'I mean, I know we're not really supposed to discourage people from being Listeners, but Samson? Can you imagine him wanting to get up at two in the morning because someone feels suicidal? Madness. I nearly laughed in his face when he said it. You know it's a trick, right? He'll manipulate people.'

A bully like Samson? Manipulate people? No doubt. He'd talk to a fragile prisoner and gain his confidence, and turn him into a slave. Or he'd stoke the fire and convince a damaged mind to end the suffering by noose or blade. Yesterday Emma would have sent word that his application was being considered, and then 'mulled it over' for months. Or outright shut him down. Today was a whole different story.

'I don't agree,' she told the supervisor.

'Really?'

The lie burned her tongue. 'I think he's trying to change. Samson could manipulate people without being a Listener. If he charms a parole board, he'll still be seventy when he gets out. He knows the gang life is over.'

'Bullshit. This guy? Bullshit. Are you serious?'

'Maybe he has benefits in mind. Listeners get perks, like extra time out of their cells. But I believe he'll take to a Listener role with professionalism. He knows we'll cut it if he messes up. Besides, like you said, we shouldn't discourage people.'

'So you *are* actually serious?'

On that other day, she would have barked at the block supervisor for his tone. Different story. 'Yes. I believe he deserves a chance. I'm going to make a phone call to the Samaritans and see if they'll send a trainer down here today.'

The supervisor grunted his disapproval, and hung up on her. Emma leaned back in her chair and cast her gaze across the moors surrounding the prison.

Then she got up and left the office. She headed to the end of the corridor, where there was a window facing south. To the southeast somewhere was Wittingham, but she couldn't pinpoint it. There were various splashes of woods and one of them could be the location of the holiday cottage. She wondered if, with powerful binoculars, she might be able to see that building. And see her daughter inside, in the hands of violent criminals.

It was best not to try, just in case. She returned to her office and made a drink, then burned a couple of minutes until her watch said it was 9.30. She used her desk phone to call the extension for Base Zero. The smarmy supervisor answered quickly. It still puzzled her how this guy had passed the prison's Crisis Negotiator course.

'We're in luck,' she said. 'The Samaritans have a Listener trainer visiting his mother in Brandon. It's so close that he can't pass up the opportunity to help. He'll be here at ten.'

Surely her lie was too far-fetched? They were in the middle of nowhere, but there was a trainer just a mile and a half away, and he was able to spare the time immediately?

'Okay,' the supervisor said. He was annoyed, but not suspicious. Why would he be? What could be wrong about this setup when you factored out a prison governor being coerced? 'I guess Samson will be getting his way. This trainer know he's going to be locked up in Zero for a bit?'

'Yes. He's done it before at other prisons. He's actually eager.'

She hung up before he could reply. She made another call, this time to C-wing. Each wing had a Watchroom manned 24/7 by an officer who watched the CCTV and responded to alarm calls from cells. The wing supervisor answered, sounding like he had a mouthful of food.

Emma said, 'Do me a favour, John. I'm being a bit anal here, but I want to make sure all your officers have the full uniform. Can you do that for me?'

Unlike the Base Zero supervisor, C-wing's head respected her authority and didn't bat an eyelid at her request. 'One sec. I'll go see.'

John was in command of five officers this morning and she heard him radio each one to ask for a uniform check. Emma didn't hear the officers' replies. John came back with, 'All good bar Smith. She's left her PAVA spray in her locker. Want me to send her back for it?'

'That's not good. Let me talk to her, please.'

John called the young, corrupt officer named Smith to the Watchroom. When she got on the phone, Emma said, 'Go back to your locker for your spray. I wrote a phone number in that paperback inside. Phone that number at 9.58am exactly. Exactly that time. Withhold your own number. A woman will answer. Just tell her that Joshua is back on the scene, then hang up. Say nothing but that. Joshua is back on the scene.'

'Who's Joshua?'

'Just do it. If this goes bad, other people's lives will be the least of our worries.'

TWENTY

After hanging up the phone on Officer Smith, Emma checked her watch. It was twelve minutes to ten. Her tension rose. The next half an hour or so would be vital, and it would decide her fate.

She called the office of the Operational Support Grade, known as OSG. Amongst his duties was receiving official visitors into the prison via the main entrance. He was her good friend, but also strict about rules. Visitors had to be handed paperwork to sign, and he would be the man wielding it. They also had to be watched passing through the portal metal detector, and it would be OSG's eyes on them.

When Emma told him a visitor would be arriving at ten, she heard him rustling papers. 'Not on the list.'

Next she filled him in on the Samson story. If he was shocked that the prison's most infamous inmate wanted to become a Listener, it was back-burner material to the fact that the meeting was impromptu.

'This ain't good, Emma. Why so quick? We should let Samson dwell a bit. Why are we giving that fool what he wants just like that?'

'A prisoner wants to do good, and we should encourage that. If he messes up, we'll cancel the plan. But he deserves that chance. We might get a pleasant surprise. I'm coming down there now.'

She was at reception with a minute to spare before ten. The OSG was in his office, which had long windows overlooking the entrance doors and the metal detector portals. She headed in and they shook hands. OSG tapped one of the monitors displaying CCTV from the visitor car park. Specifically, he jabbed at a blue Ford Mondeo. The camera quality was good enough that she could see a human shape in the driver's seat.

'I just buzzed him in the visitor gate,' OSG said. 'Guy called Louis Adley, right?'

So, that was the name of the bastard in the café, or at least the one on his fake ID. 'Yes. So, how's life since we last met?'

OSG launched into the details of his progress in building a snooker table from scratch in his outhouse. He'd been at it for twenty months. She feigned interest and glanced at a wall clock. 10.02. This was cutting it fine.

And then the office phone rang. Emma saw a flashing light from the office of her secretary, who manned the switchboard. That meant an external call coming through. And just in time.

OSG answered it in his usual professional manner, listened for a few moments, and then spoke to Emma. 'A lady's called in. You have a telephone interview planned?'

Shit. The 10am phone call from the mother of the prisoner who'd suffered bullying. She hated her next words: 'Tell her I'll call her later today or tomorrow. Tell her I'm very sorry.'

The OSG passed that message to the secretary, then hung up.

On a monitor, she saw the bastard named Adley get out of his car and walk across the car park. He would be at the entrance in just half a minute. Time was running out.

Now she could see Adley through the glass in the entrance doors. Thirty feet away. Twenty-five. Also seeing him, OSG stood up, ready to go welcome the visitor. Her plan was about to fail spectac–

The office phone rang again. One more time, OSG answered it in his almost jolly manner – but lost his composure seconds later. He covered the phone's mouthpiece. 'It's Sally. Joshua is back on the scene, apparently. She's not heard from him, though. Some anonymous caller phoned her and said Joshua's back. But she's distressed. All right if I just talk to her?'

Joshua was his daughter's ex-boyfriend. Their split had been all her idea, and he hadn't taken it well. There had been abusive phone calls, some surveillance of her walking to and from work, and suspicion of criminal damage. Joshua had been served a Stalking Protection Order and had left Northumberland. Apparently he was back.

But he wasn't. Emma felt terrible for putting OSG and his daughter in fear, but she was desperate. She said, 'Sure. Go ahead. I'll go meet the visitor.'

OSG continued the phone call, but he stepped into the bathroom for privacy, as Emma knew he would. While unobserved, she approached an electronic panel and turned a key. Through the entrance doors, she saw Adley on the steps, just seconds from entering the building. She exited the office and rushed for the entrance. She passed through the portal and stepped through the doors.

Adley stopped in front of her and held up a pack of cigarettes. He was already smoking one. 'What's this about?'

She snatched the pack and lit one. It tasted foul, but she liked the sudden wooziness in her head. 'I just needed time out here to coach you on how we're getting you inside.'

'So how do I beat that metal detector? Can you turn it off?'

'It can't be turned off except at the mains. We're not idiots.

And as you can see, you'd have to climb over a partition to avoid it, and my officer back there would call the police. So, I'm going to walk through that detector, and you better be right on my butt when it happens. Right on it. Or we're doomed.'

'You better hope you know what you're doing.'

'*You* better hope I know what I'm doing. Now let's go.'

They tossed their cigarettes and Emma opened the door. She walked inside. She saw that OSG, phone call over, was back in the office, his eyes on them. She turned to Adley. 'Arms out.'

Adley obeyed, but, through frozen lips, he said, 'Be very careful here.'

'Just remember to stay right on my back when we go through the portal.'

She gave him a quick pat down. She felt solid bumps and edges around his waist, and saw his steely glare when he realised that she knew he carried hidden items.

Pat down over, she walked through the portal, and Adley followed with barely six inches between them. The machine didn't alarm.

His phone call done, OSG exited the office. 'Sorry about that,' he said, approaching Emma and Adley with a handheld metal detector. Adley looked horrified, but so did OSG when Emma took it from him.

'I've never tried this. You mind?'

OSG paused, thought. It wasn't protocol, but she was the governor. 'Go ahead.'

Emma tested it on OSG's metal badge, which made it beep. She laughed. Then she ran it over Adley, who put out his arms and did his best to not look scared. She played the device across his whole body, and it didn't beep once.

'Good,' she said. As she held out the device for OSG, she slyly flicked the power switch from OFF and back to ON. The

OSG looked at it, confirmed the device was on, and even tested it again on his badge. Another beep.

'I need you to sign in,' OSG said to Adley. The visitor was led to a nearby desk to scrawl his name and show his fake driver's licence.

And that was that. He was in. But Emma was very worried about whatever contraband she'd just allowed a criminal to sneak into her prison.

TWENTY-ONE

When they left the lobby and were alone, Adley demanded to go to Emma's office. As they headed there, he said, 'How did we just beat those detectors?'

She told him about the simple action of turning off the handheld device. The portal had been a trickier affair. The machine had 350 detection parameters, which could be set according to what kind of items it needed to focus on and how powerful the scan needed to be. These couldn't be changed by the staff, but a key had been installed that allowed them to alternate between the highest, medium, and lowest sensitivities.

Adley was puzzled. 'Why would it have a low sensitivity instead of just being on high all the time?'

It was all about throughput and reset. The machine needed to reset after each scan, and the length of time this took depended on the sensitivity level. During social visiting times, Thursday and Saturday between 2pm and 4pm, traffic was busy, so the machine was set on low detection in order for a more rapid reset time. But it might miss the odd hidden object if there was little metal involved.

'That's why social visitors get a full pat down,' she said.

Official visitors didn't come in droves, so the portal's sensitivity would be set at medium. Longer reset time, but a more thorough scan that negated the need for a full, in-depth clothing search. This was the default setting on any day other than prisoner visiting times. The high setting was reserved for VIP visitors, like HM Prison Service managers or politicians, so as to do away with an embarrassing pat down altogether.

'Because people like you, the suit wearers, can't possibly be dodgy, right?' Adley said. She ignored the dig and he moved on. 'So you changed the sensitivity to high, right? The machine scanned you but didn't reset in time to scan me?'

'Yes. And I changed it back to medium while the officer was photographing your bullshit driver's licence. So, we got away with it, and you got what you wanted. What did you bring into my prison?'

'You'll see.'

Adley remained silent for the rest of the journey, his eyes zipping about like pinballs as he took in the prison. He was especially interested in the Hub and the doors leading into the admin suite. They had to pass through many security gates en route, but nobody tried to search or scan him. They passed numerous prisoners going about their business, but none of these said a word to him, either.

He remarked on this. 'I expected to be spat on, but you've got these people cowed. Do your lot beat them like dogs after every breakfast and lunch?'

This damn dickhead. He was so gratingly frustrating that it eroded some of his prominence. Even though he might control the safety of her husband and daughter, she couldn't contain a snappy comeback. 'Black soul respect. Kinship. They smell your badness.'

He laughed. 'Nice one.'

When they reached her office, Emma's tension increased. Adley sat at her desk, looking around the room, while she stood and waited. She knew she hadn't been through the worst of it yet.

'Nice luxury here. Are there ten inmates down in the basement, riding bikes to power the lights in here?'

'Six for the lights. The other four are stoking a furnace for my radiator. Why don't you tell me what you want.'

'Very funny. Okay, I guess you already know who I'm here for.'

'Of course. Mike Samson has given up murder and drugs and prostitution and wants to be a Listener to help vulnerable prisoners. Lucky for us a trained Samaritan was nearby.'

'Run your mouth all you wish, governor. I'll give you that as long as you don't mess me about. Make a call. Get my man up here for his training.'

She gulped. 'Here? I don't know if–'

'You're the boss here. Big cheese supreme commander. Your word goes. And I told you not to mess me about. I'm sure by now you don't need additional threats, so all I'll do is say "make your choice".'

Emma folded her arms and stared at him. 'I'm not messing anyone about. I think I know why you're here, and it's not just to deliver what you're carrying to Samson. But I hope I'm wrong, because it can't be done.'

Adley flipped his legs up onto her desk. His foot caught and toppled a pen pot, scattering biros and pencils across the wood. 'What can't?'

'I suspect you want me to help a double-murderer escape prison. That can't be done, even by a big cheese supreme commander.'

Adley glared at her. 'Now I'm annoyed because I hoped not to use thuggish threats. But so be it. Mrs Catalano, listen to me carefully. One of two things is going to happen by the time darkness falls this evening. Mike Samson is going to be wild and free beyond that river out there. Or your daughter's head is going to float down it.'

TWENTY-TWO

'Your friend must think you have the stamina of Superman.'

Jek checked the time on his phone. Minny was right. He'd been up here, supposedly ravaging her, for too long. Hyde would get suspicious soon. 'I'll go check on him.'

'And my dad. Make sure he's okay. Please.'

Jek nodded. 'I have to tie you again.'

Minny nodded. Jek pulled a bag of zip ties from his jacket pocket and bound her wrist to the headboard, as before. He'd freed her earlier, while they talked, and had said he couldn't leave her loose while alone. He put the bag of ties on the bedside table, then headed downstairs.

Jek headed into the kitchen first, where he found Joel. The man was still bound to the chair at the kitchen table, but since last time he'd been forced to bend over the table, chest pressed against the wood. Gaffer tape had been wrapped around the table and across Joel's back to pin him there. Given the man's laboured breathing, he was clearly in distress.

His eyes were pleading when he saw Jek. 'Help,' he said, his voice strained because of the uncomfortable position he was in. Jek grabbed a knife from a rack and started to slice the tape.

It wasn't quiet. Hyde rushed to the doorway, holding a steak knife. 'The hell are you doing?'

Jek grabbed and displayed one of Joel's hands. 'See the blue fingertips? That's a sign of pulmonary hypertension. This guy could get ventricular failure and die.'

Hyde seemed to weigh this up. 'That a bad thing?'

'The boss needs him alive.'

Hyde moved to the back door and hauled it open, waving for Jek to join him outside. They walked a short way to be out of earshot. 'I don't trust that guy,' Hyde said.

'Well, we're hardly good friends.'

'We don't need both of them.'

Jek knew where this conversation was going. 'We can't kill him.'

'The kid's the important one. We kill the dad and the governor will still do what's needed. She won't want to lose both.'

Jek said, 'But what about grief and panic and sorrow?'

Hyde suddenly ducked behind a cage filled with firewood and ordered Jek to join him. 'Guy over there.'

Jek peeked out and saw an elderly man walking through the woods right on the edge of the clearing. He seemed to look right at them. Had they been spotted. Whether they had or not, the old man walked on and didn't seem concerned.

'She'll get over it,' Hyde said.

'Grief and sorrow at her murdered husband? In five minutes?'

Hyde laughed, and Jek knew he didn't understand. Jek said, 'No, this is serious. If we kill the governor's husband, she'll be upset. Badly upset. Enough to throw her behaviour all out of whack.'

'So what? As long as she–'

'She might do something stupid. Besides, if she starts acting strange, she might be considered unfit for duty. Relieved of her position. That means another governor brought in. You think we could do this kidnap lark all over again?'

Hyde smiled. 'Are you not thinking straight? We're here and she's there. We can kill this guy and she'll have no clue until it's too late. He's going to be a pain, I just know it. I want rid of him.'

As if to highlight this point, there was a crash from the kitchen. Both men found Joel lying on the kitchen floor, still zip-tied to the toppled chair. He looked terrified that he'd been found. 'See? He tried to escape. And he'll keep trying. A pain, like I said. Let's just kill this fuckwit.'

'The boss might need him for something. And if he asks, and we can't produce, he might be pissed.'

Hyde ignored him and hauled the chair upright, with Joel still attached. He grabbed his tape and wound it round and around Joel, securing his torso and arms and legs tightly to the chair. Joel was slapped when he moaned, which shut him up.

When the job was done, Hyde addressed Jek's worries. 'The boss won't hold it against us if he thinks this fool tried to run and fell down the stairs. He won't check.'

'It's a bad idea, Hyde. We were told not to kill anyone.'

Hyde put a hand on the back of Jek's neck, hard, a reminder of who was boss. 'Not a democracy. He's dead and we'll dump him in the cellar.'

Hyde tore off a piece of tape and put it over Joel's nose. A second piece hovered an inch from the bound man's mouth.

'It might be fun to watch him kick and thrash.'

Before Jek could respond, Hyde slapped the tape over Joel's mouth. Air cut off, he indeed started to thrash.

'Hang on, what about money?' Jek said. 'I mean real money, not some six grand out of a vault.'

Hyde looked at him. 'What do you mean?'

'This guy is a bank manager. He controls a lot of money. We could have a shit load of it.'

Joel made noises against the tape, but they weren't screams of terror. Jek ripped away the tape from the man's mouth. Hyde snatched it back, but before he could reapply it, Joel said something that gave him pause.

'Millions. Millions come through the bank. I can get it. Please.'

Hyde grabbed Joel's hair. 'What shit is this?'

'It's not bullshit,' Jek said. 'I know about this. It's SWIFT. That stands for the Society for Worldwide Interbank Financial Telecommunications.'

'Trillions get moved through Swift every week,' Joel said, his eyes never leaving the piece of tape hovering inches from his lips.

Hyde slapped him and told him to shut the fuck up. Then he grabbed Jek's arm, and again hauled him outside for a chat. Hyde wanted more details about the millions of pounds on offer.

'Bank transfer,' Jek said. 'We access SWIFT and shift money between accounts.'

'Millions? That will make alarms sound.'

'It won't flag anywhere if we take just a small amount of money from lots of different accounts. We transfer all that loot into a bogus account.'

Hyde licked his lips. 'And this guy can do that?'

'That's what bank people do. And he's the manager. I read that the transfers can be done in about four hours. So four hours from now we can have a million quid.'

Hyde gave this some thought, but not much. He returned to the kitchen, followed by his comrade, and squatted before Joel. He held up his steak knife. 'You can do bank transfers? You can set up a fake account for me and shift some money into it?'

'And I know it can be done in four hours or so,' Jek added.

Joel nodded. 'Yes. About four hours. I can set up a new account for you at the bank and–'

Hyde's hope faltered. Jek saw it and jumped in. 'No, he can do it from here. We just need a computer with internet.'

'That's right,' Joel said. 'I can do it from here. My laptop. Four hours.'

Hyde still wasn't fully sold. 'There's withdrawal limits, though. The cops will get wind if we take out too much. I know you fuckers report money laundering and then checks will be made.'

Jek said, 'But we can take out less. I think banks can instantly pay up to two grand or so. We hit all their branches in one day, two grand from each.'

'We have dozens of branches,' Joel said. 'And, yes, we do instant cash of two thousand.'

Hyde stood. He waved the knife. Joel awaited his response with wide eyes and a thudding heart.

'I'll get his computer,' Hyde said, and he went off to do it. When he was alone with Jek, Joel said, 'I can do this for you easily. I can get the cash and you'll–'

'Don't mess me around,' Jek cut in. 'I'm not on your side; I just don't want my partner killing anyone. Stop the lies. I know you can't access Swift from your home computer.'

Joel took a deep breath. 'Okay. Sorry. I understand now. I know why you said four hours. Some breathing space. Thank you. But what happens after four hours?'

'We'll worry about that then.'

'Is my daughter still okay?'

Jek nodded. 'I won't let any harm come to her. Stop asking me that.'

'Thank you. I mean it. You're a good man.'

Jek shrugged. 'I wouldn't go that far.'

Most prisoners entered the governor's office to be accused of or hear their punishment for an infraction, or to give their evidence in an investigation. Others were presented for a general chat, or to be praised by Emma for a task, or to receive an answer to a request. Regardless, if you were an inmate and you were in that office, one or two prison officers always stood by to keep the peace.

The prison's most notorious resident probably deserved a platoon of guards, but Adley informed her that Samson had to be alone. It was a problem, but one she easily found a solution for. She told Samson's two escorts that he required privacy for a conversation with his Listener, and sent them out of her office. They weren't happy because, orders or not, their necks would be on the chopping block if a prisoner assaulted the boss. And this was Mike Samson, the most violent resident of Cheviot. But they went.

There were other ways to keep her safe, though. Samson was handcuffed and the bonds were attached to a metal ring on the floor by the guest chair. The prisoner couldn't stand without bending and couldn't reach anything on the desk. The guards didn't ask who Adley was or, if they didn't already know, why Samson had been brought to her. They shuffled him in, locked him up, and departed to chat up the receptionist while they waited.

Samson was an average man. He didn't look tough, with his pale skin and short brown hair and perfect white teeth, but he scrapped like a ferret and none dared challenge him. To those who didn't know his clout, his reputation, he might appear almost nerd-like and easy fodder, just another middle-aged professional who'd been foolish and dumped amongst wild animals. People had made that mistake in the past. All had regretted it.

The moment the guards vanished, Samson stood as best he could and he and Adley hugged – again, as best they could. Emma just watched from behind her desk as two obviously good friends caught up. She was as nervous as she'd ever been and right now that robust 'compartmentalisation' mechanism of hers failed. She pictured Minny and Joel in pain and distress and it was tough not to shed tears.

The two men swore like teenagers. Samson slapped Adley's gut. 'What you got for me here, Santa?'

Adley took off his jacket and yanked up his shirt, revealing a number of items heavily taped to his torso. Emma watched in horror as Adley peeled away the tape to expose an e-cig, a mobile phone, a Swiss army knife, three little bottles without labels that probably contained drugs – and a very small silver pistol.

Her gasp seemed to remind the two men she was here. As one they looked at her. 'Any trouble with this one?' Samson asked his friend.

'No, boss,' Adley replied. They seemed to have switched from friendship to professional mode. 'Big mouth, but no hassle. She okay with you?'

Samson looked her up and down. 'Yes. And I like having a woman guv. Something nice about being dominated by a pretty woman, even though she's only half a one.'

Emma knew he referred to her missing breast. All the inmates knew, of course. Most never mentioned it, but some were verbally nasty. She said, 'If I'd known you were going to smuggle a gun–'

'You would have done nothing different,' Samson cut in. He aimed the weapon at her. She turned her face to one side, as if that might help if he loosed a bullet at her. It made Samson laugh. He lowered the pistol. 'Beretta Pico. I love this gun. Beretta has stopped making it. That's a shame. But this one still works fine. Don't worry, it will be gone by tonight. As will I. I'm sure you know what you have at stake.'

She nodded. 'I have committed many crimes today, for you. If anyone finds out, that's my job gone and me in prison. So now you have that over me. A very powerful weapon.'

'Oh, and I should let your family go because I don't need them?'

He spoke with scorn, so she knew it was a lost cause. Still, she tried: 'Yes. Let them go.'

The two men laughed, and it ground her nerves. Anger actually helped dull her distress a jot. 'I'll do what you want. You don't need my husband and daughter.'

Samson ejected the magazine from the gun and took out a round. He asked Adley for a felt-tipped pen, and his subordinate grabbed one from Emma's desk. 'So far everything you've done has been with your family under threat, guv,' Samson said. 'You could avoid prison for that. But not if you continued to help after they were released. So, the answer is no. Stop begging because it makes you look weak. Your husband and kid will be set free as soon as I am.'

She paused. He wasn't going to like her next words, but they had to be aired. 'I can't get you out of here. There's just no way.'

Samson began hiding his new property about his person as he responded. 'Horseshit. You're the governor. You just got me a gun, and that's a major achievement. Don't let that missing tit steal your confidence. Let me ease you into the big stuff with something small and simple.' He ejected a bullet from the pistol's magazine. 'There's a guy here that I need. C-wing.'

Emma's throat felt tight. Did Samson want to break another man out of prison? Base Zero was the punishment block for dangerous prisoners, but it wasn't suitable for those deemed a long-term threat to the staff and the prison. They were in C-wing, Samson's home before he trashed another inmate's cell. This was bad. Now the prison's most lethal resident wanted to break free another dangerous man.

She couldn't possibly do it, but nor could she say no. Instead, she just stood there, flustered, mouth moving without sound. But eventually she managed one word: *who?*

'David Pleasance,' Samson said. It was a name she knew. And that changed everything.

Bizarrely, C-wing didn't just house the dangerous, for it had a sub-wing, known simply as the Annex, that held prisoners under threat of attack because of the nature of their convictions. These inmates were mostly child molesters and sex offenders. It wasn't lost on her that these people faced the biggest danger from men who shared their wing, albeit separated by heavy iron gates.

Pleasance had been convicted of raping his neighbour's two young sons. No way was a man like that friends with a gangster like Samson. She asked him why he wanted Pleasance, but the answer was one she feared she already knew.

'Because I'm going to kill him,' Samson said. And there it was.

She shook her head. 'That's too much. You can't ask for that. You want out of this prison and I said I would do–'

His slowly shaking head stopped her dead in her tracks. 'Within the next hour or so, either by hand or by phone, I'll kill someone, guv. You get to pick who. That scumbag Pleasance. Or your pretty daughter.'

TWENTY-FOUR

She was as trapped and under the cosh as any inmate in her prison, but it didn't mean she couldn't bargain. There was one thing she wanted, and she would not take no for an answer.

'I want to speak to my family. Use that new phone of yours. I want to see them on video. To make sure they're okay.'

'Not yet,' Samson told her. 'But you can have proof later. If they're dead, you won't help me out of here. I'd be silly to kill them.'

Being shut down hurt and scared her, but she had to accept that Samson was correct. He was not a dumb man. Joel and Minny were not dead. As to whether that status would last the day was another matter entirely, even if she broke this bastard out of prison. This damn mess needed a solution, and quick.

'I want to go back to my cell,' Samson said, slotting the gun into his sock. 'And make sure there's no cell search today.'

She called her secretary, who sent in the guards. In their presence, the inmate and his Listener trainer shook hands.

'Thanks for seeing me,' Samson said to him. 'I look forward to helping others with what you're going to teach me. There are so many lost souls requiring assistance.'

'No problem,' Adley responded. 'You'll be a great benefit to those in need. They will be lucky to have you. You're a fine man and we need more like you.'

Emma didn't miss the stifled grins on both men's faces. Ironically, the same subterfuge was on the two guards' faces, no doubt because they bought the pantomime but believed the trainer and his pupil were delusional.

Samson held out a hand towards her. 'Thank you, governor.'

A shake? She didn't want to annoy him, so grabbed his hand. She felt him secretly thrust something into it. She knew exactly what it was, and after the shake kept her hand fisted. 'Thanks for your time, Mr Samson.'

When the double-killer and his escorts were gone, Adley sat in the guest chair and blew out his cheeks. 'Nicely done. But that was the easy prologue. How are you going to get my man next to Pleasance? It needs to be somewhere quiet, where cameras can't see. And no one can figure out my man was there.'

Emma ignored him and looked at the item in her palm. A bullet from the pistol magazine. It was small, but Samson had managed to write on the casing in small letters.

MINNY

The message was clear. A bullet meant for her daughter, if he didn't get his way. She shoved it into a drawer. Of course, the threat had always been there, but the bullet, real and touching her skin, added substance. Her breath came in stutters.

Because of her silence, Adley said, 'Oh, I'm sorry. Have you not made your choice yet?' He lifted a wooden coaster from her desk. She'd bought it from Paris five years ago. 'I'll flip this if you like. Blank side Pleasance dies, Eiffel Tower side it's your daughter.'

She was still stunned into silence by the bullet, for somehow it had added a layer of realism to this fiasco. Adley flipped the coaster. Emma stared at it. At an image of France's most famous landmark.

'Well. Minny it is,' Adley said, and he grabbed the landline phone on her desk. 'How do I get an outside line on this?'

He watched her throughout his performance, waiting for a response along the lines of terror and pleading. But she just stared at him. He slammed down the phone. 'Don't fuck about, governor. Get my man next to Pleasance or you'll need six months compassionate leave. See, another threat by me. That's what you've reduced me to. Start talking. How can you get Samson and Pleasance together? We don't have much time.'

She dumped herself in the chair behind her desk, and swivelled to face the window. It put her back to Adley, but she didn't care. She needed time to think. Time, time, time. *Come on, woman. You're good at puzzles, so treat this like one.*

'Face me, governor, and start giving me answers.'

Samson was back in his cell and clueless about happenings in this office. She could avoid his finding out for hours because he was locked in Base Zero. Under her desk was a silent alarm. If she pressed it, guards would storm the room within a minute.

'Last chance, governor. Turn that damn chair around now or your kid is dead.'

Adley could be placed in an empty cell, his detainment kept secret. She could then alert the police. The goons holding her husband and daughter would know nothing of their presence until the cottage was surrounded. They would not be able to escape, but would they give up without hurting her family? If they killed Joel or Minny, they'd get much longer sentences for nothing. Surely they'd surrender without bloodshed...

But if not, Emma would be sentenced also: to overwhelming, debilitating grief. For life.

'Listen, bitch, you need to–'

'Shut your fucking trap and let me think,' she said. Her eyes dropped from the view beyond the window, to the Top Gleam spray bottle on the sill. 'I can get him next to Pleasance. But give me a bloody moment to work out how.'

Adley, clearly shocked at her outburst, didn't know how to react. After stuttering, he settled for the words, 'Well... be quick.'

She turned again to the window and spent two minutes staring across the moors, thinking. Adley used the time to pace around the room, getting faster and faster as his impatience increased. But he remained silent. Until he couldn't bear it any longer. He grabbed her chair and spun it to face him.

'I know a way,' she said before he could utter a word.

'No playing about. A way for my man to kill that bastard Pleasance and get away with it?'

'Yes. Give me a second. Stand aside.'

Adley took two steps back, which allowed her to lift the desk phone. He watched her dial a number. Unknown to him, the number was bogus, but the first key she hit was the speed-dial button for her secretary's pager. Sarah knew she was required to attend the office when the wireless device beeped.

Emma hung up before she'd finished dialling. 'Actually, no, that that won't work. But I have a better idea. The old library.'

Adley folded his arms. 'Start talking.'

'Base Zero only takes up a quarter of the basement because there are some run-down, disused rooms. One is the old library. The space we use for Zero used to be an infirmary a hundred years ago, and you couldn't have people walking through it to access the other areas. So although there's only one entrance into the basement, there are two corridors for separate traffic. Pleasance can get to the old library without passing the cells.'

'And then you can get Samson out of his cell and to the library?'

'Yes. The other corridor also leads to the rooms, but from the other side. Like a loop.'

'Good. He can do that alone? No escort?'

'Yes.'

Adley clearly liked this plan. 'Okay, good. So tell me how you'd get Pleasance to that library.'

Emma stood and approached the window, standing just inches from the sill. She told him the basement suffered from mould and the disused rooms were cleaned once a month. The next planned session wasn't due for a week, but no one would suspect a thing if Emma sent Pleasance down there. Being a model prisoner, he could be left alone to work. 'Besides, I'm the governor. Big cheese supreme commander, remember? What I say goes.'

Adley liked the plan even more. 'Good. 'And how can you get my man into that old library?'

'I don't know yet.'

'Well get thinking hard, you damn bitch. Or call a fucking funeral director for your kid. Oh look, you made me degrade my professionalism again.'

TWENTY-FIVE

At that moment there was a knock at Emma's office door. She glanced at her watch. 'Oh, my meeting. I forgot. Just a moment.'

She got up as the door opened. The secretary, Sarah, stood on the threshold. Before she could utter a word – like a condemning *You buzzed me?* – Emma said, 'Sarah, I'll be with you in a sec. Head back to your office.'

When the secretary was gone, Adley said, 'What's this about a meeting?'

'I have to respond to a subject access request Zoom meeting. I'll be half an hour.'

On her way to the door, she was halted by a hand around her arm. 'What meeting? Is it more important than your daughter?'

She yanked her arm away. 'It is to you. Your people sent me here and told me to act normal. Do all my normal duties. This is one of them. If I ignore this meeting, I'll have an agency board director down here asking questions. Do you want that?'

'I don't like this.'

'Bad luck. Look, I'll use the time in the meeting to think of a plan for getting Samson out of his cell. If I planned to trick you,

I could have done that after I left the coffee shop. Stop being paranoid and just sit and wait. If there's a problem, I'll call this office phone, so make sure you answer it.'

Adley took a deep breath. He was obviously upset about this distraction, but knew he could do nothing about it. 'There had better not be a problem. Thirty minutes, governor. On number thirty-one, I make a phone call about your kid. Understand?'

'I've heard this threat enough times to fully grasp things,' Emma said, then proceeded for the door.

Outside, she removed the bottle of Top Gleam from its hiding spot under her suit jacket. She entered her secretary's office and said, 'I buzzed you for a uniform ordering form. Have you got one?' The secretary fished in a desk drawer and handed one over. Emma thanked her and added, 'Do me a favour and call B-wing and tell them I'm popping down.'

Next, Emma headed down to the Hub, where she collared an officer about to head into C-wing and gave him the bottle of Top Gleam. He was given an express order to put it C-wing's cleaning store ASAP.

B-wing's supervisor was waiting at the gate for her. Behind him, various prisoners moved here and there. These were men on their way to work or education, while the remaining prisoners were locked in their cells until lunchtime. She waved the uniform order form, folded into anonymity, at him. 'I need to check something in Alain Johnson's testimony.'

The supervisor didn't need clarification. He knew that Johnson had last week written a statement regarding a vape pen containing a drug called spice that had been found on a break room table – a statement that had amounted to *I know nothing*. She was taken to the inmate's cell. The guard ordered the bunkmate out, but then expressed dismay when Emma said she wanted to talk to Johnson alone. Guard and bunkmate lurked outside the open cell door.

The prisoner was in his twenties, but his excess fat and bad skin made him look twice that. He was a drug addict, sentenced to three years for dealing, and known as someone who could smuggle in illicit substances, although it had never been proved. Given the fear on his face, he probably thought Emma was here because such proof now existed.

She spoke quietly because of nearby ears. 'I know you use spice.'

'No secret,' Johnson said. 'But not in here. No way. That bottle you people found wasn't mine. Told you that.'

She sat on his bed. He shifted his feet and inched away, as if worried she might strike him. In a whisper, she said, 'I will do you a deal, Alain. Off the record. I will get you a job in the kitchen, which I know you want. I'll get you extended time out of your cell. I'll be more open to requests you have.'

He eyed her suspiciously. He, too, whispered. 'Why would you do that? What's in it for you? You want names, is that right? Who says I know any?'

'There are men in here that you don't get on with. I can help fast-track a transfer to any prison you want. I can make sure time comes off your sentence. I don't want names. I want spice. In e-cig liquid form, same as we found in that vape pen.'

Now he was more suspicious. 'You want me to admit I can get spice? Sounds like you want me to incriminate myself. I can't get hold of the stuff.'

'We found that pen out of the blue. That's what all the inmates think. And they'll think the same if I was to stumble across more of it. If that happened, I'd be very happy and I would do what I just said I'll do. That's a promise.'

Johnson thought for a few seconds. 'I can't get that stuff… but I heard some whispers…'

TWENTY-SIX

It was 10.58 when she arrived at the gym. The prisoners allocated to using it weren't due in until 11.30, so that gave her time alone. Unfortunately, solitude and silence opened the door for painful thoughts of her family.

There were three triceps weight bars and she found what she wanted in the second. The bars were hollow. When she plucked off an end cap and peered inside, she saw the end of a length of string taped to the interior. Yanking the string heaved out exactly what she was after. A 10ml vape liquid bottle. It had no label and the liquid inside was a grimy yellow. Spice. She put it in her pocket and left the gym.

She used her watch to call her secretary for a transfer to her office phone, which Adley thankfully answered, albeit without speaking. 'It's me,' she said. 'I got waylaid. I'll be back in five minutes.'

'In six I'll call the boys and—'

She hung up. She called her secretary again, this time for details of the staff due in at midday. She picked one name, found that employee's mobile number, and called it.

She asked the male staff member for a favour. She needed a

birthday present for a friend, had no time to get out, so could he please pick up a miniature bottle of whisky? Sure he could, and yes, just one. She instructed the man to take it personally to her office as soon as he arrived, and put it in a desk drawer.

After that, she returned to her office, where Adley was just about climbing the walls. He started berating her, and threatening again to kill her daughter. For a man unwilling to go down the road of threats, he seemed all about nothing else now.

'Oh, shut the hell up,' she told him.

'Are you for real?' he said, snatching up her desk phone. 'You want me to have your daughter's head cut off right now? It takes just one call.'

She folded her arms. 'Do it. Have her killed, then we'll head on down to Base Zero and you can tell Samson he's doing the next thirty-six years because you can't control your impatience. Do it.'

Adley said nothing, and she knew she had him. Stalemate. For now. But she had no illusion that she was in control here. If things went as planned, Samson would be outside this prison before long, but her family would still be captive. If he chose to kill Minny and Joel, possibly for insolence, she couldn't prevent it.

'I told you I have duties to do in this prison, Mr Adley. I need to juggle those and what you're blackmailing me to do. I need some leeway. Let me do my thing, and you'll get yours.'

Adley took a few breaths to get his anger under control. 'Well, guv, any other little tasks you need to take care of? Any emails to send? Anyone need a new toothbrush? Any blocked toilets to fix?'

'For now, no.'

'Then how do you get Samson into that old library? And have you arranged for Pleasance to be there?'

'Not yet. I haven't spoken to him. I was going to do that before I remembered my meeting. You know that.'

'Then let's get it done. Make the call right now. Tell him he's on the new cleaning schedule and then hang up.'

She told him it wasn't quite so easy. Pleasance was a vulnerable C-wing prisoner with a previous suicide attempt, and for those guys to be allowed to work in other wings, well, 'Governors need to do a risk assessment.'

'Piss off,' Adley said, all his earlier professionalism seemingly on holiday. 'Let me guess: forms to fill in, phone calls to make? You're delaying.'

'No. Relax. I just need to ask him if he's likely to try to harm himself if he's left unsupervised. It might seem silly because he could tell me anything, but that's the way of it. It's called an F10 interview, and there is a form to fill in, but I can do that within the next three days. However, I do have to speak to him face to face.'

Adley strode to the door and opened it. 'Let's go.'

Emma froze. 'You can't come. You should wait here.'

'No. I want to see the bastard.'

'That's not a good idea. My staff might—'

'Might nothing, Mrs Catalano. You're the governor. Remember what you just said about the big cheese supreme commander? Do you really think I'm going to let you talk to Pleasance alone? So you can tip him off? I'm going to stand right next to you and listen to every word so there's no tricks. Because if there's any funny business, like a warning or something, well, you know what happens, right?'

'Actually, no,' she said with a sarcastic smile. 'I don't think you've ever mentioned it before.'

With Jek back upstairs, Hyde fetched Joel's laptop from the bedroom and set it up on the kitchen table. He found a fresh roll of thick black tape in a garden storage bin and used it to bind Joel to the kitchen chair, this time around the legs and waist but with the arms free to type. Being close to the man gave him an urge to cause pain, so he drove a boot hard into an ankle, and enjoyed the yelp of pain it caused.

When the job was done, he tested the bonds for sturdiness and said, 'I just had a nosey round your room while I got the computer. I sniffed your missus's knickers. That anger you? No one-tit bras up there or padded ones. It piss you off that she's just got one tit?'

Joel shook his head. 'I'm more worried about dying, to be honest.'

'There's a massive Rubik's cube up there. That hers?'

Joel nodded. 'She likes puzzles. Tests. Anything that taxes the brain. Once she has a problem to solve, it takes over her. Solved her first Rubik's aged eight.'

'I'm thinking about smashing it and making you eat all the pieces. Would she hate that?'

He saw the disappointment on Joel's face. The fool must have thought his captor was making serious conversation. Maybe he'd hoped to make a new friend and cut the chances of getting himself stabbed up.

'Don't tell her if you do smash it,' Joel said. 'She might do something to piss off your boss.'

Hyde gave this some thought as he locked the back door and kitchen window and pocketed both keys. He decided not to destroy the Rubik's cube. Just in case the husband had a point. The governor might be madly attached to the cube, and liable to act in a dangerous way if it got busted.

'If you try any shit on that computer, like emailing someone to tell them what's going on, you'll regret it,' he said. He pinched the man's nose, driving a thumbnail into the flesh deep enough to leave a half-moon depression that welled with blood.

'I won't,' Joel promised, blinking fast against the pain.

'Any shit and I'll go upstairs and impregnate your daughter.'

'I won't. I promise.'

'She'll have a little baby me, so you'll see my face every day.'

'He'll be bald at first, too.'

Hyde understood that the man was joking, but it hinted at something he didn't like. A lack of fear? Another sly attempt to bond? Whatever the reason, that joke and the Rubik's cube crack told him this guy was getting too comfortable. Hyde changed the dynamic with a hard punch to the side of Joel's head, which almost toppled him and his chair. 'That's a reminder that I'm the boss here and you're on the edge of death. No more fucking cheek. Get my money.'

Hyde sat at the table, facing Joel. He played on his phone, but checked the laptop screen every minute or so. It was full of stuff that looked like machine code. Way beyond him, but it looked good. After the fifth check, he said, 'What are you doing now?'

'Bypassing the bank server. This bit takes about half an hour.'

Hyde nodded, happy. He had no idea that the computer was talking to no other, nor even accessing the internet. Onscreen was Command Prompt, a text-based interface for executing commands on Windows. Using this to fool Hyde had been Jek's idea, for he knew his brutish partner wouldn't know what the hell he was looking at, but the black screen and technical jargon would seem impressive.

Hyde headed into the living room, to stare out the window. Something wouldn't stop buzzing inside his head. Just minutes later, he had to yield to it. He sneaked out of the living room and up the stairs. He knocked on the door to Minny's bedroom.

'What's up?' Jek called out.

'You finished with her? My turn.'

Jek opened the door and slipped out. Hyde didn't even get a glimpse of the girl on the bed. 'Seems you're done if you're dressed. I want a piece.'

Jek shook his head. 'You don't, mate. Check this out.'

He opened the door and stepped in. Hyde watched him yank the quilt from the bed, to fully expose the girl. She was clothed, but those garments were splattered, soaked even.

'Is that shit?'

'Diarrhoea. But I ain't letting her run to the toilet every five minutes.'

'That's fucking nasty.' Hyde gagged. The quilt and bottom sheet were ruined. She looked about as uncomfortable as anyone could without suffering pain.

'You can fucking keep her, mate,' he said, averting his eyes.

'I'm hardly touching her now. Even if she showers, that stuff's going to be in nooks and crannies. How's the money coming?'

Staring at the carpet, Hyde said, 'Some server shit we're waiting for. I'll leave you two to have fun. Hey, tie her up so she doesn't run.'

'Oh, right. Yeah, I forgot. Cheers.'

When Hyde was gone, Jek shut the door and sat blocking it. 'It worked,' Minny said. 'Thank you. But perhaps we could have said I have crabs or something.'

'Wouldn't stop him. He might make you shower after all. But for now we're good. I'm sorry.'

'It's my faeces, so it's not that bad. I mean compared to the foulness of touching him.'

She sounded sincere, but it was probably an act. He knew she was a girl who prided herself on looks and cleanliness. 'I'm sorry. It was the only way.'

'Don't apologise. It stopped that animal raping me. So... who is he to you? What relation?'

Jek looked at her curiously. 'What makes you think we're relations?'

'Earlier. You called him "my", but then stopped yourself. I thought you were going to say brother.'

Jek nodded, appreciating her intelligence. 'Step uncle.'

'Okay. Brother of a man your mum married?'

Jek nodded. 'I didn't know my real dad, but I hear he died in Venezuela. Stuffed the wrong people on a drug deal. I don't even know why he was over there. I was a baby.'

'That's terrible,' Minny said.

'My mum wanted the drugs. She was on them her whole life, and they killed her. I was sixteen.'

She shook her head. 'That's horrible. I'm sorry.'

'It gets worse. Hyde took me in.'

It was a joke, but he understood why she was in no zone for laughter. He continued. 'My mum met my step-dad when I was ten. I knew Hyde from that age, and I looked up to him. He took me in when she died. I needed somewhere to live.'

'But how did you get into crime? From him?'

'He was a career criminal and for sure it rubbed off during my formative years. But my parents were drug addict criminals, so I can hardly blame Hyde for everything. However, he did show me the ropes, and he got me in with the gang he was part of. I know you probably think it's the wrong style of life, but it's all I know.'

'Have you got a girlfriend? What does she think of it? Is she worried that you could be arrested and go to prison?'

He laughed. 'Your mum might end up in charge of me. How's she finding that, anyway? Sounds like it must be hard. She's surrounded by dangerous men.'

Minny shrugged. 'She won't say much. We don't get on that well. You know that old movie cliché about cops being married to the job and sidelining the family? Yeah, that's her. But she reckons it's okay working there. Having a woman around eases the tension in an all-male environment, she reckons. Blokes are nicer around her. Not all, of course.'

'And how does your dad fit in? Get on with him better? What's it like for him to work at a bank?'

She gave him a long stare. 'You avoided my question about a girlfriend.'

He looked away from her. 'Yes, I have one. Until we agree to split up, I have one.'

He knew she found his statement strange, and that she would ask more questions. When she raised a hand to scratch her face, but stopped upon realising it was stained with faeces, he changed the subject with, 'Why don't you shower now? We can't leave you like this. I can stop Hyde another way if he comes at you again.'

Minny nodded. 'That would be nice. If you can save me until your job is done. I hope my mum can release your friend from her prison. I'm guessing he's the boss of this gang that you're in.'

'I hope so, too. And yes, the big boss. Once he's free, we'll be out of your hair. So, go have your shower.'

She got off the bed and headed into the en suite. She stripped naked and stepped into the spray, although it was cold because the boiler was busted. She made no attempt to stand out of sight. She even left the door open while she showered.

When the mess was washed away, she emerged wearing a tiny towel that barely covered her chest and hips.

Jek didn't fall for the trick. She hoped to entice him, make him like her more, to guarantee that he'd do what he could to help her. He said, 'I made you a promise that you wouldn't be hurt. So please get a bigger towel.'

She gave him a sincere smile. He headed to the wardrobe, but found it empty of anything except padded coat hangers. 'Where's your clothing?'

She walked to her suitcase and unzipped it. 'I stayed downstairs last night and never got round to unpacking.'

'Don't wear anything sexy,' he told her as he turned away so she could dress. When she said she was done, he found her standing in tight jeans and a jumper.

'I know this is probably sexy,' she said. 'But these jeans are hard to get on even when I try. So they'll be hell to get off without my consent.'

He understood and gave a nod. 'Stand back while I strip this bed.'

She watched him work. A minute in, as he was balling up the quit and bottom sheet, she said, 'Is my dad going to survive this?'

Just like before, he was silent a moment before answering yes. He realised that pause was an answer all by itself.

TWENTY-EIGHT

A couple of months back David Pleasance had chatted to Emma, in her office, about his alcohol addiction and how he was finally getting to grips with abstinence. He'd entered prison as a serious alcoholic, but the lack of it inside, he'd said, had helped him kick the habit.

She used this to attach Adley to her side when she visited him, telling officers that, as a Samaritan, he could offer Pleasance some words of advice. It was 11.45 by the time they reached his cell in C-wing's Annex, for she had burned some time by reading emails that she'd told Adley were urgent.

Pleasance was skinny but had a fat belly from years of drinking. He was bald on top but had wiry ginger hair on the sides and back. His bunkmate was at a class, so they were alone. No guard was required in the cell because Pleasance wasn't violent, was barely over five-feet tall, and walked with a limp from a childhood bike accident.

'Guv. Hello,' he said when his visitors walked in. He lay on his bed, reading a novel. He smiled at Emma but eyed Adley suspiciously. 'Any problems?'

'No,' she said. 'Pay my guest no mind. Just a visitor checking how I do things. I have some news for you. I decided to reward you with an afternoon out of your cell.'

Pleasance nodded. 'I like that idea. Did I do something good?'

'It's just a little something for being a model prisoner. I don't think I've ever seen your name on a report card.'

'I try to be good, guv. No sense making your time here, or mine, harder.'

Emma smiled. 'Maybe I made that sound better than it really is. It's not really an afternoon out. I need someone to clean the old library. Down in the basement. But it breaks up the monotony. You game? I'll call it work and pay you.'

'I'm game,' Pleasance said, sitting up. He was still eyeing Adley warily and, when she glanced back, she knew why. The man in the suit wore a face of anger, as if he wanted to attack the prisoner right then and there. Child molesters could have that effect on some, and Pleasance knew it.

'Good man,' she told the inmate. 'After lunch, okay? I'll send an officer for you.'

'Smith,' Adley said. 'It'll be Smith. She's on this wing today.'

Emma looked at him and, to her, Adley said, 'You told me Smith is a good guard. She will make sure all goes according to plan.'

'I won't try anything funny,' Pleasance said. Of course, he had no idea of the subtle message Adley was delivering.

Adley said, 'You need to keep this quiet, Mr Pleasance. You're getting a favour here, and other prisoners will moan if they know. Governor Catalano here is going to tell the wing supervisor that you're going to her office, but Smith will take you to the old library. Don't mention it to anyone or it will be the last favour you get. Understand?'

If Pleasance found it strange that a visitor was calling the shots, he didn't show it. 'Sure thing. Mum's the word.'

Adley said it was time to go, so he and Emma headed for the door. In the doorway, she stopped and turned her head. 'Do a good job of the cleaning, Mr Pleasance. No intentional half-measures in the hope that you can get extra time out of your cell to finish the job. Use Arco Floor Scrub on the floor. Cillit Bang for the mould on the walls. Top Gleam is best for the brass door handle. Got it?'

Pleasance gave a thumbs up. Adley and Emma left the cell. While walking towards the Annex gate, which would take them into C-wing proper, he said, 'What was that crap about Cillit Bang and door handles and stuff? A code?'

'You tell me. Decipher it. Cillit Bang. Can you rearrange the letters to spell *don't leave your cell?* Brass door handles – might that be prison jargon for *it's a trap?*'

'Cut the cheek. If you play any kind of trick, you'll need more than Cillit fucking Bang to get your kid's guts off the walls.'

Emma didn't respond, but inside she was in turmoil, as with every time Adley made a threat. She needed to delay their return to the office. It was lunchtime and C-wing's cells were emptying, which made movement slower. More helpful in burning time was a guard in the Hub who had a query about his wages. Emma took her sweet time answering his question and she and Adley got back to her office at 12.24pm.

She sat behind her desk and lifted a notebook, to put it in a drawer. She only wanted to see if her gift had been delivered, and it had. There, amongst the paperwork, was a 5cl bottle of Talisker whisky. She slipped it into a pocket when Adley looked at a picture on her wall.

'What's this, first day?'

The image showed her outside HMP Bronzefield, wearing her uniform for her inaugural shift as a prison officer. 'Yes. Taken in 2002.'

'Back when you had two tits, right? You actually look quite sexy there. Lord knows what happened. Bronzefield is for women, right?'

'Right. A lot of tits in there.'

He laughed. 'Now you look after men. That hard? Serious question.'

'No. The male staff treat me worse than the inmates.'

'Ever been attacked?'

'Here and there. Nothing requiring hospital. Someone tried to throw boiling water at me on my first week as governor here.'

'You have that effect. What happened to him?'

'A lot of male inmates here like me. They didn't like that that attack might have gotten me time away, or moved to another facility.'

'The attacker was attacked?'

'Yes. And no, I didn't like that, in case you ask.'

He turned to her. 'Well, if our plan goes well, there's a chance nobody will find out what you did. So you might keep your job, and get to continue keeping all this testosterone in check.' He sat in the guest chair, feet up on the desk. He checked his watch. 'You said the paedos have lunch at a different time, right? One till one forty-five. So we'll get Samson out of his cell at two, which is when Pleasance should be about entering the library. Let's hear your plan for that, smart arse.'

This guy's true personality had emerged, and she hated the sight of him. Plus, he'd had that stupid shit-eating grin on his face for the last two minutes. So she turned her chair towards the window and gave him her back. 'Why did you tell Pleasance that he had to pretend he was coming here?'

'Because he's going to be found dead in that old library. It won't look good for you if everyone knows you sent him there. We can't risk having you under suspicion. You get removed, Samson doesn't get out. So, right now, call the Annex guards and say you want to speak to Pleasance in your office at 2pm, and that you're sending Smith to collect him. Smith will detour him to the library without anyone knowing.'

Emma felt her heart thud, and she turned to face Adley again. 'Smith might be blamed if Pleasance is killed.'

'*When* he's killed. And if it's not her, it's you. Would you prefer that? Besides, Smith is going to willingly take the blame and your name won't be mentioned. She'll say she put him in that library in the hopes that he'd get killed. Case closed. She just doesn't know it yet. Now, I'll repeat my question. How will you get Samson out of his cell at 2pm?'

'I'm still working on it.'

'Work fast. Pretend your kid's life is at stake.'

Adley ordered Emma to request a meeting with the young female called Smith. When she entered Emma's office and saw Adley, the officer froze. It was clear that she knew and didn't like this man. Join the club. She did her best to ignore him as she sat in the guest chair.

Adley didn't allow himself to be ignored. He sat on the desk, his legs right by Smith's, and glared down at her. 'We have another job for you.'

Emma stood up. 'I'm going to leave you two to chat and take care of something.'

Adley grabbed her arm as she walked past him. 'Something not dodgy, I hope.'

'Something I do every day. Sign off prisoner wages. So don't ever touch me again.' She yanked her arm free and left the room.

She headed down to the Hub and into C-wing, which was empty because everyone was at lunch. She asked a guard to unlock the cleaning store before sending him on his way. The store contained all the wing's mops, brushes and myriad other cleaning products. There was only one bottle of Top Gleam glass cleaner because it wasn't on the purchasing list – she'd brought that sole item from home.

She moved it to the centre edge of a shelf, so it was unmissable. Job done, she returned to her office, where Smith was on her feet, getting ready to leave. The young officer was crying and Adley watched without emotion.

Emma knew why. To Adley she said, 'So, you told this lady she has to feed herself into the meat grinder and expect no help from you. Well done, big man.'

Adley jerked a finger at the exit, indicating that Smith should leave. When she was gone, he said, 'Don't jump the damn gun, governor. There's been a change. On your orders, which you'll give at 2pm, Smith will collect Pleasance to go to the library. For the cleaning job you gave him. Since we can't risk that he hasn't told someone. But Smith will suddenly need a shit and leave him alone there. She'll survive that, might even keep her job. I don't know why she was crying.'

'Me neither, I guess. Can't be that she's about to lead a man to his death. That would be silly.'

Her sarcasm was overlooked. 'No more messing about. Your plan for getting Samson out of his cell and into the library?'

Emma slumped in her chair. 'The guards' office is right across from the Base Zero cells so they can be watched at all times.'

'That sounds bad.'

'But the office is in the middle of the room, and it has a separate break room at the back. With a trapdoor in the ceiling, just in case prisoners take control of the security office.'

'That sounds better.'

'For his sweet intention to become a Listener and help others–'

'Less sarcasm, please.'

'–I can arrange for Samson to clean that break room. The

guard will remain in the office if I get him to do some paperwork. Samson can sneak out through that trapdoor and down the corridor unseen.'

Adley was surprised. 'All the way to the library and those other rooms? And just wander around? With just one guard down there?'

'Yes, there are portions of this prison that retain old designs that would be considered a security issue. Yes, my staff get lax sometimes and we've had people go wandering before. That said, we never allow more than a single Base Zero prisoner out at any one time, and we always have a second guard present if someone is let out for cleaning duties or exercise. But I'll arrange for that not to happen.'

'Still. It seems like you people are asking for trouble. I guess you'll only learn the hard way when one of your people is shanked.'

'There's no way out of that basement without the keys to the gate at the foot of the stairs leading up to B-wing. Even if someone had them, a B-wing guard has to open another gate at the top of those stairs. And even if an escapee somehow got through that, where are they? A locked-down B-wing.'

'Then that's going to cause you a headache when it's time to get my man free.'

Emma hadn't yet thought that far ahead. She still retained hope that she'd never have to tackle that problem.

'What about cameras?' Adley said.

'Yes, there are cameras. Samson will be seen in the corridor, and he'll be seen going into the library.'

'There's a camera in the old library?'

Emma shook her head and told him none of the individual empty rooms had surveillance. But the corridor CCTV would capture Samson heading into a place where a man would thereafter be found dead.

'Doesn't matter as long as nobody is watching in time to stop him,' Adley said. 'Samson will go inside that library, come out thirty seconds later, and then yell that he's found a body. Poor old Pleasance decided to kill himself by bashing his own head against a wall. All that guilt. Won't matter if Samson is the only one around. It's what they can prove, not what they know.'

Emma took a deep breath, but hid her upset. 'Not a slogan that worked for Samson, is it?'

Adley let the crack slide. He moved to Emma's security station and sat, and tapped one of the monitors. 'We'll watch it all unfold from here. Live and unedited. One hour to go.'

Adley passed the time by playing with the cameras and watching the prison, like a kid with a toy. Emma spent it chewing her fingernails, like a child drowning in dread.

THIRTY

Hyde paced in the living room, needing to burn energy.

No, that wasn't what itched his mind. He was worried about the plan, that it would all go wrong and...

No, that wasn't it, either. It was the girl. He wanted a shot with her, but taking it would annoy Jek and...

That wasn't the problem, either. His forearms burned and when he looked down, he saw both fists tightly clenched. He hadn't even realised he'd closed them. His breathing was also fast.

He headed into the kitchen, stopping a few feet behind Joel. The man was locked tight to the chair by tape, but his head was free to move. It didn't turn in Hyde's direction, even though he must have heard the bigger man enter the room. He did stop typing, however.

Hyde went to the fridge, grabbed a block of cheese, and took it to the chopping board. When he snatched up a breadknife, the hand holding it started to shake.

He bit off a portion of the cheese instead and circled behind Joel. His captive leaned forward as much as the tape would allow, obviously fearful of another strike. Maybe he'd seen the knife in Hyde's hand.

'I'll have your money soon,' he said, his voice cracking.

Oh yeah, he was worried about the knife. Hyde put the sharp point of it against the back of the man's neck. As if the blade was electrified, Joel stiffened. Hyde stared at where metal met flesh, fascinated by the way the point dimpled the skin. His hand vibrated even more, and the knife tapped at Joel's neck like a tattoo gun.

'Please don't hurt me again,' Joel moaned.

Now Hyde knew what had overcome him. He had to fight the pulsing desire to slam the blade into flesh. It was as if another invisible hand tried to push against the hilt. He almost lost that fight.

And might have if a noise hadn't shattered his trance. The crunch of a vehicle's wheels on the track outside.

Joel and murder forgotten for the moment, Hyde ran to the living room window and saw a motorbike closing on the cottage. It had a vintage racer-style, but it wasn't an old bike. The quiet engine, probably electric, told him that much.

Hyde bit down his panic, knowing he had an answer if this guy turned out to be a threat. Samson had been given no orders to spare bit players. He stood beside the front door to wait for a knock.

No knock came. He saw the man's shape through the pebbled glass as he walked by and probably around back. Hyde rushed into the kitchen.

'Don't make a fucking sound or you're dead,' he told Joel as he passed him. He opened the back door. The man, who wore the requisite outfit for a biker and a knapsack, hadn't been headed here, though. He'd walked past the cottage, towards the woods. The puzzle of where he was going was answered when the man stopped at the boiler enclosure and stuck a key in the padlock.

That was when the guy turned his head and saw Hyde in the doorway. He waved. 'Hey. Name's Darren. My mum-in-law sent me. Boiler on the blink? Sorry about the key.'

Hyde stepped out and shut the door behind him. He walked towards the man. 'Oh, yes. Thanks.' He had no idea what the guy was talking about.

The stranger dumped his knapsack, unzipped it, and tipped out the contents. Tools. He opened the enclosure door to expose the boiler and grabbed a penlight. 'So you're here with Joel and the family? He works with my mum.'

'They just call you?'

'Just? Nah. Got a text last night about this thing. Again, sorry I didn't leave a key.'

Last night. So nobody had gotten a secret message out after the kidnapping. Hyde realised he'd been silly to assume otherwise: what prisoner would call for help, yet for a boiler repair instead of rescue? 'No probs. Is it just you here?'

The guy got on his hands and knees and shone the penlight into the enclosure. 'Yeah. The missus is at the hairdresser. You know, this thing is more hassle than it's worth. Good for space saving and no indoor noise, but the weather messes it up all the time. Fox got to the buried pipes once. Hand me that yellow flathead screwdriver, would you?'

'Sure thing,' Hyde said. He grabbed the requested item, holding it like an inverted dagger. And then, without pause, he raised it high and dragged it down, driving the metal shaft hard and deep into the top of the man's skull. The crack of bone was louder than the man's single, weak grunt of shock or pain.

Hyde stared at the convulsing body, half in disbelief. The man kicked and thrashed for almost thirty seconds, no additional moan escaping his throat, and then lay still. There was no blood, weirdly. In the following silence, Hyde waited for a flood of emotion, for panic and fear to wreak havoc with his system.

It didn't happen.

He had assaulted, maimed, and disfigured many over the years, but nobody had ever died. Hammering someone but leaving them alive... it was akin to fucking a woman and not blowing your load. Other men he knew in Samson's crew had popped the cherry and he'd long been jealous. He had always wondered what it would feel like. Would his psyche be able to handle it? Was it like Marmite: you loved it or you hated it?

Well, now he had his answer. His first ever murder, and what was the result? Not a frozen mind, a fried brain, or a palpitating heart. Instead: contentment. Load blown.

He felt fucking great.

But he didn't have time for patting his own back. Out on the street, in everyday life, murders were highly risky endeavours. Here he operated behind Samson's armour, but it didn't mean he was in the clear. He had to hide this body before some rambler appeared. Besides, Jek would moan if he knew someone was dead. He wouldn't understand that this had been necessary.

Nor would he understand that the boiler repairman's sacrifice had probably saved Joel's life. For now.

Hyde quickly stuffed the body into the enclosure, which wasn't easy because there was little space around the boiler. He left the screwdriver sticking out of the man's head, figuring it acted like a plug that stopped blood spraying everywhere. He had to prod and fold and hammer some body parts into place, and put his shoulder against the door to close it, but he got the job done. A glance into the woods and at the windows of the cottage convinced him that the dead guy was his personal little secret.

The bike! He replaced the padlock. The key went into the

man's knapsack and that item found a new home in one of the wheelie bins by the back door. Hyde then rushed to the front of the property for the vehicle. He wheeled it into the woods and found a fallen tree whose unearthed roots had left a deep depression. In went the bike. Hyde kicked and threw leaves and twigs to fill the hole and submerge the last trace of his crime.

The immediate problem was erased, but his paranoia was up. The boiler guy had arrived unannounced and there was no telling who knew he was here or how soon he'd be missed. It was time to change things up.

THIRTY-ONE

'He's coming.'

Sitting on the bed, Minny heard nothing at first, but the banging on the door seconds later was unmistakable. Jek rushed to her and quickly cinched a zip tie around her wrist, securing her again to the headboard. He apologised for it.

When Jek opened the door, Hyde strode in and straight to the captive. 'Good, you cleaned her,' he said. He tried to yank her from the bed, but the zip tie prevented it. It bit painfully into her flesh as her arm was pulled tight.

'What's going on?' Jek said.

Hyde extracted a pocketknife and cut the zip tie, but he was careless and nicked Minny's wrist. She refused to make a noise, aware that this big brute enjoyed seeing people suffer and beg.

'Downstairs,' was the only explanation he gave.

Holding her elbow, he dragged her down the stairs so fast she almost tripped. Jek followed, asking for answers, but Hyde said nothing.

In the kitchen, she saw her father tied tightly to a chair. He was working on his laptop at the kitchen table. On that table were a bottle of gin, three-quarters empty, and her mother's giant Rubik's cube. And a steak knife.

'Minny,' he said. 'Hey, leave her alone.'

Hyde slapped her dad hard in the side of the head. 'Stay fucking silent or I'll cut her in front of you.'

Father and daughter fell mute. Hyde forced her into a chair, facing her dad across the table. He pushed her forearms flat onto the polished wood and ordered her to stay still. Then he grabbed thick black tape and secured her in place with eight or nine strips. She knew the weak bonds would falter if she pulled hard, but freeing herself would only enrage this monster further. So she remained still.

His task done, Hyde sat in another chair, facing them both. He snatched up the gin for three heavy gulps. Minny looked round to see Jek standing behind her.

'My girl just called,' Hyde said. He picked up the giant Rubik's cube and turned one edge. 'Someone came to the van in the pub car park, started badgering her about why she was here. So I don't know how long we've got before someone else comes here noseying. I want to see a bank transfer, and real soon.'

'Someone else?' Jek said.

Hyde paused. 'People walk by and stuff.' He pointed at a wall clock. 'It's one o'clock. We're going to sit here for thirty minutes. At half one, you give me what I want or your kid gets...' He picked up the steak knife and drove it into the table. Point buried in the wood, it stood upright between the two captives, a big and obvious sign.

'It takes time,' Jek said.

'And he's got some. Be quiet, Jek.'

Minny had no idea what her father was doing, but he typed on his computer. A few minutes in, all of it suffered in silence, Hyde finished his gin and got up. 'Watch these two a minute.'

When he shifted into the living room, Minny turned to Jek with pleading eyes. 'Can you help us?'

Jek's response was to her father. 'Can you access your online banking right now, without having to hunt out passwords or use your phone?'

Joel nodded. 'But I don't have the kind of money he wants.'

'Just do what I say. Load up your bank info and transfer £5 from one account to another, and then shut down the depositing account and just leave the other one open. Do it fast, but jump back to the Command Prompt window if he tries to look. Use the alt-tab shortcut.'

Hyde was soon back, a fresh bottle of gin in his giant fist. When he retook his chair, he pointed at the empty one opposite. Jek eased into it, and now all four of them were in a square at the table.

When Hyde lifted a hand, about to grab the laptop, Jek said, 'Hyde, Minny here does YouTube videos. She doesn't know you're an actor. Show her.'

Minny had no interest, of course, but she noted what Jek had done: distracted the big brute from looking at her father's laptop. So she went along with it. 'An actor? What have you been in?'

Hyde forgot about the laptop. He pulled out his phone. 'What's your channel name?'

She gave it. He clicked on a video, whose audio played to the room. She recognised the video instantly, of course. It had 19,000 views, but she felt disgusted knowing this man was watching her apply make-up.

She glanced at Jek. He had his mobile phone in his left hand, screen turned slightly so her father could see it. The laptop, turned slightly, blocked Hyde's view of it. Not that he was looking anyway, too focused was he on watching a digital Minny make herself beautiful.

'So what's this film you've been in?' she asked.

Hyde answered without looking up. 'I've got an agent. I've only done this one so far, but my acting was praised. Check this out.'

He typed something then turned the phone towards her. Another YouTube video. It was called NO COMEBACKS (2021) – WILD GOOSE FIGHT CLIP. He pressed play. The movie scene involved a bar loaded with tough-looking, leather-clad biker-types. Two handsome men in suits walked in and one kicked the jukebox, killing the music. They demanded to know where someone called Dragonslayer was.

The gang of bikers laughed, then three bruisers stepped forward and told the suited men to piss off, or trouble was a-brewing. The centre guy was Hyde, who didn't need cosmetic aid to appear mean as hell. One of his partners jabbed a finger and said, 'Who the hell are you fools?'

One of the suited men said, 'The wrong guys to mess with.'

The bruiser snarled and leaped forward to throw a punch. He was kicked in the nuts and went down. Hyde's character stepped up next and was floored with a spinning kick. There was more to the cheesy fight scene, but Hyde stopped the video there.

'Good, eh?' Hyde said. 'That's my only film, but I've got some profile videos.'

Her father and Jek were still busy working some kind of trick, and she knew she had to keep this fool distracted. 'Oh. Show me some.'

What she didn't know was that Jek was giving instructions to her father via text. It took three more minutes, and throughout, Minny was shown numerous images on Hyde's phone. His portfolio of headshots was clearly not a professional creation, but Hyde had made some effort. She saw him mostly depicted as a thug, including one photo where he was dressed as a barbarian, but there were some curious anomalies. He played a businessman in a suit, a postman, and even a smiling doctor. That one almost made her laugh.

'We've got the first transfer,' Jek said.

Hyde slid his phone towards Minny, as if believing she would opt to continue soaking up images of his nasty bulldog face. He turned the laptop and scanned the screen, and his eyebrows raised in surprise. Minny, unable to see, didn't know that he was looking at the bank account of one Ray Smith, who had savings of over £100,000.

'Jesus,' he said, laughing. 'Get typing again. Do another fake account. Put another hundred grand into it. So how do I get a bank card to get that cash?'

'You have to use the account number and sort code,' Joel said.

Hyde lost his smile, so Jek stepped in quickly. 'Oh, that's easy. We could get the first two grand tomorrow. And more every day. Two grand a day. That's awesome.'

He raised a hand for a high-five over the table. Ever suspicious and paranoid, Hyde wasn't sure this was cause for celebration. But in the end he decided he should be happy because he slapped Jek's palm. 'Okay. Go get us two grand right now,' he said.

'But his bank shuts at midday on Sunday,' Jek said.

'No, it's open until four,' her father responded.

Minny clearly saw the concerned look on Jek's face. She knew there was a big problem.

THIRTY-TWO

Minny's father had just made a big mistake. Jek had tried to prompt him into agreeing that the bank was closed, but the man had missed it and ruined everything. Now Hyde expected Jek to go out and return with two grand in cash. That posed a pair of problems. First, he didn't want to leave the husband and daughter alone with Hyde. And second...

He'd often considered scamming people, which was preferable to dangerous robberies and street muggings. He'd done some research and learned all about something called the refund scam.

It involved contacting someone out of the blue with a claim that you wanted feedback on a recent purchase. When the customer said no such purchase had been made, the scammer would trick them into believing otherwise, then offer a refund. The hapless soul was swayed into downloading certain software that allowed the scammer remote access to their computer. Then the victim would be required to load up their internet banking, at which point the scammer would work some trickery.

This 'trickery' was what Jek had guided Joel through via text written on his phone. Using the Inspect Element tool, you could edit a web page's HTML and change its structure, like border shape, image size, font colour. And, crucially, alter text. However, the changes only applied to the page as displayed on the screen, not the website itself – a simple click of the 'refresh' button would undo the edits.

Jek had made Joel change a couple of simple values on the page of one of his accounts. The holder's name from Joel Sharpe to Ray Smith. And the Incoming Payment amount from £5 to £100,000. The supposedly bogus account now appeared to have £101,045. By the very same method, scammers would fool victims into believing they had erroneously been refunded too much money.

Many people had been conned into transferring real money to scammers. The deception had easily misled Hyde into believing he was a rich man.

And second? Jek had wanted to delay his partner by prompting Joel to announce that the bank didn't trade on Sundays. But not only had the man missed this trick, his damn bank was open and ready for business, wasn't it? And now Jek didn't have an excuse why he couldn't pop on down there and haul out £2,000 that didn't exist.

THIRTY-THREE

2.05pm. Emma sat at her security station, Adley standing behind her, both sets of eyes fixed on a camera in C-wing's Annex. They watched the young female officer called Smith as she unlocked Pleasance's cell. It was happening.

Happy to be free for an afternoon, Pleasance had a skip in his step as he walked down the wing with Smith. They reached the gate between the Annex and C-wing proper, and were let through. Pleasance seemed to lose his happy gait here, for now he was in the lion's den. The prisoners here were banged up, but that didn't stop them yelling through their cell doors. Pleasance stared at the ground, trying to block out the insult blizzard.

'Seems almost wrong that he has to walk through there,' Adley said. 'Or do you people do it on purpose to scare the paedos half to death?'

Emma ignored the insult. She watched Smith and Pleasance walk through the wing. All of a sudden, the pair became a trio as another officer joined them for God knew what reason.

Adley didn't like it. 'Who's that bozo?'

Emma called C-wing. On a camera in the Watchroom, they saw the supervisor pick up the phone. 'It's me,' Emma said. 'I need to know if Raymond Jackson needs overtime.'

'What's this overtime shit?' Adley said.

Emma gave no response. On another screen, the supervisor stepped out of his office and yelled, although the camera didn't have audio. The man with Smith and Pleasance turned around and walked back the way they'd come.

'So that's Jackson,' Adley said. 'Nice one.'

The supervisor was soon back with an answer: no, Jackson didn't need overtime. Emma thanked him and hung up.

Smith escorted Pleasance to the cleaning store, and she waited outside while the prisoner fetched what he needed. He brought out a wheeled mop bucket with wringer, then returned for more. He dumped products like cloths and bottles into the bucket, and the pair were on the move again. Emma could see the distinctive bright blue of a Top Gleam glass spray amongst the items.

Smith and Pleasance were let through the C-wing exit gates, into the Hub. They crossed to B-wing, which was also locked down post-lunchtime. At the far end of that wing was a door marked o: Base Zero.

Once through and down the stairs, prisoner and officer would hit a junction. The left route headed to open area containing the row of ten cells, but they would take the right fork. This dusty, brick-lined, weakly-lit corridor would lead them past various doors for defunct rooms, to the library at the end. Pleasance would be at the kill zone in about five minutes.

'Make the call to get Samson out of his cell,' Adley said.

'Not yet,' Emma replied. 'It takes ten minutes to clean the guards' break room. The guards will get suspicious if he's in there too long. And we need some time to pass with Pleasance in the library.'

'What? Why?'

'He's supposed to smash his own head open on a wall. Who does that immediately? We need to give the impression he was alone and stewing with his thoughts. Don't worry. Pleasance will be in the library for at least an hour.'

Adley put a hand on her shoulder. 'Bullshit. They'll think he planned this all along. Get Samson out now.'

Smith and Pleasance entered B-wing. Emma picked up her phone and called Base Zero. When the same unpleasant man from earlier answered, she said, 'I've decided to let Samson have some time out of his cell. I've decided he can clean the break room.'

Of course, the supervisor didn't like this, probably because it meant his TV chill time would be interrupted. 'Not a good idea. The break room is clean anyway and...'

While he made excuses, Emma continued to watch Pleasance and Smith walking down B-wing. Suddenly, Pleasance wrong-footed and tripped over the mop bucket he was pushing.

'Last time someone cleaned the break room, something went missing,' the supervisor said. 'So it's not wise to...'

When Pleasance got up, he was wobbly. He put his hands to his chest, as if in pain.

'Besides, Samson's happy in his cell with his music and–'

'Hang on a mo,' Emma said to the supervisor. She and Adley watched as, onscreen, Pleasance doubled over and dropped to his knees.

'What's he doing?' Adley said.

'I don't know,' was Emma's reply.

Onscreen, Smith seemed to have a better idea, as she moved in to try to grab Pleasance. He pushed her away, but the effort made him overbalance and collapse face down. When he hit the deck, he started convulsing, his legs and head vibrating against the floor.

'What the fuck is going on?' Adley said.

Emma grabbed a radio and leapt out of her seat. 'Stay here. It looks like a medical emergency.'

She headed for the door. Adley was right behind her. 'I'm coming.'

'You can't. Just stay and don't be a dickhead.'

'What about Samson?'

'Does it look like Pleasance is going cleaning anytime soon?'

As she left the office and rushed along the hallway, she radioed the B-wing supervisor, demanding to know what was going on. He already had a theory: 'David Pleasance is having a drug seizure.'

'Call the hospital. Get an escape pack and a bed watch pack ready. I'll be there soon.'

The aforementioned items would go with the officers who escorted Pleasance to hospital. The latter contained everything the officers would need to keep an eye on the prisoner overnight, if necessary. The former would be utilised if Pleasance fled the hospital. He wouldn't be the first inmate to fake illness to get beyond the prison walls.

Emma rushed down the stairs and entered the Hub, but her destination wasn't B-wing. She chose C-wing. Since no panic button had been hit, nobody here was yet aware of events next door. When a guard let her in, she told him about Pleasance's seizure and demanded to see the cleaning store, to check for anything left behind by the prisoner.

He led her there and unlocked it. His next order was: 'Go search his cell for drugs.'

When the officer was gone, Emma walked into the cleaning store and threw her eyes around. She peeked behind bottles on shelves, under the shelving itself, and stood on a mop bucket to check the empty top shelf.

And there found what she was after. She stuck it in her pocket and left the cleaning store. She got another guard to lock the room up, then made her way to B-wing to check on Pleasance. In the Hub, she passed by a staff bin and, when nobody was looking, pulled the empty miniature of Talisker whisky from her pocket and hid it inside.

THIRTY-FOUR

Seven miles east, on the edge of Alnwick, Jek parked his Kurtz RT1 in a chiropractor's car park and secured the helmet to the back wheel with a combination cable lock. He took a stroll down Main Street, checking out all the shops for one that fit the mark. He saw Joel's bank, open for business as promised, and wondered if the staff knew yet that their manager had robbed them. He walked past, along the entire length of the road, and turned to come back.

He'd seen four stores that looked good, but one he'd missed got all his attention on this return journey. It was called Broken Records and seemed to stock nothing but music on CD and good old-fashioned vinyl. He headed inside.

The place was old, but given the stock, that seemed fitting. Thousands of records were on shelves and towers, they were in racks and dump bins and hanging from slatwall hooks, and they were even stacked in towers four feet high in the aisles. There was barely space to walk around, which was handy because the grizzled, elderly owner and Jek were the only ones present.

'Got whatever you may need, pal,' the guy shouted from behind a counter also crammed with records.

Jek finished his glance around the walls. No CCTV cameras. 'How do you know? No idea what I'm after. You can't have everything in here.'

'Got even more stock in back. Try me. What you looking for? Chart stuff is on your left there.'

Stock in the back, eh? Perfect. '"Running Up That Hill". Kate Bush. Gatefold twelve inch version.'

'Ah, another one of those *Stranger Things* people.'

'No, actually. I've been into her stuff since before that show made everyone a fan.'

'No probs. Over by the window. B-section, third of the way up.'

Jek checked. The rack by the window was marked A-F, with at least a hundred records in each row. Sure enough, Bush was there and so was the limited edition he'd requested.

'*The Platters Greatest Hits*,' he called to the owner.

Behind a desk of CDs, apparently. Not Row P, as Jek thought, but in a giant section marked 1980-1981. And there it was.

'"Queens of Noise" by The Runaways.'

Not so quick this time. The owner shuffled over to a wobbly aisle tower, where he rifled before coming up short. Telling his customer he couldn't find it seemed to pain him, as if he was informing a sick son that there was no more medical help available.

Jek laughed. 'Is there a prize for guessing one you don't have?'

The owner waved a hand. 'Nah, it'll be in the back, that's all. Just a mo with the horses there.'

He pushed through a curtained doorway behind the counter, into a hallway with no carpet or wallpaper. There was a set of stairs heading up, probably to a bedroom. One door led to a kitchen, another to a bathroom, and a third to a larger room again filled with records and CDs, although here the stock was all over the place, as if someone had dropped a grenade.

Jek saw all of this because he rushed in behind the owner, and collared him in the stockroom. Unbelievably, the man actually had The Runaways record in his hand.

'Hey, you can't come in here. Staff only.'

Jek had brought a fire poker from the cottage, which he now withdrew from his jeans. 'I know one you've got. Money, by the Royal Mint. The sign on the window said cash only, so don't lie.'

Jek led the old man back through the curtain, into the shop area, and forced him to open the till. At first glance, maybe £400. It went in his pocket. When they returned to the stockroom, Jek noticed something as they passed the kitchen. He wasn't dreaming. In a clear glass coffee jar by the kettle were more banknotes, which he counted to the tune of £690. His total was now £1,195.

'I need more. I need about two grand. Give it me or you'll be hearing ventilator beeps, by Medtronic.'

The old man had more cash in his wallet, and some secreted in a book on a shelf in the bathroom. Jek's total was now £2,155. He put two grand into one pocket and left the rest behind.

He brought the owner back to the stockroom, where he made his captive sit in a corner. 'Look, I'm sorry, okay. But I need this money. I'm going now.'

He made to do so, but stopped at the door. 'I know you'll call the cops, but I need you to stay here for a bit first until I've gone. Don't leave this room until you've found "Blackboard Jumble" by Barron Knights.'

'That's out front in the two-for-one section.'

THIRTY-FIVE

It was an hour later that Emma returned to her office, where Adley had been watching events with Pleasance on camera. He was very worked up. The cameras would have shown Pleasance be stabilised and then removed to hospital, but it didn't tell much of a story.

'What the fuck happened?'

'It looks like an overdose,' she said as she slumped in her desk chair. 'Given the symptoms, the doctor thinks it might be from synthetic marijuana. He also smells of alcohol.'

'Spice? How did that dickhead get spice?'

A wave of guilt overcame her. She prayed Pleasance would be okay. Knowing he failed often in his alcohol recovery, she had been certain he would drink the whisky she'd planted behind the cleaning store's sole bottle of Top Gleam, which he'd been instructed to pick up. He couldn't risk being caught with alcohol, so he had downed it fast, right there in the cleaning store, and hidden the empty container.

Only 40ml of the fluid had been whisky, though. The rest had been liquid spice.

At some point she'd make it up to Pleasance. She could only hope he survived. Saving a man's life by killing him achieved nothing.

'You sound so shocked,' she said. 'I'm sure your people know how to smuggle drugs into prison. And I think you have some experience behind bars. Based on a few things you've said.'

'But that would make me a bad man,' Adley said with a grin. But he quickly lost it and got back on track. 'So what about Samson?'

'Still in his cell.'

Adley slapped the security station desk. 'You know what I mean? How is Samson supposed to get to Pleasance now?'

Was his anger a show of strength? This fool was just a pawn and no longer scared her. 'Beyond being sneaked into hospital? He can't.'

Adley approached her desk and picked up the phone. 'Make a call. Get Samson up here for more fucking Listener training.'

When the double-killer was brought in, he was laughing and joking with his two escorts. He seemed like a man content with his lot. She wasn't fooled and, as soon as the officers had left the office, Samson's jolly mood abruptly shut down.

'I heard what happened,' he said. 'Lucky man. But I'll get to him another time. So we skip that and get onto my escape from here. But first, I need to take care of something. Go into your bathroom and shut the door, and plug your ears.'

Emma was reluctant to leave them alone to discuss her, but she obeyed. Inside the bathroom, she put her ear to the door in hopes of hearing what was said. But the wood was too thick, and she could only guess.

There were no raised voices, though, and that gave the impression that, while annoyed about the torpedoing of his plan, Samson didn't blame her for the Pleasance problem.

But she was about to get a shock. About five minutes later, Adley fetched her, and when she re-entered the office, Samson had Adley's phone held up and turned towards her. What she saw almost made her collapse.

THIRTY-SIX

When Jek returned to Peach Cottage, he found the living room and kitchen empty. A bad sign. But he spotted that the pantry door was ajar.

When he opened it, he saw shelves of small tools and household supplies. And something he hadn't realised existed: a smaller door at the back. When he opened this, it exposed wooden steps leading down into darkness. A cellar.

He found a light switch and lit the place up. The area had been turned into a bedroom, with wardrobes and wallpaper and a double bed sans mattress and sheets. Joel lay on the bare slats, spread-eagled with his hands and feet zip-tied to the four corner posts. There was black tape over his mouth and eyes and ears. He seemed to have trouble breathing through his nose for it came in stuttering rasps.

Jek ran down the wooden stairs, crossed the room, and ripped the tape away from Joel's mouth. The man took giant breaths before saying, 'Don't hurt her, please. I'll do anything.'

Joel thought he was talking to Hyde. Shit. Jek bolted from the cellar as fast as he could and didn't slow until he reached

Minny's bedroom door, which he shouldered open so hard that it hit the wall.

Minny was on the bed in a mirror image of her father, with the addition of complete nakedness. Her tight jeans had indeed been hell to drag off, because they lay in tatters on the floor.

Another change from the scene below was the presence of Hyde, who knelt by Minny's suitcase, the contents of which had been tipped on the floor. In his hands was a purple vibrator. Jek knew he'd arrived in the nick of time.

Hyde had been caught in the act, but there was no guilt on his face. The opposite, actually. He laughed and said, 'Get the fuck out, Jek. Don't just burst in like that.'

Although her ears and eyes were covered, Minny obviously realised Jek had returned. She began writhing to get free, yelling incomprehensible words against the tape over her lips. Jek was as angry as he'd been for a long time, but he knew he had to act calm.

'Can I have a word outside?' he said.

Hyde sighed and tossed the vibrator onto the bed. He stormed past Jek and hauled the smaller man into the hallway. Jek shut the door behind him.

'It's my turn with her,' Hyde said. 'I got nothing. The bitch mum isn't here, is she?'

'But she's mine.'

Hyde put his hand on Jek's shoulder and squeezed hard. That old I'm-the-boss hint. 'Sounds a bit selfish. I've not got a toy.'

'But I love her.'

Hyde laughed, but he cut it short when he realised his comrade wasn't taking the piss. 'Love? Are you fucking for real?'

'You don't understand. I've spent a lot of time with her. We've had sex. You said she was mine.'

'What you saying to me? You want her as a girlfriend? Look how we got here, pal.'

'JoJo was the only other girl I ever had sex with. Sex is special, isn't it? The bond and stuff, the intimacy.'

Hyde looked flustered. He wasn't a man experienced in sincere and meaningful conversation. 'Not always. I mean... I...'

'It means a lot to me,' Jek continued. 'I'm not like you. I can't just sleep around and wash it away. I think I'll probably fall in love with any girl I have sex with.'

Hyde shook his head, which seemed to clear the cobwebs. 'Get this stupid shit out of your head. Girlfriend? You think you two can be together? Go on dates? Laugh about how you met? Hey, at least you've already met the parents and got that awkward shit out the way.'

Jek shrugged. 'I don't know. I thought... I don't know.'

'You didn't think, except with your dick. Remember, JoJo's gone. And now you want another one who's gonna be out of your life soon.'

Jek gave an intentional, long pause. 'Maybe we don't have to kill her. But I do love her. It hurts me that you want her. I don't want you to have sex with her while she's alive.'

Hyde laughed. 'Eh? You think I want to fuck her after she's dead? Jesus, dude.'

'No, no, I didn't mean... I just...'

Hyde squeezed Jek's shoulder again, but this time it wasn't a show of power. It was reassurance. 'Okay, boy. I won't touch her. I'll suffer while you get all the fun. She's all yours.'

'Thank you.'

'But I mean *all* yours. You watch her. You stay with her. She's all down to you and you deal with her till the end.'

'Okay. Thank you.'

The next shoulder squeeze wasn't brotherly. 'I mean the

very end, dude. We're probably going to have to kill these two. And if it comes to it, you get to do her.'

Before Jek could respond, Hyde's phone rang and he yanked it from a pocket. 'It's the boss. Keep quiet.'

Hyde answered the call, but he said nothing. He listened then hung up.

'Did he tell us where the meeting place is?' Jek asked.

'Not yet. Sorry, boy, but the boss wants these two brought together and tied up, and he'll call back in two minutes. For a video call.'

Jek had a bad feeling. 'What for?'

'My guess is the mum isn't playing ball and someone's going to pay. So go get your little girl there and bring her to the cellar. Oh, and you might want to say your goodbyes first.'

The camera wobbled badly, but Emma had no doubt what she was looking at. Adley's phone showed her husband and daughter in a cellar, lying face up on a bed that had no mattress. Bound with their hands behind their backs, probably with the same black tape wrapped around their crossed ankles and plastered over their eyes. Minny wore only knickers and was topless.

It appalled her to think that all the time she'd been here, those two criminals called Jekyll and Hyde had been at the cottage, doing God knew what to her family. The atrocious scene threatened to buckle her legs, but she would not show Samson her grief. However, it was impossible to keep the distress out of her voice.

'Please don't hurt them. I've done what you asked for. You can't blame me about Pleasance. I don't know what happened to him. It's the truth.'

Still holding that phone for her to see, Samson spoke to whoever was filming the cellar. 'Get ready to break someone's arms.'

A hand entered the shot, grabbed Joel's arm, and flipped

him onto his front. She recognised the limb as belonging to the hulking brute called Hyde.

Emma leaped forward, tried to snatch the phone from Samson, as if killing the video call might end her family's torment. Adley leaped in to block her path and pushed her backwards.

'Stop,' she pleaded. 'Don't do this. I've done what you wanted.'

Onscreen, the bald bastard brute turned the phone so his face was in the foreground, with poor naked Minny as a backdrop. His hand patted her breast, making it shiver. 'How about this one?' he said.

'She can't abide being manacled,' Emma said. 'She's manacled. Manacled! I can't take this.'

'The husband,' Samson said.

Hyde turned the phone so he was lost from shot and Joel filled the screen. The brute's tattooed arm reached down and grabbed the tape binding Joel's wrists behind his back, and pulled upwards. Both of her husband's arms bent backwards painfully, causing him to cry out.

'I did what you wanted,' Emma yelled, not consumed with anger. 'Pleasance wasn't my fault.'

Samson was grinning. 'I don't believe you. You're being obstructive and you need to know there's consequences. Break his arms.'

Hearing this, Joel flipped onto his side, wrenching his wrists free of the brute's grip. It earned him only two seconds of respite. The camera bounced all over the place as Hyde struggled to get his prisoner under control. When he again had Joel where he wanted him, the addition of a foot placed on the buttocks guaranteed no repeat of the previous escape.

But those same two seconds gave Emma time to do the only thing she could think of. She quickly ran around her desk and stuck her hand underneath it. Her fingers grabbed a metal box attached to the underside with Velcro, and ripped it away. She slapped the box onto the desk.

'Cancel it right now or you are fucked,' she said. Adley was moving towards her, so her next words were for him. 'And stop right there, you piece of shit.'

Both men knew that the bright red button on the box was a panic alarm. Adley paused and Samson ordered Hyde to do the same. Then the gang lord said to Emma, 'I'll kill them both right now if you touch that button. You'll watch it happen live.'

'I press this button and ten guards will be here in seconds.'

'And they'll see a cellar with two dead people. Is it really worth it?'

Her palm hovered just an inch above the button. 'A good question. Is it worth doing the rest of your life in prison? Will knowing you killed a couple of innocent people make the next ten thousand nights go quicker?'

Adley said, 'You think I couldn't kill you before the guards get here?'

'Won't stop them kicking in that door. This is your last chance.'

'I'll give you five seconds,' Samson said. 'After that, you'll regret this moment for the rest of your life.'

'No, you sack of shit, *you've* got five seconds,' Emma said, and hit the button.

THIRTY-EIGHT

'Don't hurt them.'

'Okay,' Hyde said to Samson, but inside he was fuming. When Samson killed the video call, Hyde lobbed his phone to Jek. He released Joel's arms, but not before giving them a yank upwards that caused his victim to moan.

'Seems your wife's got some clout.' He flipped Joel onto his back and ripped away the tape from the man's eyes, which elicited another moan of pain. Meanwhile, Jek carefully peeled away the tape that barred Minny's sight. 'But it won't last. So don't go thinking you've got any say-so of your own.'

'Can we untie them now?' Jek asked.

'You mean your little girlfriend here? Sure. And get her back upstairs. But this guy stays here.'

Jek used a small knife to cut free Minny's hands and feet and helped her up, and towards the cellar stairs. Hyde also sliced the bonds around Joel's wrists, but then secured each hand to a bedpost.

Seeing this, Minny objected, but Jek warned her to keep quiet and dragged her out of the cellar. In the kitchen, she struggled against him. He let her go and said, 'Please don't run. Hyde will hurt your dad.'

'I won't. But that monster will do it anyway.'

'I'll try to help, I promise.'

She seemed calmer now, so he allowed her to walk without aid. She headed upstairs with Jek behind her, and wasn't in a rush despite her nakedness. In her room, she dressed in clothing pulled from the pile Hyde had created – tracksuit bottoms and a green T-shirt – then fell on the bed. As before, Jek sat with his back to the door.

'Your mum's certainly got clout,' he said. 'Standing up to the boss like that. It's a first.'

'Clout in that prison, sure. Not out here. She can't save us.'

'Really? Seems like a tough cookie to me. That wasn't standard prison stuff. No governor has been through what just happened. I think she's tough.'

Minny shrugged. 'But she can't save us, can she?'

It was the second time she'd said that. He now figured he knew what she was hinting at. 'You think we won't let you go when this is over?'

'Why would your boss risk us talking? It seems safer to kill us all. That's the plan, isn't it?'

'No.'

'You're just hired help, though. Maybe you're not in the loop.'

She was obviously worried. And she was right: he didn't know Samson's plans for the family after he was free. He would not lie and gave it to her straight. 'But I will try to help,' he added. 'If I've got anything to do with it, you'll all live. We have to hope your mum can do the right thing.'

The way Minny snorted spoke volumes. He said, 'You seem to be a bit pissed off at her.'

'Well, look where we are.'

Jek hadn't expected that. 'You think it's her fault? Because she's a prison governor?'

'This wouldn't have happened if she wasn't.'

'I think saying that's out of order. She didn't ask to be part of this. It's just circumstance. At first we made you believe we were here to rob your dad's bank, right?'

She nodded.

'So did you blame him when you still believed that?'

No answer. Minny just stared at the ceiling. Jek said, 'Your mum is going to break a killer out of prison. That's the end of her career. She might go to prison herself. And she's doing that to save you and your dad. You understand that, don't you?'

Minny nodded, but it was slight.

'So give her a hug when you see her again. Promise that?'

'Easy enough,' she said, 'because we're all going to die and I'll never see her again.'

THIRTY-NINE

Emma was wrong. Three guards burst into her office, not ten, and because they'd had to run up the stairs from the Hub, they took ninety seconds instead of thirty. Their vigour was commendable, but it evaporated in a flash when they saw their boss in her chair, feet on the desk. Samson, in the guest chair, and Adley, standing by the security station, looked equally at ease.

It was all for show, of course. Hiding the despair consuming her, Emma dropped her feet from the desk and feigned surprise. 'What's going on?'

'Your office alarm,' one guard said.

Emma reached under the desk and lifted the cable with the alarm attached. 'Oops. It came loose and I must have caught it.' She faked a laugh. 'Well, let's call it a drill. Well done, guys.'

The guards were trained to be suspicious, so they eyeballed Adley and especially Samson. The prisoner and the visitor said and did nothing. One of the guards said, 'Okay, guv. Sure all's okay?'

She nodded. 'False alarm, fellas. Sorry. But that doesn't mean you shouldn't come running next time.'

The officers weren't in a rush to leave, but their boss gave no secret signal or any other indication that there was a problem, and soon they were gone. Emma approached the door and cracked it open, just to make sure the trio weren't lurking in the hallway to listen for suspicious noises.

They weren't. She shut the door and turned to Samson. 'Look, I don't know what happened with Pleasance, and I promise you I wouldn't do anything to risk my family's safety. I said I would help you get out of this prison, and I will. But no more threats. At the moment we're both on a path that gives us what we want. Let's not deviate and both end up losing everything.'

'Was that a warning?' Adley said. 'That crack to the guards about it not being a false alarm next time?'

'No, that was for my safety in the future. I have prisoners in here all the time. I'd rather not get attacked and have my people roll their eyes and think I've knocked the button with my knee again.'

Adley wasn't fully convinced, but it didn't matter. Samson told him to chill and ordered Emma to take a seat. When she was in place, he said, 'Here's the deal. Four o'clock. That's when the afternoon gardening shift starts. I'm not on that work detail, so change that.'

'Okay.'

'Make sure I'm given the task of cleaning the staff memorial.'

The memorial? Now she had a suspicion about how Samson intended to escape the prison grounds. 'Okay.'

'When we're done here, go out to that memorial with Adley and show him around.'

'Okay.'

'That young woman officer, Smith. Get her onto the gardening rota. You know prisoners have to be searched before they go outside, so make sure she's the one I get. I'll have things on me that can't be found. Also, no handcuffs for me.'

'Anything else?'

'Yeah, cut the attitude with me. Anyone would think we're not good friends.'

She offered no response. Samson said he wanted to go back to his cell, so she called the guards and soon he was away. Alone with her, Adley said, 'So let's do it. Let's go check out your prison. I'd really like to see this memorial.'

'Just curious, eh?'

'Weren't you warned to cut the attitude?'

Emma picked up her desk phone. 'With him, not you. You're just a dogsbody and you get both barrels.'

Adley looked hurt, and for once he didn't have a comeback.

With a smidgen of satisfaction at knocking him back a step, she made a call to inform staff that she'd be taking Adley on a tour of the grounds.

When she hung up, Adley approached a wall safe and stood with his arms folded right next to it. 'Get the key.'

She knew exactly what key he meant, and he knew she knew, so a lie would be wasted, even dangerous. Instead, she said, 'Now I know how Samson plans to escape, I guess.'

'More key, less words.'

She input the combination and retrieved the key in question. They left the office and ventured to the Hub, where they accessed a spur between wings C and D, the latter of which was the remand/induction wing, where the not-yet-convicted were housed and the new bloods spent their first two weeks. Their route took them outside and along a path that zigged and zagged past various small buildings.

Once beyond the perimeter of the wings, they passed the garden centre and faced open land ahead, most of it grass and used for sports. There was a long-jump pit, a boxing ring, tennis courts, and more.

A hundred metres away was the inner boundary. This barbed-wire-topped fence followed the entirely of the high perimeter wall at a distance of twenty metres, with a gate at each major compass point. The space between wall and fence was known as the Orbit, for a prisoner could walk a full revolution of the prison buildings, and feel like a satellite flying around the earth – or so one inmate had said years back.

In the Orbit were numerous gardens and vegetable patches, a beehive and chicken coup, alfresco workshops and greenhouses. All of that was elsewhere in the ring, though, for here on the western side there was a feature that nobody alive had cause to use.

It was a graveyard filled with the resting places of long-ago inmates. Off to one side, on a neat lawn, was the memorial Samson had mentioned. It was a stone statue of a prison guard, dedicated to officers who'd passed away.

Emma and Adley crossed the grass to the gate in the fence, which had a keycode lock. 'Shall I avert my eyes in case I help someone escape?' Adley said, and laughed at his own joke.

Emma input the code and they were through. 'By the way,' Adley said. 'My time here is done after this. I can't be here when Samson escapes because the place will be locked down. So you'll be rid of me.'

Again she made no reply.

They walked alongside the graveyard, to the memorial. However, when they stopped before it, the statue was not Adley's focus. Emma saw that he was looking at the imposing five-metre-high perimeter wall just ten steps away. And the western corner tower.

It had a large, heavy iron door that had been in place since the 1920s. Prisoners in the Orbit could walk up to it, touch it, but that entryway into the tower was solid, unmovable. Many had tried over the decades, but no one, except perhaps the Incredible Hulk, could breach it. Unless you had the key...

'Unlock the door,' Adley said.

The key would give easy, immediate access to the interior of the tower, which stood just metres from the river. It seemed like the perfect place to mount a prison break, and over the years the staff had gotten wind of many a plan to do just that. However, all had failed because of a lack of knowledge and planning.

Emma believed the same applied now. She pulled the large key from her pocket, then said, 'Has your man thought this through? That door is alarmed.'

'I know. Just unlock it. We're not opening it yet, so no alarm will go off.'

The inmates respected the dead and nobody had ever damaged the gravestones, but that didn't apply to the surrounding areas. Pristine new graffiti and the remnants of old art covered the lower bricks in the perimeter wall, perhaps for its entire length. The tower wasn't unblemished, and the old iron door was also coated in scribblings and scratches. Emma deciphered some of them as she inserted the key and, needing two hands because of grime or rust, turned it.

Nobody had opened this door in three years, since her first shift as governor. On that day she had wanted to explore every nook and cranny of the prison, and that included the four towers. She knew exactly why Samson was going to face problems if he thought he could escape via this structure.

'There's no door out onto the other side,' she said. 'That would be silly.'

Adley said they should return to the nearby memorial, just in case eyes were watching. He sat on the grass and bid Emma to do the same. It would feel too much like old friends enjoying the summer, so she refused.

'I know there's a riverside doorway, if not actually a door,' he said. 'I know that in the early years prisoners used to arrive by boat, and that's the way they came in.'

'Yes, but that doorway is now blocked by heavy steel bars. It's more like a window. The bars are as thick as my wrist and only inches apart. And don't think that Samson can jump off the roof of the tower. The stairs were blocked off a hundred years ago, so there's no way up. No way out. Like I said, we're not silly. Samson needs a new plan.'

Adley grinned at her. 'Don't worry about it.'

'But I do, because you have my family. We have cameras on the wall that watch the land all around this prison. It's empty and bare out there and we can see for miles. But if you're thinking of the river, well, there's tangles of barbed wire on both sides and cameras aimed at the water. We sometimes get people coming right up to the towers and throwing things through the bars.'

Adley's grin widened. 'Don't worry about it.'

'An electric metal saw of some kind would take ages to get through the bars, and my people would get to you before you had even one cut. Not that they'd get anywhere close to the tower before we spotted you. And those camera feeds, by the way, aren't just in my office. They are watched by my OSG in his station and by someone at HM Prison Service, so don't go thinking that I can just turn them off and–'

'Don't worry about it,' Adley said, his grin now a thing of the past.

'Look, you need to think about this plan because my family can't be made to suffer if it fails. Even without the problem of escaping the tower, it's ludicrous. You think I can sneak Mr Samson out of his cell? Through the prison when it's locked down? Across the prison grounds, which have guards walking about? Through the inner fence, which is alarmed? And do all of this while cameras film everything?'

Adley stood and brushed grass from his trousers. 'One last time: don't worry about it. Or do, actually. Because if Samson isn't on the far side of that wall by the end of this afternoon, you're going to need a couple of new plots in that graveyard. Now, that's a threat I actually enjoyed making.'

FORTY

'Hyde seems to be fuming about not being allowed to hurt my dad.'

Jek nodded. Neither of them could fail to hear Hyde downstairs, vocalising his upset with her father. In any other hostage scenario, that would terrify the witnesses. But Minny was no longer as worried about Hyde's violent nature because his boss, whoever he was, had given express orders to hurt nobody. Yet. Surprisingly, her mum had seen to that. Minny couldn't imagine the conversation that had taken place to achieve this result.

Jek said, 'He never struck me as that kind. I mean, I've seen him hurt people, but never like this. I think it's because he's been given more power. This is a big step-up for us. He's never done something so... major.'

'He's unpredictable. Can you go check on him? In case he disobeys your boss. You could get me some food, please. I've not eaten since late last night. My dad, too.'

'Sure. Okay. But I'll have to zip-tie you again, I'm afraid. In case Hyde checks.'

'Okay. I understand.'

'If he finds out I've been leaving you free up here, he might–'

'I get it, Jek. What's your real name, by the way? I don't want to keep calling you that.'

Jek paused, but he opted for safety and said he couldn't yet give her that information. He tried a joke – 'Being secretive proves we're not going to kill anyone' – but she told him the line was a cruel thing to say to a kidnap victim. He apologised.

He grabbed a zip tie from the bunch on the bedside cabinet and secured one of Minny's wrists to the headboard bar, just like before. When he left the room, Minny leaned in to bite at the plastic bond. She didn't have the jaw power to bite right through because she could only snatch it between her front teeth. She had to wrench at it, which caused a flash of pain as a tooth seemed to twist in her gums. But soon she was free.

She moved slowly, not wanting to make the bed or the floor creak. She knelt by her pile of clothing and hunted inside.

FORTY-ONE

Jek found Hyde in the kitchen, just finishing up taping Joel to a chair at the table. The laptop was before him and his arms had been left unbound. Obviously Hyde wanted him to continue transferring money between bank accounts. Jek didn't think this trick would work for much longer.

When Hyde saw Jek, he pointed to the back door. They headed out for a private chat. 'I'm going to kill them both,' Hyde said without pause. 'Sorry and all, but that includes your new girlfriend.'

'The boss said no.'

'The boss only needs them until he's out of that prison. You think he's going to want the cops knowing the plan? Talking to the witnesses? Think again.'

The escape of the head of a major organised crime network was going to burn the entire UK's law enforcement overtime budget. As people directly involved, the Catalano family were going to be grilled for days, in the hope of giving up a clue. Samson couldn't risk them foiling his plans for escaping the country. Only their deaths would make sure they gave the police nothing.

Jek had always known he might be called upon to end an innocent life, but there had been hope of a bloodless resolution. Now he could play optimist no more. Instead of useless faith, he needed positive action if he was going to save Minny and her father. The mother he could do nothing about...

'You understand that, right?' Hyde said.

'I do, but I love Minny. I want to be with her.'

Hyde laughed. 'Get real.'

'I'm serious. I don't want her dead. I want to marry her. But she will need her father to give her away at the wedding, so he can't–'

Hyde laughed no more. 'Stop. They're walking dead, so get used to it. The boss calls the shots.'

'Maybe there's a way he won't know.'

'Course he'll know. I know I said the same as you before, but I was wrong. He'll know. Now stop this shit.'

Jek grabbed Hyde's arm. 'Then we don't do it. I can't. And I can't forgive you if you do it. Samson will have to do it himself. We can tell him that.'

'Tell the boss what to do? You want to go in the same grave as them?'

'I'm not killing them. I won't forgive you if you do it. Make some excuse. Tell him it's a getting-out present for him to kill them himself. Tell him it's the best way to get one over on the mother. But we're not doing it.'

Hyde picked up and skimmed a stone towards a lamppost at the corner of the cottage. He missed. 'I'll suggest it. But if he says no, we're doing them. End of. Are you on the rebound? Cos you lost your other girl? Maybe you blame yourself and you're trying to replace her by... what's the word? Proximity?'

'Proxy. I think you mean I'm trying to keep Minny to make up for JoJo. But I don't blame myself for JoJo. I know who's to blame.'

FORTY-TWO

Minny thought she had to be wrong, that she was fuelled by blind hope. During the video call, her mother had bizarrely said Minny was 'manacled', and emphasised that word again and again. It had to be pure coincidence that Minny had described her smartwatch as manacling her to her mother. Surely that couldn't have been a hint from her mother that they could secretly converse via their devices.

She found the watch and strapped it to her wrist, then grabbed a zip tie from the bunch on the bedside table. She bound herself as before, to the headboard. She was able to work the watch and was about to call her mother's device when she paused.

Had she got this wrong? She had used the word 'manacled' out of the blue, and maybe her mother had done the same? Maybe it wasn't a clue at all. Maybe her mum was in no position to take a call, and what Minny was about to do was dangerous.

Well, she would soon know. She found her mother's number and called it.

FORTY-THREE

When they returned from the gardens, Adley promptly left the prison. His parting gesture was a salute. Maybe that was for the benefit of the guards. Her return salute certainly was. Sans witnesses, she would have flipped Adley the bird.

This time he went through the metal detector portal without contraband, and without incident. The moment he was outside, Emma felt as if a great weight had been lifted. It was fleeting, though, because nothing had changed. Her family was still on the chopping block.

Back in her office, Emma sat at the security station and accessed the cameras that covered the visitor car park. She watched him drive from the grounds. Adley's registration plate was visible, but useless. It was probably a clone. These people were too smart, had planned this too long, for any of them to be outdone that way.

She grabbed her desk phone to make some calls. First, to C-wing, where she got hold of Smith. 'Go to Base Zero at ten to four. Samson is joining the garden crew, and you're going to search him. I'm sure you already understand that you'll find nothing. Put your boss on so I can tell him.'

That job done, she called Base Zero, where she said to the supervisor, 'Mike Samson. As part of his Listener training package, I'm authorising some extra time out for him.'

'I just cleaned the break room, so there's no need to have him do it.'

'You can calm down. I'm taking him off your hands for a while. Have him ready for movement at 4pm, please.'

'Sure thing,' the man said, after a doubtful pause.

'I shouldn't do this, but... well, I want to show how grateful we are, and that we trust him, and respect his progress.'

'Samson? Progress? I'd like some of what you've been smoking, boss.'

She gave a fake laugh. 'Yesterday I would have said that was true. But I think he really wants to change his ways. So, I'm putting him on gardening. And I'm to authorise that he can be out of his cell without restraints.'

Another doubtful pause from the supervisor. Zero prisoners always travelled in handcuffs. 'You sure?'

'Believe me, he knows his Listener training will be out the window if he messes about. I think we're all good.'

'Okay. You're the boss, boss.'

Her next call was to the head of the Garden Team, someone else she didn't get on with. She had once overheard him gossiping about her breast cancer, and not in a good way. She had torn him a new arsehole for it. She vowed to keep her tone sweet until he darkened his. 'Your 4pm shift. I'd like to add a new man just for today.'

'We're full. Like a coach.'

'Make it like a tube train and squeeze him in.'

He gave a sigh she was absolutely meant to hear. 'Short notice.'

'It's gardening, not surgery.'

Another sigh. 'What's his name?'

Watch this. 'Samson.'

No sigh this time, just a long pause. Her staff were getting good at expressing their feelings via silence. 'You're messing with me.'

'No. I don't want to hear it, Mr James. Samson won't start trouble. I'm also sending over Officer Lucy Smith to be his escort.'

'Wait. Just one? You know we always have two or more for the Zeroes.'

'I know. But that doesn't send a Listener trainee the right message of respect. And Samson won't be cuffed. Goodbye.'

She hung up and walked to her window, to stare across the sunlit land. There. All done. She'd just arranged the escape of a violent prisoner and spat upon her oath of allegiance. She would be charged with misconduct in public office and jailed. But these things didn't matter next to her family.

She sighed with relief, but checked herself immediately. What was she thinking? Samson wasn't yet free, and even if he escaped the prison, it wouldn't guarantee the safety of her husband and daughter.

But even if they were released, mega damage would have been done. A double-killer would be on the streets, able and likely to cause more harm to the innocent. And it would all be her fault.

She put her hands over her face. Her smartwatch rested against a cheek, which highlighted its vibration a moment later. A call.

The ID said MINNY 2.

It was from Minny's watch.

Did one of the brutes back at the house have it? Were they calling with more instructions? With a nervous hand, she tapped the screen to take the call.

'Mum,' said Minny.

Emma couldn't believe it. Minny. Her massively unlikely plan to alert Minny to the idea of using their watches to secretly talk – it had worked. She answered with, 'God, baby, are you okay? How did you– I mean where is– Are you okay?'

'Yes, yes, so far.'

No trick, no dream. It really was Minny. 'Oh, baby, I'm so glad you're–'

'Look, Mum, just listen a moment. I don't have long. I know what they want you to do. You can't do it.'

Emma was desperate to know how Minny had acquired that information, but asking would burn valuable time. 'I have to. They'll hurt you if–'

Minny cut her off and, in little more than a tearful babble, doubled-down on her order. The two men were still at the cottage, she said, but the younger one, the nicer one, he wasn't an evil brute like his friend. The man called Jek had promised he would do his best to make sure Minny and her father were not hurt. But she had overheard the other bastard say they would be killed as soon as their boss was released from prison.

'So you can't do it, Mum. You can't. They'll only keep us alive until he's free. But I think we might be able to escape.'

'I hope so. But how?'

Minny claimed she was winning Jek over. He liked Minny and now trusted her to be alone without restraints. She believed she could convince him to let her have even more freedom, and she might then be able to make a run for it with her father. If so, Emma could leave the prison, and then they'd all be safe.

Emma didn't want to feel too much hope, but into her mind popped a scene: arresting Samson once her family was safe. How sweet it would be to let him get halfway escaped, and then dump ten guards on him and have him dragged back into–

'Shit. Coming back. Gotta go, Mum. Will call later.'

And with that the line went dead. Emma stared at her

watch, which now displayed only the time and date. It was great knowing Minny was alive and well, but the call had left her more scared and confused than ever. Could Minny and Joel really escape? The thought tried to embolden her, but it failed when her eyes noted the time.

Forty-five minutes until the planned escape. Not nearly enough time for Minny and Joel to get out of the cottage and to safety. She needed to delay Samson, but he would surely suspect a trick and make her family suffer. She had no choice other than to let his prison break play out.

But if Minny was right and he planned bloody murder once free...

FORTY-FOUR

'Cops!'

Jek thought he'd misheard. The police? Were they here?

Next, footsteps on the stairs, Minny's bedroom door bashed open before Jek had fully moved out of its way, and he took a heavy smack in the shoulder.

Hyde was in the doorway, seething. 'You fucking bitch.'

Jek had no time to tell his partner he was wrong. Hyde launched himself at Minny, who couldn't escape because she was bound to the headboard. Hyde jumped onto the bed and latched a tattooed hand around her throat.

'You called the fucking cops, you slag,' he said.

Minny tried to speak, but her throat was pinched and allowed nothing in or out – including air. Jek knew words wouldn't work here, so he leaped onto Hyde's back. He snapped an arm around the bigger man's neck from behind, doubling the number of people in the room who now couldn't breathe.

Hyde tried to buck him off, but when Jek toppled, he didn't let go of the chokehold. Both men fell onto their flanks on the bed, with Minny's leg trapped beneath them.

'Think about this,' Jek said, his lips close to Hyde's ear. The man was gurgling. 'Even if she did call the cops, they're here and they're coming in no matter. We can talk our way out of this, but not if there's bodies. Think!'

He wasn't sure Hyde had been swayed by these words, but he couldn't choke his friend unconscious. He released the stranglehold. Hyde scrambled off the bed and turned on him. He was enraged and looked ready to attack. Maybe he would have, and maybe not, but the decision was stripped away by a loud knocking on the front door.

'I'll have to kill the fucking cops as well,' Hyde said, now a little calmer because of fear. 'And then I'll be back for you, you bitch.'

Jek got to his feet and grabbed Hyde's arm as the bigger man went for the door. 'No, we send her out. She gets rid of them.'

Hyde slapped Jek's hand away. 'Don't be a dickface. She'll tell them.'

'She won't. She would have already. Look, I'll be honest with you. I've been letting her out of her restraints. She's been free to move about in this room. She would have tried something already. She won't risk anyone getting killed. And she didn't make any calls. We've got their phones.'

Hyde thought about this, and he was aided by a slowing heartbeat. He then pulled out his pocketknife. Minny moaned and closed her eyes as he leaned over her. Jek did nothing this time, for he knew his step uncle well.

Hyde snipped the zip tie around her wrist, freeing her from the headboard. It surprised her. He grabbed the same wrist in his meaty hand, closing his fingers over her smartwatch. 'I'll gut your dad if the cops step one foot in here. Get down there and get rid of them.' He yanked her right off the bed by her arm.

She landed on her feet and would have collapsed if not for his grip on her. The giant tug on her wrist had bust a strap on her watch, and she saw it go bouncing across the carpet.

'I need to go with her,' Jek said. 'They're here because someone complained. You told us that Denise said someone moaned about the van being in the pub car park. They know there's men here. But you can't go because you've got form. I'm not known to the cops.'

Hyde knew he was right. 'Let's go.'

The trio headed downstairs. Once in the kitchen, Hyde shut the door behind them and forced Minny into a chair, then ordered Jek to help him with Joel. They snipped the tape holding him to the chair, then Hyde put a blade to his neck. Minny didn't move.

'Cellar, now,' Hyde ordered Joel. 'No funny moves or I'll stick your baby. Jek, get her to the door. Don't fuck this up.'

Jek guided Minny into the living room. 'Be careful answering their questions. Don't let them in. Please. I'm your boyfriend if they ask about men seen out back.'

She nodded. The living room door was at a right angle to the front door, so he hid just inside, close enough to overhear everything. His position gave him a profile view of Minny as she opened the front door.

He heard two voices, one of them female, as the officers outside introduced themselves as Northumbria police constables and gave names and shoulder numbers. The female asked who else was in the house.

'My mum and dad,' Minny said. From what Jek could see, she seemed calm and wasn't giving any coded distress signals. 'Well, not in, but staying with me. Mum's at work and Dad went to a friend's.'

The male said they were here to investigate a report of two suspicious men seen by the cottage and at a nearby pub.

Minny nodded. 'Yes, my boyfriend came down. He was given a lift by his step uncle. Have they done something?'

The female spoke. 'Your boyfriend. Describe him for me.'

Minny outlined the clothing Jek wore. Alongside her detail about his relationship to Hyde, it made him edgy. But he knew lies were riskier.

'And his name?'

Minny paused, and Jek's gut seemed to churn. He hadn't given Minny his real name.

Thankfully, she was sharp. 'Look, officers, no offence meant here. I know you got a report. But why do you want to know who he is? I told you the men you're referring to are with me. They're legit. Why is that not the end of it?'

Now the male spoke. 'And where are they?'

'My boyfriend is in the bath. His step uncle went home after he dropped him off. Why?'

'Can we have a word with him? Your boyfriend?'

Jek had no clue what he should do to fix this pickle. But Minny did. She turned towards the stairs and yelled, 'Babe? Pop down here. Police at the door. They want a word.'

Shit. A good plan, but with a serious fault. Jek couldn't get to the stairs without the police seeing him. He thought quick and moved through the living room. He grabbed the throw from the armchair and entered the kitchen. Hyde wasn't here.

Joel stripped naked and threw his clothing into the washing machine. He ran a tap and soaked his head with water, allowing it dribble over his torso and legs. After he'd wrapped the throw around his waist, he grabbed the kettle and opened the door to the hallway.

Now he took his first look at the two officers, and they him. Both were young and good-looking. Beyond them, parked at the end of the trail through the woods, was a marked police car. They said nothing until he'd walked down the hall and stopped by Minny's side.

'Oh, I thought you were upstairs,' she said to him.

'Just came down for a drink,' he replied, holding up the

kettle. He hoped bringing it out of the kitchen wasn't a step too far. 'Hello, officers. What's the problem?'

'What's your name?' the female said. 'And put the kettle down, please.'

Jek laid it aside, on the floor. He knew he didn't have to identify himself unless he was suspected of a crime. But it would raise suspicions. Worse, it was a criminal offence to give a false name. So, he said he was Tom. She wanted a surname, so he added 'Cupton'. Next, his date of birth. He knew right then a search for him would be performed on police databases. The male stepped away and got on his radio.

The female asked questions already posed to Minny. How did he know her, and had he travelled down here in the company of another man. He gave the same answers.

'And your uncle's name?'

Here, a problem. Jek had no criminal record, but Hyde absolutely did. Once this pair knew Jek was related to a hardened criminal, they might want to hang around and delve deeper. But if he lied and they found out anyway...

No choice. He gave his step uncle's real name – which was actually Hyde, preceded by Rory – and his date of birth. The male officer ran it through his radio while the female made small talk about what sights the couple had visited. It was part fishing and part delay. When her partner came back, he whispered to her. Now they both knew.

'So where is Hyde now?' the male asked Jek. His attitude had toughened a little. Their suspicions were up.

'Back home by now,' Jek said. 'He dropped me off. Look, is there something wrong?'

The female pointed at Minny's wrist, where there was a red welt from the zip ties. Jek hadn't noticed it before. He couldn't get his damn eyes off it now. 'How did you get that mark?' the officer asked.

Minny looked at the welt. She answered almost immediately. 'I... er... can't say.'

Jek's heart nearly dropped out of his ass. The two officers looked at each other, then devised a plan. The male wanted to chat to Jek: 'Let's take a little walk.' The female wanted to talk to Minny: 'How about you and me go inside to talk?' A standard trick to make sure suspects couldn't confer or threaten each other.

Again, no choice. The two pairs split. Jek followed the male officer away from the house, even though he was barefoot and wearing only a throw around his waist. At his car, the officer said, 'Sit in the back seat for me, would you?'

Jek obeyed. The car had a mesh screen separating the front from the back, and the rear doors wouldn't open from the inside. He was caged, as planned. The male paced outside, chatting on his radio. Jek stared at the cottage, concerned about what was going on inside. He worried even more when the male also vanished into the house without a word to his prisoner. Jek fought the urge to bust the window.

Now Minny was going to deal with two coppers alone. She could sink the mission in moments.

FORTY-FIVE

Inside, the female followed Minny to the kitchen, where she immediately spotted the tape-covered chair. 'Everything okay?' she asked Minny.

'Sure. Apart from you two treating my boyfriend like a criminal.'

'We're not. We had a call, that's all. So, you said Mr Hyde, the step uncle, was here?'

'No. We told you he went home.'

'Oh yes. And your parents? Both back home?'

'One at work, one seeing a friend. That's what I said. That a problem?'

'No. That's definitely the case, then? All's good here?'

'Yes. Nobody is committing crimes. It annoys me that someone called you. If they were close enough to see two men in the backyard, then they were too close. You should have a word with them about trespassing.'

The front door opened, but Minny saw only the male officer enter. She had no idea where Jek was. The man joined them in the kitchen, at which point the female spoke again:

'Nobody is accusing you of a crime. We just want to make

sure everybody is okay. If there was something untoward happening, a sign of that would be great. With such a sign, we'd leave here as if everything checks out, and then we'd work on getting you help. Just a sign.'

A sign. So simple. One little sentence, one second of her time, and she would be saved. But her brain wouldn't compute the scene. Earlier today she would have celebrated the arrival of the law enforcement, yet here stood two saviours and her next words were:

'Am I supposed to give a wink or a codeword to let you know I'm unable to talk? You want to check the house for kidnappers?'

She told herself she was doing the right thing. Hyde was down in that cellar with her father. If something went sour here, he might be hurt. Just as bad, news would get to Jek's boss and he would hurt her mother.

'Can we?' the male said. 'I mean search. Not for kidnappers, of course. Just a general look around.'

'Actually, no. I saw you both looking at the chair covered in tape. That was a sex game, like the handcuffs that hurt my wrist. That's what boyfriends and girlfriends do.'

'True, but–'

'No buts. Just because my boyfriend's step uncle is a criminal, that doesn't mean they both are. It doesn't mean they're here causing no good. You came here for nothing and I'm offended at the way I've been treated. I'd like you to skedaddle.'

The officers looked at each other. A silent message was passed. They thanked Minny and said they'd see themselves out, and turned to do so. And, just like that, it was over.

And then it wasn't. The officers got halfway to the door, then there was a heavy thud from the cellar. Unmissable. Both officers turned their heads towards the pantry door. Minny needed a quick excuse to–

She didn't get the chance. The male, without warning, darted for the door and yanked it open. Beyond was a scenario that would have provoked giggles in a sitcom: Hyde crouched in the pantry, head cocked to one side as if he'd had his ear to the door. But nobody would have laughed at the giant steak knife in his hand.

FORTY-SIX

At 3.29pm, Emma left her office with a radio. In the Hub, she ordered a guard to open A-wing. She walked towards the nearest set of stairs. All the other wings had spiral staircases between floors, but in here there were switchback stairs. On the middle landing, her radio slipped from her hand. She retrieved it and moved on.

When she emerged onto the top floor walkway, she saw a laminated paper wall sign that said PRISONERS MUST NOT LOITER ON STAIRS. It was in place with BluTack but a corner had come loose and was folded outwards.

She ignored it and walked past various cells, to visit a lifer who had last week asked her to read a fantasy novel he'd penned. He was eager to give her a copy and she soon returned to her office with 350 handwritten A4 pages. She sat at her security station to watch the CCTV. She took her cordless desk phone with her. It was 3.49pm.

3.50pm. The young female guard called Smith enters Base Zero and speaks with the supervisor. She doesn't look happy with him, so maybe he's being insulting or unfunny. Maybe he's telling her that Governor Catalano wants her dead by giving her

Samson to escort by herself. All other cells are unlocked by key, but in Base Zero the doors are electronic. Smith goes to Samson's cell and the supervisor jabs a button on his control panel.

3.52pm. Samson waltzes out with a grin on his face. Smith gives him a search that looks so sloppy Emma expects the supervisor to pull her up. He doesn't. Maybe he wants her dead. Smith and Samson, who's not cuffed, start walking.

3.55pm. Samson and Smith enter the Hub. Because it's gardening time, there are numerous other guards present in case of trouble, and if they are worried that a Zero has just a single escort and no restraints, they don't show it. Prisoner and officer make their way to the spur between wings C and D, where other inmates have congregated in readiness for getting out into the sun. Samson seems to know and is friendly with a lot of them. There are five gardens department staff, who wear blue T-shirts and black trousers.

4.03pm. Twenty prisoners and six staff, including Smith, walk outside and make their way to the toolshed. Nine minutes later, they emerge again. The prisoners now wear purple gardening jumpers and pocketless blue trousers. They were searched before leaving the Hub, before entering the toolshed to change clothing, and again before heading back outside. In all three instances, Samson's frisk was sloppily performed by Smith. If Samson has contraband on his person, he must have transferred it unseen when swapping outfits.

Now that they're ready for work, the group crosses the grass, heading for the inner fence. Today the prisoners are working at the north end, which means Samson is a few hundred metres from the western tower with its unlocked door. However he's planning to get out, it could happen in the next five minutes.

4.14pm. Emma switched from the outdoor cameras to those in A-wing. The northern stairwell that she'd climbed earlier was empty of life. Another camera showed three guards chatting in the Watchroom. She called it. Despite the tension pulling at her innards, she smiled upon seeing the three guards play rock-paper-scissors to nominate who'd answer the phone.

When one did, she said, 'Do me a favour. I hate to nitpick but there's a sign at the top of the north-end stairs that's come a bit loose. Can someone go stick it down properly? Thanks.'

She hung up and watched the three guards. Their body language and laughter suggested she was the subject of ridicule. One guy confirmed it with a middle finger aimed at the phone. Well, he'd be getting a Christmas Day shift for that. The trio then played their game again to determine who had to get off his ass and go fix the sign. The winner – or loser – was a man who had a moustache that belonged in a 70s porno.

4.16pm. The prisoners on garden duty reach the inner fence. At the same time, 70s porno reaches the northern stairs and saunters up. One of the garden staff addresses the crowd to give the usual warnings about tool safety – and the futility of running away and hiding.

4.16pm. 70s porno reaches the landing where Emma dropped her radio and turns to take the next set of stairs. And stops dead. He then takes two steps towards the middle of the landing and bends down, looking at something small on the floor. A second later, he hauls his radio and yells into it.

Emma lifted the plastic cover on a recessed red button on the security desk. Her hand hovered above it while her other, holding the phone, paused with a finger on the answer-call button. She watched one of the officers in the Watchroom take the radio call from 70s porno. Immediately, the callee grabbed the wall phone. Hers rang a second later.

'We just found a bullet,' he snapped. 'North-end stairway in A-wing.'

'Get ready to receive your prisoners,' Emma said, and then

hit the big red button. An alarm immediately started ringing throughout the prison.

She watched the camera covering the inner fence, where those on garden duty were about to file through the open gate. Hearing the alarm, the lead officer suddenly slammed it shut. The prisoners instantly became irate. They knew the score. There was no gardening to be had today, or classes, or association, or dinnertime. Or escapes.

HMP Cheviot was being locked down.

PART 3

FORTY-SEVEN

Just minutes after Emma called the National Tactical Response Group, three vans were aiming towards Cheviot prison. They ferried fifteen members of a Tornado Team, who were armed and clad in full riot gear, and highly trained in stamping out uprisings. They were called out to prisons just a handful of times each year, although they'd never been dispatched to HMP Cheviot.

All prisoners were locked up by 4.36. When the Tornado Team arrived ten minutes later, they entered a serene environment. But the calm mien didn't dampen their vigour or speed. A guard had found a bullet and there might be a gun in the hands of someone who should never be allowed near weapons. Every inch of the grounds would be picked over for that firearm. Every cell would be tossed and its occupants searched. Even more than the firearm, they wanted someone to make an example of.

The National Tactical Response Group was overseen by HM Prison Service and not responsible to a governor. As soon as she made the call, Emma had effectively handed over control of her facility. Someone else was now in charge and she would be little more than an observer. On any other day, it would have felt like a kick in the teeth.

She held a meeting with her supervising staff before sending them out to assist the Tornado Team by searching various outbuildings. One of them was Smith, who had managed to take Samson's gun and phone – the contraband he'd hidden in his clothing – before he was locked up. Emma learned this at just after 5.30pm, when Smith visited her in her office. With both items.

'Jesus,' Emma said. 'Why did you bring these here?'

'Because they'll search staff lockers. But they won't search your office. You're probably the only one they'll trust. You have to take it. He told me to give them to you.'

Smith dumped both items on the desk. Emma didn't want to touch them, but knew she had to. They couldn't just sit there. There was no hiding place that she trusted, for she wasn't absolutely certain the Tornado Team wouldn't search her office. Governors weren't above suspicion. She locked the items in the safe for now.

'He's not happy,' Smith said.

'No shit. Nobody is.'

'Look, he told me to come here because he wants to rearrange the escape for tomorrow morning. He's waiting for an answer and he'll be pissed that it took me over an hour to get to you. You have to go see him. And take his phone.'

She knew that she would have to face Samson. Adley had told her that the deadline for Samson's release was 6pm. Twenty minutes from now, it would be too late. Adley would order the deaths of Joel and Minny if he didn't get word from his boss. Not having a phone wouldn't be a problem for a connected individual like him.

The Tornadoes would search Base Zero and the entire basement, but it wasn't a priority because it was the prison's most secure zone. Currently they were in A-wing, and she knew she'd find the supervisor alone.

She called ahead and he met her at the gate at the bottom of the stairs. 'I want to talk to Samson,' she said. 'Just in case he knows something. I might be able to get some clues about this smuggled gun, if there is one.'

No argument from him. Maybe he knew any objection would be countered with more talk of Listeners and respect and changed souls. He headed into the Watchroom and she approached Samson's cell. The door had a window of toughened clear plastic about the size of a standard chessboard.

Samson was lying on his bunk and reading a book, as if he didn't have a care in the world. He didn't look angry, but his chest rose and fell with rapid breathing. He kept his eyes on the book and his back on the bed. But he knew she was there.

'Quarter of an hour until my people expect me,' he said.

'There's nothing I can do. At least not until the prison has been searched. I couldn't possibly have foreseen this. You know the policy if there's a suspected firearm in the prison.'

He slowly nodded. Still he didn't look away from his book. 'Fourteen minutes until your husband and daughter die.'

'Look, I can't do anything. These things happen. Bad timing. We can rearrange it. You can't hold this against me.'

'Really. I'd like it back.'

'What?'

'The bullet I gave you with your kid's name on it.'

She kept sudden anxiety out of her expression. 'I threw it down a drain. Why do you want it?'

He sat up and dumped his book. 'If you were anyone else, I'd kill your kid slowly for that.'

She thought quickly. 'Wait. You think the bullet that was found was the one you gave me? You think I'd be stupid enough to carry that around and then lose it?'

'Don't play dumb. You planted it to delay things. That was a lethal mistake.'

'Fuck you,' she snapped. 'You've got my child and my husband. I wouldn't risk that. This wasn't down to me. If I wanted to delay you, I could invent any number of reasons. You think I'd lock down my whole prison?'

He paused. He'd probably expected her to admit he'd sussed it all out. Now he wasn't so sure of his own theory. 'If I find out you did this–'

'I didn't.'

He held his hand out. 'My phone.'

Making sure the guard wasn't looking towards the open cell door, she opened the food hatch and slid the device inside. Samson grabbed it and said, 'I'm calling someone, so go make small talk with the guard and come back in three minutes.'

She waited exactly three, but she spent the time looking over a log in the Watchroom rather than talking to the obnoxious officer. When she returned to Samson's cell, he was waiting, phone call over.

'No more fucking about, guv, or I'll start lopping off people's fingers. When the dickheads out there have left the prison, you come see me. ASAP. Okay?'

'Yes.'

'I told Adley to stand my boys down. But they're going to sit with your husband and kid until the morning. That's the new appointment. Garden duty at ten tomorrow morning, but without hitch this time. And if I'm not on the outside by the end of the morning, well, you get one guess as to what happens.'

It was hardly good news, but she was happy that she had more time. Time in which Joel and Minny could hopefully escape. 'Yes. Okay. But make sure they're not harmed, because you're going to put them on the phone before I get you out of this cell. If anyone is harmed while you're still here, well, you get one guess as to what happens.'

He understood, she saw. Both their worlds would be ruined if Minny and Joel died. But something bothered her. 'Why are we meeting tonight if you're escaping in the morning?'

'Because you're going to bring me something. And then you're going to arrange for a guard to come and get that something and hide it out near the tower, ready for my escape tomorrow.'

'Smith clocks off at eight tonight, so she can't–'

'Not her. She's not the only guard I have in here. No names till you come get me.'

That made Emma's breath catch. Another guard. This was real bad. 'What am I bringing tonight?'

'My gun.'

A weapon was the last thing she wanted him to have, but she didn't have much of a choice. She agreed because she was all out of plans.

FORTY-EIGHT

The Tornado Team had a fairly easy day. Their presence was required because a gun was a danger to the whole prison, but they were used to riots and sieges. Nobody in Cheviot had taken a hostage or damaged anything or threatened violence. The prisoners were safely locked away and, bar those who'd missed showers or work or classes, nobody was kicking up a stink.

Accompanied by two of HM Prison Service's Dedicated Search Teams, the Tornadoes went into each cell fast and loud, in case that elusive gun was pulled and aimed, but most inmates submitted without issue. A few authority-haters required restraints, but otherwise it was a walk in the park.

The gun wasn't in a cell, which was actually bad news. Searching the rest of the prison grounds would take the DSTs many days and until it was found, or deemed not to exist, all prisoners on the move would be carefully watched. Extra guards would be present during association and exercise periods. Cheviot would for a time feel more like an A+ rather than a category A facility.

For the Tornadoes, though, there was little work and by 8.30pm they had gone. A calm descended on Cheviot. Since evening bang-up was at eight, little felt different from any other day. Emma's own case notwithstanding.

One prisoner in particular felt an impact, though. Allersby, who'd sought a phone in order to remotely watch the birth of his son, started banging on his door, demanding to see the governor. Only when she heard his name did she remember his appointment.

'Has his wife given birth already?' she asked the officer who'd called with the news.

'Yep. Two hours ago. Some midwife called the prison. His missus is none too chuffed.'

'And no one told me?'

'Guess not. We were kind of busy. Besides, no one...'

Of course. Everybody had been locked down, no phone calls at all permitted. But that wasn't going to make Allersby feel better. She decided she would make it up to him somehow and got the officer to pass that message in the hope that it would calm him down.

'How about I tell him instead that he should have thought about this before he started dealing drugs?'

She wasn't sure if the officer was serious. 'Just my message, please.'

After that call, she made one to Base Zero. This message was for Samson: that she would come see him at ten tonight. The supervisor passed it on and returned with one. 'He says if you don't come on the dot of ten, that's it for him being a Listener. You had your chance. He says everyone can suffer. Ha. You believe this guy, thinking he's the bees knees? These threats are just what I was talking about. Selfish sod is out for what he can get. He doesn't give a toss about helping people to...'

Emma was no longer listening. Unlike the supervisor, she knew Samson was talking in code, and she knew exactly what he meant. If she didn't come for him at ten o'clock on the dot, her family was dead. She hung up the phone while the supervisor was still rabbiting.

The past few hours had been hectic, not a moment to think. Now she had that moment, and her thoughts were in one place. The western tower. She'd worried about getting Samson out of his cell and into that tower, with little consideration given to his plans thereafter. Now she could think of nothing else. *Just how is that bastard planning to get onto the other side of the wall?*

Her desk phone rang. It was her secretary, with an outside call. From Darren, Cheviot's duty manager. Emma took a deep breath as the call was put through. Darren, too, was a victim of this fiasco, and she had no idea what to say to him.

'I guess you heard,' he said. 'What did you hear?'

He was worried that somehow she knew he'd been lured into a honeytrap. 'You got attacked by a pair of muggers. I'm so sorry about that.'

'Yes. That's right. But I had no money on me, so they broke my legs.'

He described how, and it was a terrible story. Two men had held him down on his back with his legs bridging a stream, then added weight until they snapped at the knees. A mental video of the scene made her shiver. That poor man. She knew his attackers were the animals calling themselves Jekyll and Hyde. The same men who had her husband and daughter.

'Did they say anything to you?' she asked.

'No,' he said after a pause. 'Except they said they wanted something, but they went ahead and broke my legs without telling me what.'

The broken legs were what they wanted, to guarantee he'd be off work and Emma would replace him. She felt a wave of guilt, but didn't know why. She hadn't caused this.

'Anyway, I'm calling to apologise and to say I've gone ahead and written the impact statement about the cell fire. I'll email it across when I get a chance. I didn't want to leave you extra jobs.'

'Oh, okay. Thank you. Again, I'm sorry about what happened.'

'Thanks. Look, I also called just to say... well, I don't want to scare you. I just wondered if the people who attacked me had another reason...'

Her breath caught. How much did Darren know. 'What reason?'

'I don't know. This line of work... we get threats. I wondered if one of our inmates sent them. You know, payback for something. I guess I'm just saying watch your back. But I don't want to make you paranoid. I'm sorry.'

She relaxed a little. He didn't know the truth. 'I'll take care and keep my eyes open. Thanks again. I hope you get better real soon.'

After the call, she looked at her watch, wondering if she should try to call Minny again. It was risky, though. It might endanger her family. She couldn't do it. She had told Samson she wanted to hear from them before she helped him escape, and she had no choice but to hope he kept his word. If he got out.

If.

FORTY-NINE

Just how is that bastard planning to get onto the other side of the wall?

The answer was elusive, but if it was around to find, it lay in only one place.

She made a call to D-wing, where she asked for an officer to accompany her outside. She was sent a woman called Tasker, who was overweight and a twenty-year veteran of prison service. They met in the Hub and Emma explained what she wanted.

The search teams hadn't yet been into the grounds proper, although they were in some of the outbuildings. Emma had a theory: what if the unsearched towers were the conduit between the outside world and the inside?

Tasker wasn't so sure. 'I know we've had people throw things into the towers from outside, but how would a prisoner have gotten a gun into the prison? The tower doors are locked and alarmed.'

'Still, it's burning a hole in me. I want to go check. We'll start with the western tower because of the river. I've already turned off the alarm.'

And so it was. She and Tasker headed out. Emma had the

key to the tower and pretended to turn it in the door lock, even though it was already disengaged from earlier. Like the stiff lock, the door required the strength of two to push inwards against rusted hinges and an accumulation of dust.

Tasker stepped inside first. The interior was gloomy, but it received illumination through the barred doorway at the back. That would soon depart because night was coming. The place stank badly for some reason, and not just because of windblown detritus and even a few dead animals on the grimy floor.

Twelve feet above them was a newer, reinforced concrete ceiling. It sliced the stone staircase, which curved against around the wall, in half. These steps were the only indication that there was space above. Samson wasn't getting out through the roof, that was for sure.

'I wonder if they entombed anything up there,' Tasker said. 'Like a prisoner or some treasure.'

Emma approached the barred window. It had once been a doorway, but its height was only four-and-a-half feet. She wrapped her hands around two of the six bars. They were flaky and sharp from peeling black paint, but thick and sturdy. They were spaced just five inches apart, so Samson certainly wasn't squeezing himself through without a year of hunger striking behind him.

She was no engineer or craftsperson, but surely it would take Samson's men a long time, perhaps an hour, to cut through these thick bars, just like she'd told Adley. Everyone would hear it. The exterior cameras would see it. So that was out.

Then how?

Emma put her face close to the bars and looked left and right. Three of the prison's towers had a chain-link fence curved around them to stop the people getting close. Here, because of the river just three metres away, it was a little different. Five metres to each side, barbed-wire-topped fencing ran out from the walls, down the riverbank, and dipped into the water. The ten-metre section of riverbank between them was also lined with thick tangles of barbed wire. Emma was looking at a wedge-shaped, secure area of grass.

The barbed wire at the edge of the riverbank prevented access from the water, but not the opposite way round. A leap from the top of the embankment would clear the barrier. If Samson escaped the tower, reaching the water would be easy – but then what?

From where she stood, facing the corner of the breakers yard across the water, she had an arrow-straight view through the fence and down a long aisle created by two rows of busted vehicles stacked four high, to some kind of office at the end. She had seen the yard on Google Earth and knew it was a maze-like warren of car-lined alleyways, good for losing yourself as a fugitive. Could this be his plan?

There were problems, though. The far riverbank was also lined with barbed wire for fifty metres in each direction. If that didn't stop an escapee who was determined to enter the breakers yard, he would then face high iron palisade fencing topped with rotating spikes. It seemed too much.

So, Samson had other plans. If he had people coming for him, a car could whisk him away in no time. If he had no help on the outside, he could swim with the current and, if he stayed below the surface for extended periods, make speedy, unseen progress through the open land. Out there were woods and villages he could get lost in, allowing him to make his way anywhere.

Or, he could swim against the current until the barbed wire ended, climb out, and run towards the nearest populated place: Ingram. Her home village. Did he have a safe house there? God, what if it was the empty house across from hers?

For the first time in seemingly a long time, she gave a little laugh. Now she was just being silly. Samson would be picked up by car and taken back to London, his home turf. He wasn't going to live on her street!

The officer named Tasker came to her side and stared at the grassy no-go zone directly outside. 'No footprints or anything. I don't think anyone came this way to lob a gun in.'

'No,' Emma said.

'I'd say it's best to check the other towers. No river there. Easier to get to.'

'No. Even if the gun came in that way, the doors are locked and I have the only key. Besides, the gun might now be in the prison. We'd see nothing. Footprints wouldn't mean a thing. I think this was a wasted journey. Let's get back inside.'

'Eager to get home?' Tasker asked with a grin. 'You've been on since early this morning, right?'

'Approximately twelve hours. Feels like fifty.'

'Tell me about it.'

That was one thing Emma could never do.

FIFTY

Somehow, the blood avoided her.

It crept across the tiled kitchen floor, towards her. Minny took a step back, then another, until she bumped into the corner created by the sink unit and the tall fridge. The blood cut off her escape as it touched the far edges of the unit and the fridge, But there it stopped, as if wary of her. She sat down in her clear wedge of floor with her knees against her chest.

As the one who'd opened the cellar door, the male policeman had zero chance to defend himself. Hyde's big knife had sunk into his throat even before the danger could register. That first blow had staggered him backwards before buckling his knees. Before he'd even hit the deck, the knife had given the first wound two partners in the chest.

Hyde had then launched himself at the female officer. With more time to… not think, but react, the female had managed to unholster her yellow taser and fire. But panic had voided her aim and the probes had missed their target. That had been the extent of her own defence. In the next second, Hyde's blade had been hilt-deep in her chest. She had fallen backward, fast and hard, and Minny had heard the crack of bone when skull hit tile.

Clearly the woman had had no capacity for a comeback at that point, but Hyde hadn't been finished with her. There would be a single scenario from this terror that would haunt Minny for years: the monstrous brute bent over the female officer, stabbing downwards at speed. Each blow must have caught on bone, for when Hyde had withdrawn the blade, it had sucked the torso off the floor a few inches, giving the impression that his victim was bouncing.

Minny had tried to close her eyes, but they would not obey her.

Now, sitting in the clear wedge of floor, trapped there by the blood flood, Minny finally managed to shut her eyes. Her ears, though, would not help wrap a bubble around her.

'This is your fault, you bitch,' Hyde yelled at her. 'Skedaddle? That some kind of code word? You could have sent them on their merry way. But no. So look at what you did.'

His hand grabbed her hair, and the fingers of the other dug into her eyes, trying to force the lids open.

'Look at your work, bitch.'

His fingers were painful and might just blind her, but still she kept her eyes screwed shut. Sight she could live without, but if she looked again at the carnage, her mind would shatter.

New sounds: the front door slamming open, and footsteps.

'What the Jesus fuck?' Jek screamed upon entering the kitchen.

'Don't, he's got a knife,' she said, fearful that Hyde's bloodthirst wasn't yet satisfied.

For the next few minutes, she did her best to plug her ears as the two men screamed at each other. But she heard it all. She waited for Jek to moan in pain. She waited for blood to invade her wedge and soak her feet and butt. She waited for stabbing pains all over.

None of that happened. The voices got quieter, and quieter, until all she heard was a standard conversation. Normal words exchanged between the relatives. No threats. The two men simply discussed what to do next. The first item they agreed upon was to get Minny back upstairs.

A hand took her arm and Jek said, 'Stand up. I'll carry you. Keep your eyes shut.'

She let herself be raised to her feet, then lifted off the floor. She planned to keep her eyes shut until Jek dumped her on her bed, for that was a safe distance from the gore. But when that happened, she chose to continue living in a black world. She felt his hand raise her arm and zip-tie it to the headboard. Only when he was gone did she re-enter the real world.

There was little to hear from downstairs for a few minutes. The first sound was Hyde's voice, and it seemed to come from outside. 'Grab his legs, you dick, it's easier. And be quicker. And don't say he's heavier because this bitch has puppy fat.'

She wanted to throw up. The two men were obviously removing the bodies from the house. Hyde she could easily imagine doing so, but her brain couldn't – or wouldn't – construct an image of Jek dragging a dead man. She wondered if he was acting under threat after all, or in a state of shock. Or if his previous niceness had been an illusion.

FIFTY-ONE

'...And don't say he's heavier because this bitch has puppy fat.'

As if he was doing nothing more grotesque than carrying a sack of potatoes, Hyde hauled the wrapped body of the female police officer off the blood-greased kitchen floor and heaved it over his shoulder. And then he stood there, waiting, as if he believed Joel could do the same with the deceased male.

The madman had already found bin liners and enveloped the bodies. No portion of clothing or skin was visible, but the tightly wrapped gaffer tape highlighted curves and straights, clearly defining the packages as human bodies. Nauseous with fear and disgust and disbelief, Joel had to clear his mind of everything except his wife and child. Front and centre, they gave him the impetus to push on, and he grabbed the dead male's legs.

Hyde carried the woman out the back door, where he stood and waited for Joel to follow. Waiting would be a theme because while Joel's arms were free, his ankles were still taped together. He could move only by hopping. This foul episode would not be swift.

'Run and I'll be turning your kid into one of these

Christmas presents,' Hyde said as Joel dragged the body towards the door. In a gruesomely ironic twist, the slippery blood all over the tiles made the going easier.

Even if he'd had the ability, Joel would never run and abandon his child, but Hyde didn't understand this and continued describing the abuse he'd unleash on Minny if an escape was attempted. Joel barely heard. Terror and fatigue had powered down his brain into the equivalent of a car's limp mode.

Jek had collected the police car from the end of the track and it was now parked alongside the house, both rear doors open. Jek stood by it. Hyde dumped his package half-inside, then accessed the opposite door to drag it fully onto the back seat with his partner's help.

Joel had barely dragged his own load ten feet. Free to help, Hyde barged him out of the way, which caused Joel to trip and sprawl in the dirt. Hyde lifted the corpse into his meaty arms. Joel lay where he'd fallen and stared at the tree canopy.

Contents aboard the car, Hyde shut both doors. 'You go inside now and check on Miss YouTube,' he told his comrade.

Jek paused. 'Is killing just as cool as you always hoped?' The question wasn't rooted in genuine curiosity. Joel knew the kid didn't like what had happened to the police officers.

'Off you go now,' Hyde said.

When Jek was gone. Hyde approached the wheelie bins by the back door and delved inside one. He extracted a backpack, and from that a bunch of keys. 'Go stand by the boiler box thing.'

Puzzled but fearful, Joel obeyed. He hopped his way there, by which time Hyde had overtaken him and used a key to open the enclosure door. 'Get him out,' Hyde said, stepping back.

Him? Another body? Loath to do so, Joel bent to see inside the metal box. The scene inside was more terrible than anything before: another body, but this one unwrapped. A man was curled around the boiler, wedged tightly in there.

'Who is he?'

'Mr wrong time, wrong place. And he did you a major favour. Now don't make me ask again. Get him out.'

It was a tough task because, dead or not, Joel didn't want to damage the body any further. Every second of it piled more misery upon Joel. When he saw a screwdriver sticking out of the dead man's head, he jerked away and, thanks to his taped ankles, fell on his arse.

Cursing his weakness, Hyde took over. He hauled the body out of the tight space with zero of Joel's care for its well-being. Joel was pretty certain he heard something fleshy tear, although it might have been clothing.

Hyde chose to drag this body, perhaps because it wasn't wrapped up. This innocent victim went into the boot of the police car. After slamming shut the lid, Hyde returned to Joel.

'Jek's like you: a pussy. Can't handle the bodies, so we'll keep this one on the quiet, okay? You mention this guy, even by mistake, and I'll have one of your kid's fingers off. Got that?'

So, Hyde suspected that Jek would be unimpressed by a third murder. Could that pose a future opportunity to fracture their friendship further? 'You like killing people, don't you?'

Why had he said that? A numbed brain? A moment of bravado? Sheer incomprehension? Hyde didn't care for mitigating circumstances and thudded a boot into Joel's jaw, which seemed to loosen at least one tooth. It made his head buzz and the world shimmer.

'This is work, business, that's all,' Hyde said. 'Not that I have to explain anything to you. I kill the people I need to, and your big mouth is probably gonna put you top of that list before long.'

FIFTY-TWO

When Jek entered the room, she could still hear two men outside, doing something godawful. Now she knew she'd been wrong about who had been issued instructions by Hyde. 'You are both bastards,' she hissed at him. 'My dad.'

Jek sat on the edge of the bed. 'Not my choice. None of this crap was.'

'But Hyde didn't drag you here. You chose to do this.'

'I chose parts of this, yes.'

'The part that involved breaking into this house and kidnapping a family.'

He nodded. 'But if I hadn't come, Hyde would be here with one of his cronies. Trust me, you got lucky with me. At least I'm trying to make sure nobody dies.'

She wanted to spit at him. 'Well done with the two police officers.'

Jek paused. He looked down, and that was when he saw her smartwatch on the carpet. He picked it up, looked it over, and put it in his pocket. 'I was locked in a police car, Minny. Besides, I have a mission, and nothing will ruin it.'

She turned her head from him, unwilling to talk any more.

He didn't push it and left soon afterwards. Minny tried to ignore the sounds from outside, but it was impossible. She knew her father was burying the two police officers, and she felt for him. She wondered if the kidnappers planned to somehow blame him for the murders. Even if that wasn't their plan, he might get in trouble, threatened or not, for helping them dispose of the bodies. And she wondered if this nightmare would ever end.

About half an hour later, some ten minutes after the noises outside had stopped, Jek came to her room again. 'We have to go. We have to leave this place. The police will come looking for their people soon. Please don't object or resist.'

He sounded machine-like now. She didn't like it. The old Jek seemed to have gone. Or he'd removed the mask that had fooled her.

So she did as asked and didn't object, didn't resist. Willingly, she went downstairs behind him, and outside. The sun was setting, which put the woods in darkness. The urge to run was as great as the desire to yank a hand from a fire, but her feet stayed put. She couldn't abandon her father.

Her father's car wasn't here, and nor was he, but she saw an old, yellow van with Hyde and a woman standing by it, a motorbike parked nearby, and a police car on the track. Jek led her to a sliding side door of the van and told her to get in. That part she did eagerly, for her father was here. His arms were zip-tied behind his back and his ankles were bound. There were no windows, so it was pitch black when Jek shut the sliding door behind her.

'No talking in there,' Hyde shouted. 'And don't undo your dad, or else.'

She heard three engines start within a second of each other. She guessed Jek was taking the motorbike, and Hyde would probably drive the police car. The van was cranky and loud, probably on its last legs. In the blackness, she fumbled for her father and hugged him. His bound hands meant he couldn't hug her back. But he could speak.

'I'm sorry for this,' he whispered, loudly enough to be heard over the engine, but not by those riding up front.

'It's okay, Dad,' she said. She reached behind him, for the zip ties, but he objected. 'I have to release you.'

'No. He'll hurt you. Just leave me for now. I'm hurting and I don't think we could tackle two men. We'll have to wait for a better chance to escape.'

He was right. 'We'll be okay, I promise. I spoke to Mum.'

'What? How? When?'

She told him about the phone call via the smartwatch, if only to reassure him that her mother was okay. But she mentioned nothing about overhearing Hyde's plan to kill them once their boss had escaped prison, or her instructions to Emma to delay that breakout. It would only make him worry that she was taking dangerous risks.

'Your mother's a clever one,' he said. 'She'll know what to do. Don't be scared for her. She'll be fine.'

Minny believed it now. Her mum was as sharp as a needle and had gotten her role as a prison governor by knowing how to play people. She would see trickery and lies coming a mile away. There was every chance that her mother could sideline the escape plan and save herself. But, given her distance from them, rescuing Minny and her dad from the evil clutches of Hyde might prove a task too much.

Minny might have to save them.

FIFTY-THREE

As he followed the van in the police car, with Jek's bike at the rear, Hyde tilted the mirror so he could see between the front seats. To the bodies stacked along the rear bench.

Is killing just as cool as you always hoped?

Ever since that moment when, as a kid, he'd watched a man get beaten to death outside a pub, he'd wondered what it would feel like to get some of that juice. To plan a kill, take his time with it, and stare into a victim's eyes as the heart shut down.

He'd never chased that buzz, but life had forced him headlong down a path towards it. The old standard broken home scenario: abusive father, a mother who didn't give a shit, and a social circle composed of all the wrong people.

Without the infrastructure in place to give him a sweetly normal upbringing, he hadn't managed to succeed in school or learn a code of conduct accepted by the moral world. Nobody gave him respect and nobody opened doors for him. He was street-smart, but not educated. Learning came by way of experience, not tutoring. For some reason he just couldn't take on board what people told him.

It had held him back and by the time he was a young adult,

he had none of the skills or knowledge that people required to make a positive mark on the world. But he did have mass and power, and a fuck-you attitude. He had long ago found out that any argument, any obstacle, any difference of opinion, could be swung in his favour with a fist. He couldn't increase his brainpower, but he could increase his bulk.

Everybody had labelled him an outcast and a problem-child and said he'd never achieve a thing. But those streets smarts and bloated muscles would ultimately send him to high places. By spilling the blood of those who got in his way.

'You like killing people, don't you?'

Hyde tilted the mirror again, this time so he could see his own eyes.

No, he didn't like killing. He wasn't a monster. A callous streak was the backbone of the world he was embroiled in, that was all. The boiler repairman and the cops had all threatened the plan, so they'd had to go. Their deaths had been necessary. He hadn't really enjoyed whacking them. He was all business, and murder was part of the game. He couldn't swear it wouldn't raise its head again, but he had no intention of adding it to his portfolio.

'He's no doctor, but it remains to be seen if I'm a monster.'

He looked away from the mirror, unable to face the reflection of his own accusing eyes.

FIFTY-FOUR

Five or ten minutes into the journey, the van stopped. When the sliding side door opened, Minny saw only Jek standing there with a crash helmet in his hand. 'I'm sorry about this,' he said. 'Hyde wants you to see what happens next. I'm sorry. Blank your minds if you can, or stare slightly above so you don't see.'

He stepped aside to expose a new part of the world. It was now quite dark. The van was on a flattened dirt road running through woods. Behind, and parked in the grass, was the police car. Hyde was at the back, by the open boot, and in his hands was a jerry can. He was splashing petrol into the boot, then inside the car, now all over the exterior.

That done, he came to the van and held up a lighter. 'Who wants the honour? One of you will, or you'll both suffer.'

Minny realised that the two police officers hadn't been buried at all. They were dead in the boot of the car. This was about destroying evidence by fire – including the bodies. She would have no part of it.

But her father, perhaps to save Minny from the ordeal, said, 'I'll do it.'

Hyde shook his head. 'No, you did the dragging. You, young

miss. Out you come. Film this for your YouTube channel if you want.'

She didn't move. Hyde lost his grin. He reached into the van and grabbed her father's legs, and dragged him towards the door. 'Right, he's going up in flames, as well.'

'No,' she said as Hyde hauled her father out, to land hard on his front on the dirt track. She got out after him and snatched the lighter from Hyde.

'That's a good little g–'

Just then, all three of them reacted as light blasted the darkness. The police car was suddenly aflame. Jek stood by it, a lighter in his hand.

'You dick,' Hyde yelled. 'I wanted this bitch to do it. I said that.'

Jek shrugged. 'I didn't hear you.'

Hyde swore again. He pushed Minny into the van, then picked up Joel, with surprising ease, and lobbed him inside. Minny stuck out her legs to help break his fall. She saw that his face was scratched and dirty from stones and muck on the track, and then saw no more as the door shut and plunged her world into darkness once more. They were on the move again shortly afterwards. To God knew where.

FIFTY-FIVE

For a long time, Emma sat in her office and stared at her watch, trying to pluck up the courage to call Minny. There was every chance her daughter was alone and could answer. But if not, if one of her captors was with her, their communication line would be dead. And Minny might get hurt if the men suspected they'd been secretly communicating. She was desperate to connect with her daughter again, to know she was okay, to say *I love you* in case she never got another chance. But it wasn't worth the risk. She would wait for Minny to call.

This prevarication burned a lot of time. When she noted that it was 9.40, her heart started to race. Samson wasn't planning his escape until tomorrow, so why did he want her to visit him in twenty minutes' time? The fact that he wanted his gun could be a clue. He might have another target now that Pleasance was out of reach. And her presence by his side – could that be so she would escort him to his new victim's cell?

She was loath to release him from his cage, but what choice did she have? He would have her family killed. He was locked up, but he had a phone. She could send in guards to take it and then leave him to rot, but that, too, was a risk. He wouldn't be able to give the kill order, but what if he already had? He'd hinted as much when claiming that Minny and Joel would be dead if he wasn't free by 10am. His men might have instructions to start blasting if they didn't hear from him.

10am was twelve hours away, which was ample time for her to send the police to the cottage. But what if her family had been moved? What if Samson was supposed to send his thugs a message every half hour, and one failed contact meant the knives would come out?

Her phone rang. It was the A-wing supervisor. 'Allersby is crying his eyes out. He wants an explanation. He wants to see you. I thought I'd mention it, that's all.'

'I really should apologise,' she said. 'I could have authorised his video call without affecting the lockdown, but it slipped my mind.'

'You had a lot on. Don't worry about it.'

'Allersby will rue missing his kid's birth forever. Giving him a face-to-face apology is probably the least I can do. Tell him I'll be down to see him shortly.'

Allersby, a tall, skinny and prematurely balding man of about thirty, was sitting up on his bunk when she arrived. His bunkmate was standing.

'Guv. Thanks for coming. I want to ask you about possibly getting a video chat with the missus tomorrow. Can my mate step out so he doesn't hear this?'

She checked her watch. 'Sure.'

The bunkmate squeezed past her, and past the wing supervisor. But as he stepped out the doorway, he reached back and grabbed the supervisor's arm. Before Emma knew what was happening, the bunkmate had hauled the officer out of the cell.

In the next moment, Allersby leaped up and kicked the door

shut. Before she could react, he grabbed her and put a stubby pencil to her throat.

'Anyone comes in here and I'll stick you,' he yelled into her face.

The time was 9.51. In nine minutes she was supposed to be at Samson's cell, or he'd order her family to be killed.

FIFTY-SIX

Hyde peeked through the lit kitchen window of the farmhouse. He saw an elderly couple inside, both in dressing gowns, both with cutely matching curly grey hair. The male had a towel over his shoulder.

Beside Hyde, Denise said, 'They should be easy to restrain. But, baby, you're not going to kill them, are you?'

After hearing about the two dead police officers – not the boiler guy, for that little tale might annoy her – Denise had been pretty withdrawn. It was frustrating because he'd told her this mission might involve deaths, and she'd just about begged to be involved.

He said, 'Sweets, I thought you understood. Coppers are a big threat. I had to put them down.'

She looked glum. 'I know. I just... these people are no threat.'

He moved out of sight of the window and pulled her into his arms. 'Exactly, so nobody needs to die. I told you, we just tie them up. We only need the house for a few hours. If they're senile they probably won't remember this come tomorrow.'

She nodded against his chest. 'Okay, baby. But let's not hurt them.'

'Of course not. That's why we're going with your plan.'

Her plan was softly-softly bullshit. He wanted to boot down the door and rush in, a blitz attack that would probably remind the old farts of a Nazi invasion and freeze them dead in their tracks.

She kissed his bald head, pulled away from him, and went around the house to the front door. He followed.

On the step was the jerrycan used to burn the police car. Her idea was to knock on the door and claim she needed water for an overheating engine. He waited out of sight beside the door while Denise banged on it. Once they were inside, Denise would zip-tie the wife and Hyde would restrain the husband. Easy.

He glanced over at the road, where Jek stood by the parked bike and van to make sure the prisoners didn't escape. They swapped thumbs ups. Jek was another one who'd been eager as hell at the outset and now moaned because people were getting hurt. Why play a part if you didn't have the balls for it?

The old dear came to the door, but opened it with the security chain in place. Good practice, but the follow-up was weak. Denise gave her line about water and a hot engine, flashed the jerrycan, and the chain dropped away a second later. Trustful people, the bumpkins out here.

Even better, when the woman fully opened the door, she walked away into the house. Denise followed her towards the kitchen and both of them were out of sight by the time Hyde put his first shoeprint in a stranger's home.

His target was the husband, but he had no idea where–

'Do you want this bath after me, Maggie?' came a yell from upstairs.

Thanks, pal. Hyde thudded up the stairs. On the top

landing, he saw four doors, all open, all dark beyond except the one dead ahead. He was in there a half second later, meeting eyes with the husband, who was naked in the bath.

Downstairs, he heard a moan from the wife. *Well done, Denise.* The old guy reacted as any bloke should when hearing his missus in distress, so Hyde moved quick and had to abandon his planned joke about being their long-lost son. He grabbed the man's scrawny throat with his big hand and pushed him against the slanted back end of the bath.

'Don't make a damn sound,' he said. The old guy did all his screaming with his wide eyes.

To prove he was serious, Hyde pushed down harder still, forcing the man's head under the water. Wrinkled fingers scratched at his hand, but inadequately. Hyde decided to let the man breathe again.

Or he tried to.

Instead, his body remained locked in place, straight arm holding the head under the water. If he let the old man go, he might pull one of those emergency cords with the red triangle that all old people had. Or grab a shotgun. Too risky.

Hyde held fast until the flailing arms dropped away and he saw the mouth open for air that didn't exist. The eyes stared up at him through four inches of water, pleading for mercy.

Which also didn't exist.

When he went downstairs a few minutes later, he found Denise and the wife sitting at the kitchen table. The old woman had her arms zip-tied behind her back. Denise was apologising and the old woman just listened. They both seemed calm, as if they were old friends having afternoon tea. Maybe home invasions were run-of-the-mill out here. *Oh, here we go again,* with a roll of the eyes.

That calm disintegrated when they saw the dripping, naked body over Hyde's shoulder.

Denise moaned and the old woman shrieked. Too much noise, even though they were out in the boondocks. Hyde dropped the body onto the floor as the old woman jumped to her feet, still screaming. Denise was frozen to the spot, eyes and mouth wide, but the old lady had a plan: run for the back door, even though her arms were out of the game and she wouldn't be able to open it.

Hyde snatched a butter knife from a finished food plate as he ran past the table. He caught the woman at the door. He tried to stab her in the back, but she half turned and the dull blade hit her arm. It didn't even puncture the skin, but the pain elicited a mighty yelp.

He grabbed the same arm with both hands and yanked downwards, forcing the skinny woman to overbalance and face-plant the tiled floor. He then raised a boot and dropped it onto her head like an anvil.

Denise, still seated, gave a mighty grunt when the blow landed, as if the exertion belonged to her. She loosed another as his foot struck again.

In total she made the sound thirteen times.

FIFTY-SEVEN

When the van had stopped, Minny expected the rear or the sliding side door to open. She had heard Hyde and his girlfriend exit the cab, but nothing thereafter, and not a peep from Jek.

'What are they doing?' she had said.

Her father had held up a finger, an instruction to be silent and listen. She had heard nothing. After a short while, her father tried both doors. Locked. 'Maybe they've run off.'

Minny had thought of her mother. Perhaps she had somehow saved the day, forcing the kidnappers to flee. She lifted the hand that had worn her smartwatch, but it was gone. She remembered that Jek had pocketed it. Damn.

The silence had seemed to last ages, but now it was terminated by voices outside. The cab driver's door opened and shut, then the engine started. Minny thought they were going to drive again, but the sliding side door grated open. She backed away from it.

Jek and Hyde stood there. The van was parked on a tarmac road with dark fields all around. Right behind the two men was a dirt track leading off the road. It curved out of sight beyond the van door.

'Out,' Hyde ordered, pointing at her father. 'And you stay put, girl.'

Her father started to move, but apparently not fast enough. Both men grabbed him and yanked him out. They held him down on the road and put zip ties around his ankles. More secured his wrists together behind his back.

Minny watched Jek as this took place. He didn't seem unwilling to incapacitate her dad. She had been so wrong about this bastard. He had tricked her all along to gain compliance. He was as bad as his vicious friend.

Minny was ordered out, but allowed to stand. She saw the female kidnapper, Hyde's girlfriend, in the van's driver's seat. She seemed to be crying. Just seconds later, the vehicle tore away at speed. Minny figured the girlfriend was going to hide it somewhere.

Now she was no longer in the dark interior of the van, Minny could make out a small brick house about fifty metres down the track, which wound past and towards a series of farm buildings. The front door of the house was wide open and all the lights were on. Now she knew where the trio had gone earlier. The house was to be their new hiding place.

Hyde zip-tied her hands behind her back, but left her ankles free. He dragged her father down the track by the hair, forcing him to hop while bent over. Jek led her by the arm. She wanted to spit and curse at him, but she said nothing. He played copycat.

Hyde entered the house first and led her father down a hallway. Jek aimed her for the stairs. The bedroom he took her to had a coastal theme, with pale, warm tones, exposed, timeworn beams and sea-based artwork. The king-sized bed even had an ocean-print quilt. But also a solid wood headboard that had nothing to zip-tie a prisoner to.

'I'm sorry about this,' he said. 'Hyde isn't happy that I was being nice to you. So I'm pretending I don't care about you anymore.'

That made sense. She believed him. It dampened some of her hate and anger. But only a little. He was still her abductor. 'Who lives here?' she asked.

'I don't know them. They're not here. Sit there, please.'

He meant a wicker egg chair. She sat and he said he had to secure her in place, in case Hyde came upstairs. She understood and said so. When that task was complete, he went for the door with a promise to be back shortly.

'I don't think I trust you anymore,' Minny replied. 'I don't matter to you at all. Nor does my father.'

He paused before giving his answer. 'You do. Both of you. But someone else matters more.'

'A murderer in prison? Each to his own, I guess.'

Jek exited without another word.

FIFTY-EIGHT

Jek found Hyde in the kitchen, doing something astronomically unsound.

He hadn't yet laid eyes on the homeowners, in part because he hated to see people suffering. Any suffering here was a part of history, because they were dead. The male looked almost at peace, but his soaked body told a story of drowning. The woman, however, had suffered a far more violent demise. Surviving head trauma like that would put her in Ripley's Believe it or Not.

Now he knew why Hyde had insisted on using Denise to infiltrate the house: he'd planned to kill both occupants.

The murders themselves, however, didn't hold a candle to the aftermath. Hyde had laid the couple out parallel, just a foot of space between them, and forced Joel to lie down in the gap, sandwiched between corpses. Hyde was using tape to bind all three of them together, nice and tight. Joel's head was just inches from the busted skull and lacerated flesh of the old lady's. He moaned against the tape across his mouth. Hyde seemed to find it all very funny.

'You're losing your mind,' Jek said.

Hyde continued binding corpses to the living and didn't even look at Jek. 'I'm showing the boss that I have skills and can do what's needed. I've been held back too long. That's why I'm in charge and you ain't. Too weak.'

Sure, Hyde had always been low-rung in Samson's gang, but this wasn't his attempt to prove his worth. He was a tiger made docile by a cage, now loose and able to bite and rend. A dangerous mind given free rein. Samson had probably sensed it and had given Hyde this job because he needed someone a little crazy. 'Whatever you say.'

'This is the endgame. After today, we're away and free, my man. It won't matter how many dead we leave behind.'

He meant Samson's plan, Jek realised. For their help, the boss intended to whisk them overseas, to a Spanish hideout he had prepared and waiting. 'So if you were going to the moon and you had your finger on the nuclear button...'

Hyde laughed. 'If I could have my mates with me, hell yes. I'd nuke the planet. You want to help me here?'

'Let me think. No. Did we find out yet where the meeting place is?'

'No. Stop asking that. It could change. When it's time for us to know, we'll know. Now off you go and take care of Miss YouTube.'

Jek was happy to. When he entered the bedroom, Minny asked how her father was.

'He's not hurt. But he's not happy.'

'How long will we be here?'

Earlier, Hyde had had a phone call from Adley, one of Samson's right-hand men. There had been a problem at the prison and Samson's planned 4pm escape had gone up in smoke. Now they were in for a wait, and that was all he knew. 'I don't know. Hopefully it's not too long. When the call comes, Hyde and me go and you'll be released. That's the plan.'

'Yours, maybe. Not Hyde's. He won't let me and my dad live. And you know it, so don't lie to me.'

There was a chance Samson would not order their deaths, but the original plan had been to kill all three Catalanos once he was free. He would not lie to her, but his answer came from another angle. 'I will try my best to make sure none of your family is hurt.'

'But what about Hyde? What if you have to hurt your own family to do that?'

Again he would not lie to her, but this time he chose silence.

FIFTY-NINE

'That was my kid's birth, you bitch.'

Emma tried to lean back, away from the pointed end of the pencil at her throat, but Allersby had her against the wall and she could go nowhere. 'I'm sorry,' she said. It was that or *At least you know you'll see her at some point in the future, dickhead.*

'My kid's birth!' he yelled again. 'He only gets one, and you made me miss it.'

'I know. But it was out of my hands. Put the pencil down, please.'

'I should put it deep in your neck.'

A crowd had gathered at the door. Four or five officers, all peering through the thin, vertical plastic window. They tried to appeal to Allersby, telling him he was making a mistake, that nobody had intentionally tried to stiff him, that he should let the governor go. Backing vocals were given by prisoners shouting their opinions, none of it helpful or pleasant.

'I'm not letting her go,' he yelled back. 'And no one come in or I'll stick her. Stay out, you bastards.'

'I'm okay,' Emma shouted. 'Don't rush in. Shaun doesn't want to hurt me.'

'Tell them to back away,' Allersby said. 'I don't want their faces at my window.'

Someone outside said they couldn't do that, but Emma wasn't having it. 'No, back away. Everyone. Do it now.'

The faces departed, but neither she nor Allersby were fooled into thinking the immediate area outside the cell was clear. She met Allersby's eyes. 'How about I sit by the door, so no one can come in? You don't need the pencil.'

'Fuck you. I'll tell you what I want. My wife and kid, brought right here. Here into this shithole.'

The kid was newborn, which made it impossible to grant that wish, at least for a few days. But she'd had some hostage negotiation training and knew the word *no* was one to avoid. 'We can see what we can do. But first—'

Angry, he drove a knee into her thigh, which hurt like hell. 'Fuck that. First, you're bringing them here. You ain't getting out of here until then.' He turned to the door. 'You fuckers better not call the hostage people in, or I'll stick her.'

Now, he went with her plan and forced her to sit with her back to the door. He knelt by her, the pencil ever at her throat. He yelled through the door again. 'Go get my wife and kid. You've got two hours to get them here, or I'll stick her.'

Two hours? A glance at her watch showed her she had less than two minutes before everything perhaps turned to hell.

SIXTY

The Base Zero supervisor, surname of Warren, was a bit of an anomaly. He was cheeky, sarcastic, and pretty much disliked by all. But he had a werewolf-like ability to change his attitude when needed. This had allowed him to become the prison's Crisis Negotiator. Luckily, he was working twelve hours today and was punching into his coat in Base Zero Watchroom when he got a call for service.

His replacement was already present, so Warren immediately left Base Zero. The replacement went to Samson's cell. 'The governor's been taken hostage. She can't get away.'

Samson had his phone in his hand. He had been about to make a call and have her husband killed. He jumped off his bed. 'Bitch. This better not be another trick. Get on the phone to Markham and get him to Peterson's cell on C. I want him to get Peterson's phone, then this is what he's going to do...'

SIXTY-ONE

Back at Allersby's cell, a guard informed Emma that Warren was on his way. She was hardly enthused. Nor was Allersby, who yelled, 'No one's talking till my wife and kid get here. And they better be on their way.'

Warren was at the cell door a minute later. Allersby told him to fuck off, and wouldn't say a word after that except to count down the minutes.

Emma glanced at her watch.

10.06.

10.09.

10.12.

She wondered what Samson was thinking. Had he called his people and done something stupid? Her gut had been throbbing ever since this mad fiasco had begun, but now a headache had joined the party. She had taken risks by poking at Adley's ego, by foiling Samson's attempt to kill David Pleasance and to escape during his gardening shift, but what she was doing now was so much more dangerous.

Before, she had had the freedom to make changes, adapt on

the fly, for she was the governor and in control of this world. Here, right now, the balance had tipped away from her. A bit player with a pencil and too much anger had erased her power. By the time she got it back, if ever, it could be too late and all that was dear in life might be gone.

Just then there was a commotion outside the door. Someone told someone else to stay back, stop, get away from the door. There was a short scuffle of feet, as if the officers had tried to prevent someone getting close. A new voice then said, 'You wife's on the phone.' Something was pushed through the hatch before Emma heard more scuffling, presumably as the deliverer was removed.

The item that fell inside bounced off Emma, who still sat with her back to the door, and skittered across the floor. She and Allersby stared at it. It was a tiny mobile phone.

'Hello there,' said a voice from the phone.

'Who the fuck is this?' Allersby shouted at the device. Clearly, being male, the voice wasn't that of his wife.

Emma recognised it. Samson. One of his bent guards must have posted the phone for him, and probably under threat since he would now doubtless lose his job.

'It's Samson,' said the voice. 'Mrs Catalano was supposed to visit me at ten. Not good this, Shaun.'

Allersby's bravado evaporated. He sounded scared when he said, 'I'm sorry. But it's my kid. She made me miss–'

'Boo hoo. Let her go, Shaun, or you'll be off my Christmas card list. And you know I make the best cards.'

That simple, innocuous line contained an unsaid threat that nobody missed. Allersby immediately dropped the pencil and stepped away from Emma. A second later, officers stormed the cell, so fast and hard that the opening door sent Emma skidding across the floor. Four men dove on Allersby and pinned him onto his bed.

But even above all that racket, Emma heard Samson's voice again ooze from the tiny mobile phone.

'It's time for our appointment, guv. See you in a minute.'

SIXTY-TWO

The officers were worried about her health – mental and physical – after the scare. The facility doctor gave her a check over – brief, at her insistence – and sent her on her way.

From an officer, she learned that the phone had been shoved through the cell door by an employee called Markham, who was now suspected of being corrupt and serving Samson. She contacted his supervisor and told him to suspend him pending investigation. Samson had also had his cell searched and his phone confiscated. But they could hardly shift him to a worse place than Base Zero, so they simply left him alone thereafter.

Eighteen minutes after release from Adley's cell, she opened her office safe and extracted Samson's gun. It fit nicely in her suit jacket pocket, although there was a bulge. Her nerves were on fire, mostly because she didn't know Samson's plans with the gun, so hadn't yet figured out what to do.

She phoned ahead to request a visit with Samson. Given that he was now in the bad books, no lie about Listener training would fly. So she pretended she wanted to quiz him about the officer he'd sent to deliver the phone to the cell.

A new guard, called Yonkers, was on shift in Base Zero. He

was in his sixties, nearing retirement and eager for days without stress. All the prisoners and staff liked him. He also wasn't the suspicious type, and he didn't question her when she asked for Samson's cell to be opened. He remained in the Watchroom, eyes on paperwork.

She entered Samson's temporary home. He was dressed and in his shoes. 'Gun?'

'Not if you plan to kill someone.'

'Like I said, I'm having it hidden until tomorrow. Gun, now.'

Out of sight of the Watchroom, she pulled the weapon from her pocket. He snatched it and checked it over, possibly for damage. He declared it all good. 'You sold my man down the river.'

'Markham? I was waiting for that. I had no choice. He threw a phone with you on the line into the cell. You did that to him.' Then something struck her. 'How did you know that?'

Samson laughed. The he yelled one word: 'Yonkers.'

No. Surely not. But it was real. She knew from the dejected way that Yonkers came over. 'You're near retirement,' she said to him. He wouldn't look at her.

'He's also got twin sons down in London. My neck of the woods,' Samson said. 'Yonkers here will let us out and say nothing. You'll do the rest.'

Another terrible realisation hit her. 'You said the escape was tomorrow.'

'I did. I also said I wanted that knobhead Pleasance dead, and you fucked it up for me. Then I wanted out during gardening, and you played some silly trick there, too. I'm even wondering if you set that thing with Allersby up.'

'Are you serious? I set up being taken hostage?'

'You fucked up his dream to watch his kid being spat out. You knew he had form for taking hostages. And then you went into his cell alone. You knew he'd do that or you're an idiot. Which is it?'

Emma said nothing.

'Yep, another damn trick,' Samson said. 'No doubt you would have had some more trickery ready for me come tomorrow morning. You fucked a lot of people over to get your way.'

'Get my way?' she snapped. 'You're threatening to kill my family, you bastard.'

Samson pulled a phone from his pocket. She figured Yonkers had sneaked it in somehow. 'And I still can with a single phone call. So, guv, now I'm the one doing the tricking. I'm not going out tomorrow, but right now. And you're coming with me.'

SIXTY-THREE

Samson knew he'd be giving up his bent officer when he sent Markham to Allersby's cell to rescue Emma, but he no longer planned to use staff for his own ends and, more important, didn't want the governor hurt. To prove himself further, he was now going to divulge the whereabouts of hidden contraband.

'Starting with a tobacco stash he knows about,' Emma told the C-wing supervisor by phone. 'It's in the graveyard. I'm going to take him out there. I'll have Yonkers with me, so send a man down here to watch the other Zeroes, please.'

The supervisor said he'd do just that, no questions asked. Emma hung up the phone and took a deep breath. Samson had been right: his plan for getting outdoors and to the western tower was simple, and would work a treat.

'I didn't want to do this,' Yonkers said. 'He's got me by the balls. Some thugs approached my sons at their university. I–'

'I understand,' she said. How could she condemn this man when she was in the same boat, acting under threat to help a criminal? 'But we're doomed after this.'

'Even if I don't go down for this, even if nobody ever found out, I'm getting out after this. I'll steal something if I have to and get fired.'

A good idea, but possibly useless. Samson's kind didn't give up their golden geese without cause. Yonkers could retire and join a bowling club, and Samson would force him to steal pins. But she wasn't about to worry the officer any more.

They returned to Samson's cell, whose door was open. He was ready to go.

Ten minutes later, the governor, officer and prisoner exited the Hub via the spur between wings A and B. Their movement would be watched all the way to the inner fence on building-mounted cameras, and thereafter by CCTV devices attached to the top of the perimeter wall.

Emma told Samson this and added: 'So I hope you plan to escape quickly. If you have people coming to saw through the bars in the tower, they won't get chance before people come running.'

'Don't you worry about it,' he replied. 'And if it all goes wrong, I have six bullets.'

They continued walking. The inner fence approached far too quickly for her liking. Once there, Yonkers input the code and opened the gate.

Samson told Yonkers to head back. 'Go lurk around outside somewhere. Don't go back into the prison for half an hour.'

The officer looked at Emma.

'She's staying with me,' Samson said.

'It's fine,' she told Yonkers. 'Go back. I'll be okay.'

Then something happened that Emma didn't like. Without instruction, Yonkers removed his radio and gave it to Samson. This action had been pre-planned – but why?

When Yonkers was on the other side of the fence. Samson shut the gate. They both watched the officer walk away.

In the dark, the graveyard and the tower created a spooky

scene and added to Emma's distress. Samson walked amongst the graves and squatted before one to read the inscription.

'What are you doing?' she said.

He stood and shook his head. 'You want your tobacco stash, right?'

He moved to another grave and perused a second engraving. Now she understood. There was a camera atop the tower, staring down at them. If someone was watching, they were supposed to think that Samson was looking for the correct grave.

'When are your people coming?'

'Eleven minutes,' he said. 'Eager to have me gone?'

For six minutes, Samson pretended to hunt for a certain dead inmate. Emma followed him around, just watching. Neither of them spoke.

The silence was broken by the radio given to Samson. A voice said, 'Yonkers?'

'It's me,' Samson answered.

'Jacoby went to the toilet, so I didn't have to touch him. You're good to go. Camera is off.'

Samson didn't reply. He threw down the radio and grabbed Emma's arm, to lead her fast towards the tower. She realised what had just happened. Yonkers, Markham and Smith weren't the only officers in Samson's pocket. He'd also gotten to one of the two staff who tonight manned the security station in the Hub. That man, whoever he was, had obviously been tasked with getting rid of his colleague and shutting down the western tower camera at a precise time.

'Just how many of my staff have you forced into doing your bidding?' she asked.

'Fuck it, I'll tell you. Seven. Four new ones and three who got transfers here. And they're not all operating under duress. Now, open the door. If the alarm goes off, you'll badly regret it.'

The tower door was already unlocked and, because it had

been opened earlier, it wasn't so stiff this time. Emma pushed it wide all by herself and stood back. 'Now let my family go.'

'I'm not out yet. Later. Get inside.'

She paused. 'Why? Let me talk to my family.'

Samson shoved her through the doorway and quickly followed. He slammed the big door shut with a kick. Because it was dark outside, there was very little illumination save for moonlight that bounced off the river beyond the waterside opening.

'What are you doing?' she said. 'Why am I in here?'

Samson pulled out his phone a dialled a number from memory. When someone answered, he said, 'It's me. You guys in place?'

The phone was on speaker. She heard Adley's voice. 'Sure, boss. Good to go. She there?'

'She is. And you're on speaker.'

'Hello again, guv. Be seeing you soon.'

Emma's breath caught. A pause, then Samson said, 'Get the beers ready, dude. Catch you soon.'

Samson killed the call and pocketed her watch. Emma said, 'I said I want to talk to my family. And what did he mean by that? See you soon?'

'You're coming with me, I said. I need insurance in case it goes wrong. Once I'm free, I'll let you go back to your family. You can hear from them soon. But I'm not messing about with phone calls. If you think they're dead, scream for help and blow my plan.'

Scream from all the way out here with an iron door in the way? Nobody would hear. 'I don't trust you.'

'What am I, a criminal?' He laughed. 'No choice. Besides, you'll be arrested for this shit, as you well know. So you wouldn't see your people until court. This way you can hug and kiss them. It might be your last chance.'

Feeling flat and lost and hopeless, she sat on the cold floor, in the dark, while Samson went to the window and peeked through the bars. She could just about make out the fence belonging to the breakers yard for it reflected moonlight. The yard and the rest of the land out here was pitch black.

Her attention was snagged by movement beyond Samson. She ran to his side for a better look. He laughed at her inquisitiveness.

The movement had been a man in the breakers yard. He was dressed in black and stood by the fence, in the arrow-point corner directly across from the tower. As she watched, he lifted a tool that suddenly buzzed. A metal cutter of some kind. He raised the device above his head and started to cut a metal coupler connecting the two corner panels of the fence. When it split apart, the man bent down to work on the second remaining coupler.

She didn't understand. The tool surely couldn't get through the tower's bars, not in less than an hour or so, and how would the man cross the river anyway? Were there no other people? This was surely a Sisyphean task.

'Keep watching and you'll see,' Samson said, as if having read her thoughts.

She might be clueless as to the full method of Samson's escape, but she knew one thing for sure. It was really about to happen before her eyes.

SIXTY-FOUR

Hyde sent Jek a text, ordering him downstairs. The big man was in the living room, watching TV and drinking a can of bitter. The governor's giant Rubik's cube was on the coffee table, having been rescued by Hyde. Empty cans were scattered around his chair. Hyde hadn't seen him yet, so Jek poked his head into the kitchen, where he saw things had changed for the better.

The fun of binding Joel to two corpses had run its course and now Minny's father was taped to a chair at the kitchen table. The laptop was before him again so he could transfer money that didn't exist into an equally illusionary bank account. Déjà vu.

Jek returned to the living room. 'You called me down?'

Hyde jumped, having not heard his comrade enter the room. 'Funny bastard. Look at this TV. Two grand at least. But check out the wallpaper, the carpet, these nasty chairs. Fifty bloody years old at least.'

Jek didn't even look. 'You called me down for that?'

'No, I got a call. Samson should be out by ten. That's when we go. There's a big barn on the farm out back. We might need it if Samson doesn't get out, though. The old woman told Denise they have ten labourers coming. We can't stay here all night because the hired help will be here early. Go have a look at the barn. Take some photos. Samson wants to see it. He ordered you to go.'

Jek said nothing. He headed out the front to avoid the kitchen and walked down the track in the dark, deeper into the fields. Security lights created bright pools here and there, but most of the farmland was in blackness. He could see the barn beyond a couple of other dark buildings.

The reason for checking out the barn made sense, but Jek doubted Samson had ordered him to find a new hideout. Hyde was just being lazy.

SIXTY-FIVE

Hyde had indeed lied to Jek about who had to undertake the scouting mission, but it wasn't because he was lazy. In fact, the moment the younger man had gone, Hyde decided to spend some energy.

He went upstairs and into the main sleeping quarters, where Minny was lying on the bed. And she wasn't tied up. Seeing him, she sat up and her eyes widened. He was yet to get bored of seeing that reaction to his presence.

'Don't worry, I won't be raping you yet. Maybe later.'

He walked around the room, poking here and there. She just watched. He said, 'Want to show me your pussy?'

She shook her head.

'Even if it saves your dad from a broken nose.'

She said nothing. Made no movement.

Hyde shrugged. 'Okay, I'll go break your dad's nose.'

He reached the door before she reacted. She slid her tracksuit bottoms down, and wore nothing beneath. She then lay back, privates exposed, staring up at the ceiling.

He nodded. 'There it is. That's mine later.' Trailing laughter, he left the room.

SIXTY-SIX

Jek headed round the back of the house, to get his Kurtz. The bike was equipped and registered for road use, but it was also a fine vehicle for blasting off-road. He chose to ride with the light off and hope the engine noise, if heard by neighbours, couldn't be pinpointed at this farm. He also left his helmet behind.

He rode down the track to a gate in a galvanised wire fence surrounding the farmland. It was unlocked, so he nudged it open with his front wheel. While still some way out from the barn, he realised it was actually a cowshed. Closer, he saw apparatus for milking cows, but no animals themselves. Maybe they stayed outdoors in summer. A big place, but ultimately was no good for a hideout because it was open fronted.

Still, orders were orders, so he snapped photos with his phone and returned to show Hyde, who was still in his chair. That was good, for he'd worried that Minny might be targeted in his absence.

Jek had been gone only five minutes, but Hyde had added two empty cans to the mess around his feet. He sounded quite drunk now. 'That's no good for a hideout,' was his diagnosis. He lobbed Jek's phone back to him. 'I saw a grain silo. Go check that.'

'Why?'

'Just go check. In fact, photograph inside all the buildings.'

'Samson's orders?'

'Yep.'

Sure. Jek walked out. He rode around the farmyard for half an hour, snapping away with his camera. He enjoyed his time out because he hadn't ridden his bike off-road much in the last few weeks. He took photographs – exteriors only – of eight different buildings, including a portable toilet – that one was for a joke. That was number three. The fifth item he aimed his camera at wasn't a building, but he had a very good reason for wanting Hyde to see it.

When Jek returned to the farmhouse, he handed his phone to Hyde and told him to scroll through the images. Hyde was angled so that Jek couldn't see the phone, so he watched the big man's finger carefully.

Hyde swiped twice, which put him on photo three, the portable toilet. 'You're a funny bastard, Tom.' He swiped twice more, which gave him photo number five. He looked at this for a long time. And then he lobbed the phone back, the final three photographs ignored.

'So what was that for?' Jek asked.

'I told you. A place to hide if we can't use this joint tonight.' Hyde lobbed his empty can and cracked another. 'You better get back to the girl.'

Jek paused. 'I was thinking. Now that me and her are going to be boyfriend and girlfriend, maybe she should meet the boss.'

Hyde laughed. 'You're being a bit silly there, lad. Like I said, don't get too close to her. It won't last.'

Jek left the room. Hyde had sounded pretty confident of his *it won't last* claim, and Jek knew why. Photograph number five, the one Hyde had lingered on, was of a green box-like machine, as tall as a man and half again as long, with a chimney and 'Addfield' printed on the front. A quick search of Google had confirmed Jek's assumption: it was an industrial incinerator for disposing of agricultural waste and fallen livestock.

And now his fears were confirmed. Hyde hadn't wanted photographs of buildings in order to find a hideout, but rather a place to dispose of something. Hence his joy at discovering a large incinerator.

And what did he plan to dispose of? Not sheep, that was for sure.

SIXTY-SEVEN

When the second and final coupler was split, released tension threw the two fence panels apart about ten inches. A wide enough gap for the man to push through. Instead, he turned and ran, disappearing down an alleyway created by a gap in the left wall of vehicles.

Emma heard another noise now: an engine. Staring down the arrow-straight corridor created by two vast walls of cars, she saw movement at the far end. Within two seconds, she understood what she was looking at. A truck. It raced down the corridor, fast, lights off. A hundred metres away, then eighty, then sixty, which was close enough for her to recognise it as an articulated lorry minus a trailer. So this was Samson's escape vehicle.

But that theory immediately died. The lorry came at them like a missile, with nothing to stop it. But stopping wasn't the plan. She knew its intention was to ram the already weakened fence. The foolish driver thought he could leap across the river, but there was no chance.

She was about to run, but Samson had moved behind her and now clamped his hands over hers, welding them to the bars.

His body pushed against her back, forcing her chest against the cold metal. 'Stay and watch the show, guv.'

'You're insane,' she yelled.

The engine sounded like war, like the end of the world. Emma screamed as the truck crashed into the fence, throwing the two panels wide like doors. They ripped free from other couplers and spun away to left and right.

The lorry veered upwards slightly, as if launching from a shallow ramp, and blasted across the short expanse of grass and out into thin air above the river. It seemed to expand to fill her vision, close enough that she recognised a Mercedes badge on the front... and that it had no driver... and then the missile dropped away at the last second.

Just two metres from her, the truck was hauled down by gravity and slammed into the riverbank, crushing the tangle of barbed wire. It sounded like a nuclear bomb right in her ear and the whole world seemed to shudder. Water and dirt splashed through the bars, coating her and Samson. Instantly, an alarm began whining throughout the prison. The impact had triggered the perimeter wall's seismic sensors for the first time ever.

Samson roared with laughter. Emma was too numbed for any response. But her eyes worked just fine. The lorry was mostly submerged in the dark river, just its empty window frame and crumpled roof visible. She saw some kind of machinery attached to the steering wheel – had the vehicle been controlled remotely?

Now she also saw that it had a flatbed trailer, which she'd been unable to see as the lorry raced dead-straight towards her. It rose out of the water at an angle, its end propped up by the top of the far embankment. It created a handy ramp for Samson to stroll up to his freedom.

His plan had failed, though. Samson had a route into the

breakers yard, but no way to reach it. Thick steel bars were determined to keep him deserving of the title of prisoner.

'Time to go,' he said.

'Go where? You're trapped still.'

He peeled her hands off the iron bars. 'Go because we can't watch the next bit, unfortunately.'

At another sound, her eyes lifted from the truck to the track running dead-straight down the centre of the breakers yard.

Where another vehicle, smaller but much faster, was thundering towards them.

SIXTY-EIGHT

Samson grabbed Emma's arm and yanked her away from the bars. 'Come on or die,' he yelled. He dragged her towards the exit. Unsure of what was about to happen, but aware that it was dangerous, she helped him haul open the iron door enough to squeeze out. Once they were free, he pulled her against the wall, away from that door.

And just in time. A second sound tore apart the skies, this one like a meteor striking the tower. She felt the edifice vibrate like jelly against her back and brick dust rained onto her head and shoulders. But before the dust could land, the door slammed shut, struck by something with weight and momentum.

And then all was still, and silent. Still utterly confused, she didn't object when Samson pulled her towards the door again. He put a shoulder to it, and for some reason she helped. Something inside scraped against the floor as they pushed the barrier open, and they were in. She moved on legs that felt like someone else's.

Someone else's eyes saw the damage inside the tower. Bricks whole and smashed littered the floor, amongst them six great

251

steel bars, torn free of the wall and bent and still retaining stone encased at their ends. One of these lay against the bottom of the door, obviously the item that, propelled at speed, had slammed it shut.

But there was more. The wall where once the bars had been now had a great hole in it, plugged by some kind of 4x4 vehicle. She recognised a Toyota badge. The vehicle had a thick exoskeleton and looked like a machine from a Mad Max movie. The cage encasing it was for strength, she knew, to offset the crumple zone and guarantee the maximum impact force of speeding metal against ancient stone. And it had worked. The tower had been sliced through like cardboard and, dents and scratches aside, the vehicle was undamaged.

There was no driver – remote controlled also? She didn't get much time to examine the wreckage. Samson pulled and pushed her across scattered bricks, alongside the 4x4 and outside through a gap between its flank and the wall. He hauled her across the grass, and they leaped three feet down the embankment, onto the sloping, twisted roof of the lorry. Another shove forced her down again, onto the wood-panelled trailer, this end of which was under two feet of water. He landed next to her, took her arm once more, and now they were running up the incline.

A short leap of two feet put them on the far embankment. They moved across land that had been shaved and the soil packed down hard, to create a slight ramp. Almost impossible to discern from afar, but adequate to launch a speeding vehicle across the river.

They ran through the gap in the fence, onto the straight track that bore between high walls of trashed vehicles. Samson still had her arm, and now he yanked her backwards. She understood why when a dark van, no lights, suddenly reversed out of an alley in the left wall of cars. It screeched to a halt just feet away. Had she continued running forwards, it would have slammed her.

The rear doors blew open. Two men were right there, ready with hands. They took Emma first, roughly, then Samson, with care. She was pushed into a corner. The doors slammed. The back of the van was lit by a ceiling bulb and bare except for a bean bag, which Samson took. Emma sat on the grimy floor. She and the two unknown men slid to the back as the van burst down the track.

She watched Samson fist-bump and hug his masked men. Things had moved so quickly that it took her a few seconds to adjust, to realise where she was, what she had done, and to fathom that she had a serious problem. Not the prison break, but its aftermath. Samson was out, but he still had Joel and Minny. And now he had her, too. She had lost the fragment of control she'd wielded.

Still, he might be a man of his word. It was all she had left to cling to. 'My family. You're out. I did that. Time to honour your promise, Mr Samson.'

The three men looked at her as if she'd materialised out of nowhere. Samson asked one to get him a line to the boys at the cottage. Emma watched and hoped.

When the man, who had a Welsh accent, was on the phone to the kidnappers, Emma reached for the device. But the man handed it Samson.

'Let me talk to them,' she said. 'You made a promise.'

The Welsh guy said, 'Why'd you bring her anyway?'

Samson replied, 'Because she's annoying.'

'My brother's wife is annoying. So I stay away from her.'

Samson slapped the man's chest. 'But you killed her dog and dumped it in the front garden, didn't you? And then parked over the road. Why?'

'To see her face when she found it. Why?'

'Ditto,' Samson said, and then he spoke into the phone. He told the man on the other end that the mission had been a success, then ordered them to the 'hideout'. There was a pause while the other man spoke. Emma wanted to snatch the phone. She prayed she'd be speaking with her family in the next few seconds.

But Samson spoke just two more words and hung up.

'Kill–'

'–them.'

Hyde stared at his phone, a smile on his face. Sweet music. He had never heard a better pair of words put together. He'd worried that Samson might release the prisoners, and Hyde had even considered killing the Catalanos and risking the boss's wrath. Samson wasn't a fan of letting his foot soldiers end lives because it lit a fire under the cops, although the rule didn't apply to the man himself. He'd been convicted of two murders but Hyde knew of five for certain who were six feet under, and then there was that rumour about the missing girl.

Restraint had been hell, but patience had rewarded him. He had a go for two more killings, with blessing, and he was going to enjoy it. Why hide what was inside him? What fight the monster within? Embrace it. He liked to murder and enjoyed watching people suffer – so fucking what?

For too long he had failed to progress up the ranks, no matter how vicious or loyal he was. But things were different now. Hyde had finally been entrusted with a big job and had performed well. He'd surely get a place in Samson's inner circle for his loyalty and professionalism. That would mean more money, more clout, and endless opportunity for letting his hair down.

And he could take Jek up the ladder, too. The kid had never shown an affinity for anything other than petty crime, but that changed when he lost his girlfriend, JoJo. It snapped something inside him, changed his whole personality. He'd wanted to join Samson's crew with a desire to also get promotion to the inner circle. That would be helpful.

Secretly, Hyde hadn't wanted Samson to escape, for it increased the chances of his losing his empire or handing its reins to someone else. But he was more clued-up now. Hyde knew he wasn't smart or calm enough to run the gang, but Jek was. And Jek was loyal to him, looked up to him. If Jek became heir one day, it meant Hyde would effectively run things.

But all of that was for the future. Right now they had to get rid of the Catalanos and, once they had a location, go meet Samson at the hideout. He yelled upstairs for Jek, who came running.

'He's out,' Hyde said. 'Free man. But there's...' He nearly said the word *good*. But Jek wasn't going to think this was good. '...bad news.'

He saw Jek's shoulders slump. 'There's no need to.'

Hyde knew he didn't have to explain. 'Can't have witnesses. Or the bitch mum must have pissed Samson off.'

'We could just tie them up, make sure they don't get free until we're long gone.'

Oh, Jek looked so forlorn, so hopeful. The kid really liked the girl. Hyde felt pity.

But not much. 'No can do. If we let them live, he'll know. Even if they tell the cops nothing, that's disobeyed orders right there. And if Samson doesn't kill us for it, that's his trust out the window. No promotions, maybe no money. He's going to be pissed off enough about those two police fuckers we killed back at the cottage. I really wish it didn't have to be this way.'

Did he hell. He would have chosen no alternative.

Jek took a deep breath. 'I don't want you to kill her.'

'But we have to because–'

'I'll do it.'

That, Hyde hadn't expected. 'Really?'

'Yes. It's the best way. Besides, her dad says she can't be with me. She's not allowed a boyfriend until she's twenty.'

Hyde wanted to laugh. Jek was willing to cut Minny down because she couldn't be his girlfriend? This sounded like one of those if *I-can't-have-you, nobody-can* stories in the sort of magazine that was bloated with incest and murder but had smiling, attractive women on the cover. 'For real?'

Jek nodded. 'So I'll kill her. I'll make sure it's quick. But not here. It's not a nice place. I still love her and I want to take her somewhere special.'

Somewhere special? What, like the Eiffel Tower, to propose to her before lobbing her off the heights? But Hyde bit his tongue. 'Okay. And I'll do the dad.'

'But not yet. That bastard told me I can't be with his daughter. So I want to watch him die. Can you wait until I'm back?'

Hyde could spare the time. He'd use it to think of a thrilling way to off the dad. 'Sure. And then we can go burn the bodies. All four. There's an incinerator on the farm. The perfect place.'

SEVENTY

'Perfect,' Jek said in response to Hyde's mention of the incinerator in photo number five. 'In fact, I'll do the girl next to it. That way we don't have to carry her there. Then we can walk the dad out there for the same reason.'

Hyde nodded, liking it. 'Okay. So go do her and come back. We'll give the dad time to do one more transfer and then we'll do him. Give me your phone a sec. I want to see the incinerator again.'

Jek handed it over. Hyde tapped and scrolled, then killed the screen and handed it back. Jek slotted it into a pocket and turned to leave. 'Don't fuck this up,' Hyde called to him. 'The plan is too important.'

Jek agreed. The mission was all that mattered.

He headed to Minny's bedroom. 'Up you get. We're taking a walk. Outside. Don't ask why or where.'

She came willingly, and it was obviously because she thought her father would be along for the trip. Because when she got downstairs, she asked where he was.

'He'll be right behind. Please don't stop.'

'No, he's hurt, isn't he?'

'He will be if you don't do as I say. Please.'

She took a few moments to consider her options, which amounted to just a pair. Leave or stay? He knew she wasn't sure what to make of his previous sentence – threat or warning? She eventually started moving, although that didn't answer his question.

Jek led her to the back of the house, where his bike was stored. His helmet and combination were beside it. He didn't bother with the safety equipment, but the lock went into a pocket. He threw a leg over the vehicle.

'What's the lock for?' Minny said.

'Don't ask. Let's go. Get behind me on the bike, and hold tight, and please don't run. Hyde will kill your dad.'

She looked around, as if indeed planning to run. But then she climbed on the bike. She latched her arms tightly around him and he started riding. After the bike passed through the gate in the fence, heading deep into the farmland, she tapped him on the shoulder. 'Where are you taking me? I don't know if I trust you.'

'I promise you'll be fine.'

He rode across the dark land, past the cowshed, and to a tall, open-fronted corrugated steel shed. Parked outside was a small backhoe whose boom was missing an attachment. A collection of attachments lay in the shed, like giant toy pieces. Jek parked and they got off the bike.

'What's here?' she said, again looking around for help or an escape route, or just an answer. 'Why isn't my dad here?'

He took her arm and pulled her. She knew he wanted her in the shed and fought against it. He was stronger, though, and in they went. She bellowed for answers, but he gave none. He forced her to sit by a bale handler attachment, which looked like a giant mouth with three pointed spikes on each side. She had stopped struggling and shouting and was now crying.

He pulled his steel-cabled bike lock from his jacket and fed it around her waist and a bar on the bale handler. It was a tight fit. When he locked it, she was stuck fast.

'Please tell me what's going on.'

He knelt before her. 'I'm sorry for this. Your mum came through. She got our man out. But that means we don't need you or your dad. He wants you both dead–'

He had to cover her mouth here because she loosed a wail louder than any of her demands for answers. 'Nothing can stop my mission,' he said.

And with that he pulled out a knife.

PART 4

SEVENTY-ONE

Not long after the van started driving away, it stopped so Samson could exit and sit in the cab, where Emma heard him laughing and joking loudly with the driver. Samson's Welsh goon had a syringe, and a sorrowful look on his face when he pulled it out of a small first-aid box. The other guy lounged against the side wall, playing on his phone and ignoring everything else.

'This is kind of a must,' Welsh said, meaning the syringe. 'You can't see where we're going.'

That sounded like good news. These people wouldn't worry about her pinpointing Samson's secret burrow if they planned to kill her. Unfortunately, she knew this guy was lying. 'No, it's simply to make sure I go from A to B without issue. Give it here.'

That threw the man off. 'Do you know what this is?'

'Some kind of sedative to knock me out. I know I can't avoid it. But I'll fight like mad if you try to stick me. Hand it over and I'll go out peacefully.'

Welsh gave this some thought and looked back at his pal, as

if for consent. Without looking away from his phone, that man said, 'If you mess this up, I wouldn't want to be you.'

She wasn't sure to whom his warning was addressed. Welsh clearly thought it was him because he pulled out a knife. 'Don't try anything, Mrs Catalano. I don't want to use this.'

He slid the syringe across the floor. Emma picked it up and stabbed herself before she had time to reconsider. Unsure of how long the drug would take to affect her, she lay on the floor to avoid slamming her head if she suddenly blacked out.

First, and strangest symptom: her eyes burned. Then she felt her body become heavier. Her arms seemed glued to the metal floor of the van. It reminded her of an amusement ride called the Gravitron, which she'd given a whirl at Alton Towers as a kid with her mum and dad, bless their souls. It had had a spinning room that pinned you to the wall by centrifugal force. That was fun. This wasn't.

'How long does this take to...' she said, and then she was gone.

SEVENTY-TWO

When Jek returned to the farmhouse, he found Hyde sitting across the kitchen table from Joel, who had his hands taped behind his back. On the table was the giant Rubik's cube, which Hyde seemed to have grown love for, and a scattered bag of peanuts. He was flicking the peanuts hard at the captive's face.

The moment Jek walked in, Hyde pointed at the living room and they both moved to that location. Hyde shut the door behind them.

'Did we get a meeting location yet?' Jek asked.

'All in good time. How did it go?'

Jek pulled something out of his pocket. Knickers. Bloodstained. Hyde clapped. 'Was it hard?'

'Yes. But I got it done.'

'I meant your dick when you cut her open.' Hyde laughed. 'No, seriously, well done. She wasn't for you, mate. There's bigger, better fish in the sea.'

'It still hurts. I think her face will haunt me for a long time. I put her in the incinerator. Do we have to burn her dad now? And the elderly couple?'

Hyde nodded. 'Actually, first come with me.' Hyde led him

into the kitchen and got him to sit at the table, across from Joel. Jek had the horrible feeling Hyde was about to tell Joel that his little girl had been killed and cremated.

But he didn't do that. He said, 'Let me have your phone.'

Puzzled, Jek handed it over. He saw Hyde wake it up and start tapping the screen. The bigger man then stepped behind Jek and leaned over him to place the phone on the table. Jek saw the voice recorder app open, and his bad feeling intensified a thousandfold.

Still lurking inches behind Jek, Hyde pressed a button to play the last recording. It started with Hyde's voice saying...

```
Hyde: Don't fuck this up. The plan is
too important.

Jek: I won't. The mission is all that
matters.
```

Next, the sound of feet on stairs as Jek headed to Minny's room, where he said...

```
Jek: Up you get. We're taking a walk.
outside. Don't ask why or where…
```

The recording put bewilderment on Joel's face, but not Jek's. He knew everything that was about to happen. However, precisely because of that, he shared the fear that Minny's father surely felt.

The trio of men listened to Minny begging to know if her dad was okay. Then her trip with Jek downstairs, and outside. The motorbike ride. Jek locking Minny to the piece of heavy farm machinery. And pulling his knife on her...

Minny: What are you going to do?

Jek: Not hurt you. I never could. But I have to be crude here. I need your underwear. I'm going to put some of my blood on it. I have to convince Hyde that you're dead.

Minny: Why? Why do I have to die?

Jek: Listen, Minny. You don't have to die, and I hope it doesn't happen until you're an old woman. I'm not going to kill you or let anyone else. And I'm not going to let my partner hurt your dad. I'll save you both. I'm going to go help him now. I'll leave him somewhere where he'll also be safe. But I can't have you running to the police. My mission is too important.

Minny: I won't, I promise.

Jek: I can't take that risk. Listen to me. The bike lock has four digits. Ten thousand combinations. It will take you most of the night to work through the codes to get free. Then you can run to the police if you want. By that time, this will all be over.

Minny: But what about my mum? What will your boss do to my mum?

```
Jek: I don't know. I'll be with my boss
soon. If she's alive, I'll try to help.

Minny:  What  do  you  mean  'if'  she's
alive?

Jek:  Look,  you  need  to  be  quiet  out
here. If my partner hears you screaming,
he'll  know  you're  not  dead.  We  have  to
make him think you are, okay?

Minny: Okay. Thank you. But what if he
kills you?

Jek: Then we're all dead.
```

Hyde leaned over Jek to stop the recording. Then, before Jek could utter a word, he felt fingers grab his hair and a sharp blade touch his throat. Joel groaned. Perhaps he'd just lost the last of his survival hopes.

'I can explain,' Jek said.

'I just heard your explanation. Up you get, boy. Your tricking days are done. We're going out there to finish that bitch off, and then I'll consider whether or not to forgive you for betraying me.'

SEVENTY-THREE

Hyde zip-tied Jek's hands behind his back. Then he heavily taped Joel to the kitchen chair and the chair to the table. Minny's father looked defeated and flat, not an ounce of fight left in him.

Hyde pocketed Jek's phone then grabbed his former comrade's hair and made him stand. 'When we get back from slaughtering your kid,' he said to Joel, 'you're going to finish transferring money. Maybe you want to live, or maybe you want to join her in heaven. You can pick. Or maybe not. I haven't decided yet.'

He ushered Jek to the back door and out into the silent night. They ignored the motorbike and started walking down the track.

'See what trouble your dick got you in?' Hyde said.

'It's not my dick. Just my brain. It was wrong to kill these people.'

'Which ones?'

'Any of them, you fucking maniac. You're dangerous and out of control. I was just trying to save people.'

'Did that work? Two dead cops. Two dead old farts. Soon to

be two dead Catalanos. You're too obsessed with that fucking girl just because JoJo walked out on you.'

'She didn't walk out on me. You know—'

Jek ceased talking when Hyde pressed the knife a little harder into his neck. 'Listen to me, you twat. I tried to help you. You were saying some dangerous shit and I didn't want you to get in trouble. Selfish bastard.'

'But I wanted—'

Another jab with the blade. 'If you want to replace JoJo, it ain't going to be with YouTube Bitch. Because you're going to kill her properly this time, with me watching. You owe me for this shit. We're family, man.'

'No. You're just the brother of the guy my mum decided to start sleeping with.'

Hyde drove a knee into Jek's ass, hard. 'Fuck you. You'd be dead on the streets if not for me. I treated you like my own boy. Nice way of saying thanks, you dickhead. Fuck you then, okay? You don't want to be family anymore? Fine. It'll make it easier for me to put you down like a dog if you mess with me again. Just get moving and keep your mouth shut.'

A minute passed in silence as they walked to the gate in the perimeter fence. Once through, Hyde asked where Minny was. Jek paused.

'You can kill her nice and quick, boy. But if you make me hunt around here to find her, I'll bleed her out from a hundred stab wounds in each leg. I'll slice off her tits and widen that sweet pussy of hers. Make a choice.'

Jek started walking. Soon Hyde spotted the metal shed full of backhoe attachments. But no girl locked to any of them. He upped his pace, now dragging Jek. When he was close enough to realise she absolutely wasn't here, he tripped Jek to the ground and booted him in the gut three times, to ensure he didn't have the capacity to leap up and mount an offensive. Jek coughed and spluttered.

Hyde approached the bale handler and saw Jek's bike lock on the floor. He threw it at his injured partner, narrowly missing his head. 'Look. 9950, that's the code you chose. You dickhead. All night to guess the code? She figured you'd make it at the far end, so she just worked backwards. Took her just fifty guesses, and now she's probably already blabbing to the cops. When did your brain starve to death?'

Jek gave no answer. Hyde played with the combination, to change it, then dragged Jek towards the bale handler and secured him to it. The cable was tight around Jek's midriff.

'Wait here for me, boy. I'll go kill the dad and get your bike. That house is burned now, so I'll burn it for real. And while I'm doing it, I'll have a think about you. Maybe I'll forgive you for this, and maybe not. Maybe I'll call Samson and see what he wants done with you, and you know that won't be rewarding.'

SEVENTY-FOUR

When Hyde returned to the farmhouse, he found the tape that had been used to restrain Joel on the floor, amongst scattered pieces of the giant Rubik's cube. But no Joel. The bastard had free himself and–

A knife amongst the mess on the linoleum told the story. The man had been taped to the chair and couldn't have reached the knife rack. So he hadn't freed himself. YouTube Bitch had sneaked right past him and made her way back here.

Hyde checked the whole house to make sure the bastards weren't hiding. They weren't. He entered the backyard and got on Jek's dirt bike. The key was in the ignition. He'd sold this machine to Jek, so he knew how to handle it like a pro. He rode onto the track, but he turned left, not right. The kid and her dad wouldn't go bombing through the farmland, but would instead hit the road and hope to flag down a car. Even this late, they might get lucky, so Hyde had no time to waste.

He paused at the edge of the road, thinking. The farm mostly covered the land to his right, and his targets would find that too close for comfort. They'd want distance from this place, and that surely meant they'd fled to the left. That was his play.

It was so dark out in the boondocks that the bike's weak headlight illuminated only a small portion of the way ahead. The road seemed to knit itself out of thin air as he blew down it. Not good, he figured. They'd hear him coming long before he saw them, and it would give the bastards ample time to veer into a field and hide.

This way.

A faint noise, direction unfathomable. But it had clearly been a shout from YouTube Bitch, calling out instructions to her dad. Hyde stopped the bike. He turned the handlebars left, washing light over the fields that side, then to the right–

And he saw them. A flash of movement exited his field of illumination before he could diagnose what it was. But he knew. How many other people were running through the fields this late?

He kicked the bike forward, into the field, in pursuit. Almost immediately, the headlight pinned the fleeing pair as they ran through the grass, away from him. But there would be no getting away. His new bloodlust needed feeding, and it was dinnertime.

SEVENTY-FIVE

Being stuck in the van with two men was the reason Emma had been happy to knock herself out with a drug. But she woke to something much worse.

Her eyes opened to a grid of white squares with brown lines. Some kind of propeller was in the middle. There was a rumbling noise all around. Utter confusion made her chest thump with fear.

It wore off quickly. She realised she lay on her back, staring up. The grid was a coffered ceiling, the propeller a fan hanging from it. The noise morphed into voices, a lot of them. She tried to sit up, but her body wasn't ready yet. However, she could turn her head. She lay on a patch of trimmed grass, although for some reason it was inside a large room.

The source of the voices became apparent. She seemed to be in a pub, and it was busy. Men and women were everywhere, drinking, laughing, play-fighting each other. They didn't look dressed for a night out, though.

A guy sitting on the bar did a double-take and pointed a finger. 'Awake,' he said. 'Call Samson.'

Dozens of sets of eyes turned to her. An ugly woman of

about thirty materialised out of nowhere, inches away, and grabbed Emma's cheeks to give her head a shake. 'Darling, you're in hell,' she said, then laughed and vanished.

Hell? Emma wasn't certain the woman was wrong.

The shaking of her skull seemed to cast off the final remnants of the drug, like water from a dog's back. Wide awake now, strength back, she sat up. The grass beneath her was actually the baize of a pool table. She wasn't strapped to it, luckily. That item aside, the entire pub had a golf theme, which probably made it a golf course clubhouse. And the patrons, of course, would be the cast and crew of Samson's prison break, here to celebrate the return of their king. With his treasure.

She took all this in in seconds, but lingered longer on the exits. The windows had opened curtains, which allowed her to see closed exterior metal shutters. There were three interior doors – one of them behind the bar – and maybe one led to the main entrance, but each was probably locked. Between two windows was a set of double doors, above which was a sign saying COURSE ENTRANCE. These were made of glass and also clearly shuttered on the outside. A wide staircase with ornate bannisters led to a higher floor, but for sure there was no escape that way.

Knowing she was trapped did nothing to enhance her fear, for she had been a prisoner ever since men burst into her country cottage that morning.

Samson might very well kill her, but not yet, and not by someone else's hand so soon after she'd woken. This thought emboldened her and she slid off the pool table. A man with a cocktail grabbed her arm and began some kind of vocal objection to... To what, she never discovered, for she cut him short with a hard slap on the back of his hand.

'Don't touch me, dickhead.'

He didn't try again. She walked to the bar, watched by all.

People slid out of her way as if she was infected. On the back wall of the bar was a long mirror and she saw her ragged face. She looked like she'd been sleepless for days. Her nose had been daubed bright red and some fool had drawn a black moustache.

A short man was behind the bar, frozen in mid-pint-pull. She pointed at the optics mounted to the mirror. 'Gin. Triple. Put it on my tab.'

The guy looked around, unsure what to do. He then laughed, but only because the rest of the patrons went first.

'Serve her,' yelled a voice over the noise. Heads turned, including hers. At the top of the stairs stood Samson, wearing just boxer shorts. Further down the corridor behind him was a doorway with two girls lurking and watching. They were naked except for knickers. The scene suggested the trio had recently terminated some cardiovascular fun.

She watched him walk down the stairs. The girls retreated into their room. Emma turned back to the bar at a thud. A glass half-full of gin sat there. She grabbed it and turned to face the room.

'So, what are we celebrating?' she said, and downed the gin in one.

SEVENTY-SIX

Hyde had been right about Jek underestimating Minny. He had set the bike lock's combination at 9950 because he'd figured Minny would start her guesses at 0000 and work upwards. Bad mistake.

But Hyde had made the same error. He couldn't risk the tactic of picking a code near either end of the scale, so he'd opted for the only alternative. The centre. Jek started at 5000 and counted backwards. At 4450, he switched to running the numbers forward. The lock clicked open on 5012. Three minutes' work.

He bolted for the farmhouse, hoping he was in time to save Joel, but hadn't even covered half the distance before he heard his bike's engine fire up. It was a clear signal that Hyde was in pursuit of someone, and that could only mean that Minny hadn't opted to flee to get help. He knew how tough and resourceful she could be. If she had remained in the area, it was for one reason only: to save her father. Hopefully she'd gotten to him in time and they were both on the run.

He saw Hyde exit the track and turn left onto the road. Then he heard a shout from a field beyond the tarmac.

This way.
Minny. Now Jek had an idea of where she was.
But so did Hyde.

SEVENTY-SEVEN

Hyde's original plan was to blast past the running pair and leap off the bike ahead of them, cutting off their path. But as he closed on them, he realised they were bounding along at a serious pace. He was a streetfighter and had energy for days when throwing his fists, but running was another matter. If the pair turned back or got past him, his 240lbs of bulk would never catch them.

Besides, they would scrap like alley cats and by the time he'd killed one, the other might be out of reach even if he used the bike to give chase again.

New plan. With his weight atop it and serious momentum, the bike would surely incapacitate anyone it slammed into. Luck permitting, the impact wouldn't throw him off and he could simply aim at the one left standing. Once both were down, he could take his time wiping them off the earth. He hauled on the throttle, increasing speed.

The pair rushed at him fast, and they didn't look back once, but somehow they knew exactly when to foil his plan. When just feet from their backs, a second from scattering them like bowling pins, the bitch and her dad veered apart. The bike blew between them.

Annoyed, Hyde lashed out a foot at the girl, but he was already past and caught thin air. However, the sharp movement caused the bike to wobble. He tried to connect it, but the front wheel slipped on the grass and down he went, hard.

To prevent a tumble and to save valuable time, he clamped his legs on the machine and tightened his grip on the handlebars. The bike scoured across the grass with him still mounted. A pedal gouged the earth and brought the bike to a rapid stop. The runners had rejoined and were fleeing away at an angle.

'Stop!' he yelled.

Had he expected that to work? Of course it didn't. He yanked his leg from under the bike and raised the machine, ready for another go. The bitch and her dad were fleeing deeper into the countryside instead of back towards the road.

Perfect. This time he'd aim straight for the dad, who was the most likely to put up a good fight, and ram him right out of the picture. Hyde didn't want the kid bloodied and bent anyway. That would just ruin his plans for some intimate time with her.

SEVENTY-EIGHT

Samson sat across from Emma in a corner booth. It reminded her of the first time she'd encountered Adley, who was absent. It also harked back to one of her first dates with Joel, and that added a level of discomfort. Her desire was to close her eyes and ignore this man, but she needed to fathom his plans for her and her family.

There was a bottle of gin and two glass tumblers on the table between them. She didn't want to touch the alcohol, having consumed that initial trio of shots only to settle her nerves. Samson drank, though. Fast. It had been a long time and he seemed to be making up for lost ground. Good. The looser his tongue, the more information she could soak up, and the better her chances of finding a way out of this pickle.

'You shouldn't have tricked me,' Samson said, his voice a little slurry. 'Grudges are my thing. I have an unforgiving soul and my anger ferments.'

'I prefer to remain calm and move past.'

He tasted those words by speaking them aloud, but with a change: keep calm and carry on. 'A phrase by the Ministry of Information back in 1939. Part of their Home Publicity campaign when World War Two was on the horizon. Any other wartime nuggets you live by?'

'Freedom is in peril–' she started.

'Defend it with all your might,' he finished. 'Go ahead. Break free. Or is that puzzle brain of yours still working on another pantomime?'

'Where are they? You got free. You're living the high life again. Girls and booze. Why do you need me and my family?'

'They're dead, remember. I sense you don't believe it.'

She refused to. Black despair would frizz her brain. Samson had ordered his men to kill her husband and daughter, but that had been the last she'd heard of it. It didn't mean they were dead. Until she had proof otherwise, Joel and Minny were alive. If she could keep that possibility afloat, she could think clearly and work out a way to escape this man. If he killed her, her family would suffer badly.

He was awaiting a response, which she didn't have. Calling his bluff might just anger him enough to make a call to his cronies to confirm a deadly result. He might even show her pictures and–

No, no, no. They are not dead. They are–

The terrible silence between them was interrupted by a shout from a nearby man. 'It's midnight.'

Samson had something planned, for he held out a hand, without looking at it, and said, 'Phone.' He obviously expected his subordinate to gently place the phone into his hand. Instead, the device crashed into the table and skidded into the wall.

'You damn twat,' Samson said. The man who'd lobbed the phone was laughing. 'Someone stick a pool cue up that guy's arse.'

Another gang-member grabbed a cue to do as ordered. Both men fought, but Emma saw smiles and heard playful banter. These people were idiots.

'See, I can take a joke,' Samson said to Emma as he dialled a number from memory.

'Tonight, while you're celebrating. How about tomorrow when you're sober and fermentation is complete?'

He ignored the question and got up to take his call in private. As he walked away with the phone to his ear, she heard him say, 'What's happening there? The job done? They dead?'

Emma grabbed the glass before her and swallowed the gin in a single gulp.

SEVENTY-NINE

For seemingly an age now, Joel had stared death in the face. The bastard called Hyde was a raving lunatic and seemed to have a particular penchant for torment. How many times had the man kicked a shin, flicked an ear, pretended to punch, or made a show of practising stabbing and slicing motions with his knife? How many times had the bastard sat across from him at the kitchen table and talked about the ways he would kill him? How many different sexual positions had he described raping Minny in?

Joel had never been in doubt that he would die at the man's hands, and that his daughter would suffer the same fate. It had worn him thin, numbed his skull, and at times even made him wish for a heart attack to end the misery. So intense and overwhelming had been the gloom, not even his rescue at Minny's hands had brought relief.

When she had burst into the kitchen, alone, Joel's brain had refused to believe it. When she had grabbed a knife and sliced away the tape holding him, he hadn't been able to shake the notion that it was all a trick. Even when they'd fled from the house – he'd nudged the table in haste, dislodging the Rubik's cube, which had smashed into pieces on the floor – and onto the road, he had worried that the inconvenience to Hyde would only make his bullying and violence worse.

And, finally, when Hyde had pursued them on a motorbike, out here in the dead of night in the middle of nowhere, Joel had plunged into the deepest despair imaginable. Hyde had taken on a kind of immortal, even god-like shade. No beaten dog had ever feared its abusive master as much.

But that changed in a heartbeat – or rather, a peal of laughter.

Above the noise of the roaring bike as Hyde, fresh off his fall, resumed his chase, Joel heard the man's wild cackle of joy. It splashed a red filter over everything, blotting out panic and pain and fear. Enough was fucking enough.

As the bastard turned his bike to come at them again, Joel grabbed Minny's arm and ran with her. The engine grew loud behind them, until it seemed that Hyde's front wheel might catch a trailing foot any moment. The headlight drowned them in a growing pool of white. At the last moment, Joel hit the brakes and turned, dragging his left arm around in a semi-circle, adding power to create the hardest punch ever delivered by a human being.

Not quite. Joel had hoped to clothesline Hyde right off his mount, but instead his forearm hit the bike's headlight. His puny flesh was a baseball to Hyde's bat and, had it not been attached to him, would have twirled into space. Instead, Joel was hauled off his feet and dumped flat on the grass at least two metres from where he'd planted his feet.

By chance, he landed in such a position as to be staring right at the bike as it blew past him, wobbling from a lack of control by the rider, and toppled for the second time.

'Dad,' Minny yelled.

She was far ahead of him, ahead of Hyde, and growing

smaller. Joel's strike against the bike had bust the headlight, and now the world was black. Minny was soon lost in that darkness.

By that time, Hyde, some twenty metres ahead, had shaken off the cobwebs and was on his feet. He looked around and spotted the bike. Joel got to his feet. That was when he noticed his left arm swayed loosely from his elbow. Broken by the impact against the headlight. The pain now announced itself with fireworks.

But it couldn't counter his rage. The threat still hovered over them. Hyde would be on his bike again in seconds, free to hunt down Minny and do whatever evil he had in mind. Joel saw only one path ahead and he took it. He grabbed his left wrist, to stop the arm swinging and grinding bone, and then he ran at Hyde.

Perhaps believing Joel was out of action, the big animal didn't even look his way as he grabbed the bike and set it upright. As he lifted a leg to climb on, Joel crashed into him. For the second time in a quarter of a minute, all three of them hit the deck.

'Keep running,' Joel screamed as loud as possible. As the only man aware of what had just happened, he got his wits together quicker. By the time Hyde realised he'd been floored by his enemy, Joel was on the bigger man's back, throwing punches with his good arm.

But the broken limb hung loose by Hyde's head and he saw it, grabbed it, twisted it. The pain blurred Joel's mind, pausing his attack long enough to shift the momentum. Before Joel knew it, he was the one lying in the dirt with an enemy above.

'I'm gonna rip your spine out and fuck her with it,' Hyde spat as he landed punches of his own, thunderous blows like meteors striking. Joel managed to grab one of his wrists, but Hyde had a second and it continued to drop bombs.

With only one arm to shield him, Joel knew he was done. As

each thud into his face and head threatened to blacken the world with unconsciousness, he latched onto one wispy and whimsical chance to save his daughter.

Still clamping a hand onto Hyde's left wrist, he drew the bastard's hand close to his face and snapped his teeth around the thumb. Hyde screeched but did not pause his blitzkrieg. Joel didn't care, for he had never assumed his bite would end the assault. Nor did he attempt to shield his face anymore.

All he wanted with his every fibre was to keep that lock in place at the moment of death, and freeze with it in place when his body shut down.

To create an anchor that would slow the madman and allow Minny to escape.

Keep running.

Her father's words had had the opposite effect. At his shout, Minny stopped bolting across the field and turned, scanning the gloom for him.

Terrified, she saw a portion of the darkness shimmering, and it took her a few seconds to realise she was watching two men fighting on the ground.

'Dad!' she tried to scream, but the sound came out as a weak wail. She also tried to run towards him, to help, but her feet wouldn't shift. Moments later, she saw just one human shape get to its feet. The dark and the distance made it impossible to determine who was who... but she knew it was Hyde. Her father lay still on the ground.

Keep running.

Her dad had attacked Hyde to give her time to escape. As the monster lifted his fallen bike and started the engine, she turned and bolted. She would not let her father's bold, dangerous tactic go to waste. She would flee, find help, save them both.

Behind her, the bike's engine roared, and she knew Hyde was coming for her. Thirty or so metres ahead, she saw something small and square and bright white hovering in the dark. Then another set about ten feet away. More. Suddenly, she made out a wooden post between each square, and knew she was looking at a fence.

She glanced back and saw that Hyde had eaten up a massive portion of the gap between them. She pushed on at an increased pace, allowing herself a smidgen of hope. The fence would foil Hyde's vehicle, forcing him to continue the chase on foot, and her smaller, younger, fitter body would hold the aces in that race.

The engine noise filled her ears, although there was no light from the headlamp. She didn't dare look back, for seeing him up close would poison her determination, slow her speed, and give her to him. Somehow, she found another gear and added speed. But it didn't seem to achieve anything, for the fence seemed to approach agonisingly slowly.

Now, just ten metres from the barrier, she made out its design in the darkness. Wooden posts with three lengths of widely spaced strips of high tensile wire between them. The white squares, one attached to each top wire, were strike markers, there to warn birds of the danger if they flew too low at night.

Her direction of travel meant she was coming at the fence at an angle that took it away from her, and she had focused on the closet portion. Now, when she shifted her sight dead ahead, to where she'd meet the barrier if she continued in a straight line, she saw a problem that dissolved her remaining shard of hope.

The fence ended.

She saw posts running off into the distance, but the strike

markers and the wire ceased to be. Two big coils of wire sat by the final completed post and another coil next to the first freestanding wooden stake. A job in progress. It would not save her.

Knowing she would not outrun the bike, which sounded like it was right upon her, Minny turned to face it. Her only chance now was to dodge the machine, like a matador sidestepping a bull, and run back the way she had come. The manoeuvre would force the bastard to turn around and would buy her precious, but possibly futile, time.

But time wasn't her ally tonight, for she had none to react. Half a turn made towards the bike, she saw the machine invading her world, filling her vision, Hyde upon it with his leg outstretched like a jouster's lance. A nanosecond later she felt a mighty thud that lifted her off her feet.

As the bike blew past her, the world seemed to whirl and threw itself hard into her head, and everything turned somehow even blacker.

EIGHTY

Jek crossed the road and ran into the field on the far side, his eyes scanning the darkness ahead. He'd been lured by the bike's headlight some distance away, but that had now been extinguished for some reason. The bike itself, based on the engine location, had continued to move. However, he could now not hear nor see a thing.

He ran on and soon his eyes made out lumps in the darkness. Closer, he saw the shape of his Kurtz lying in the grass. Closer still, he saw a human shape about fifteen metres beyond the bike. The dimensions told him it was Hyde. Strangely, he was kneeling up straight and not moving.

It was a puzzle until he got closer, and then everything made sense. There was a fence with three wires, complete with strike markers, strung between wooden posts, but it was incomplete. The two posts Hyde knelt between had no bottom or centre wires, which lay in large spools by the stake to the right. A third spool was next to the post on the left because the top wire had already been strung, although no marker had been set to warn birds... or madmen chasing down victims on a bike.

Hyde hadn't seen it... and now never would.

Hyde wasn't actually kneeling because, while his feet were in the grass, those knees hung three inches from the ground. Only his robust spine had prevented decapitation by the almost-invisible top wire, which was deeply embedded in his ravaged neck and had left him dangling. Blood coated his clothing and a wide swath of grass all around. The birds had a collision warning after all.

Jek just stared. The scene was too surreal to comprehend. As he got within feet of his comrade, he noticed a second injury to the man. His left hand was savaged, the flesh of the thumb missing and exposing bone. What the fuck had happened out here?

He touched Hyde's shoulder. 'Sorry, my man. No one should go out like this. You didn't deserve it.'

He searched Hyde's pockets and found his phone and Hyde's, then cast his eyes around the black field expanse of the field, seeking Joel and Minny. So focused had he been on Hyde, he hadn't noticed a couple of black lumps just twenty metres past his step uncle's body. Minny and Joel. But they weren't moving.

Halfway to them, he read the scene. Minny sat facing him, with her knees up to her chest. She was staring into the sky. He could hear her sobbing. Just inches behind her lay Joel. Silent. Still.

Dead.

Just then Hyde's mobile rang in Jek's hand. Unknown number. But he knew who was at the other end.

Samson's voice, with a chattery background, said, 'What's happening there? The job done? They dead?'

'Half-done. But Hyde is dead.'

Samson paused. 'Right. How?'

'The dad put up a fight. Got him with a knife.'

Another pause. 'Right. Burn the place down with the bodies inside. Then go hide out with Jonas for a bit, until I contact you in a few weeks. For the Spain thing. Jonas will look after you. And I'll get your money to you.'

Samson was in the middle of relaying this Jonas's address when Jek interrupted. 'Your plan was crap and things went wrong. We had to leave that cottage. Now we've also got two dead cops and two dead old farmers.'

If Samson was curious or horrified, he hid it well. He also seemed to let the insult slide. 'Burn them as well. Good Job, Tom. Forget the hiding out. I've got an early payment for you.'

'I'm not in trouble?'

Samson laughed. 'No, my friend. Come see me. Then I'm going to send you on your way. Where are you? Someone will collect you. It'll take about an hour.'

On the trip to search for a suitable residence to seize, Jek had spotted a pub about a mile away, whose name he gave to Samson. He said he'd be in the car park in one hour, then added: 'I'll have a present for you. I heard the mum was a pain in the arse, so you'll like this.'

'What is it?'

'I said the job was half done, remember?' He looked at Minny to find her staring at him. 'The daughter is still alive and well. And you can have her.'

EIGHTY-ONE

His phone call done, Samson looked around, saw the man who'd lobbed him the phone, and pitched it right back at him, hard. It missed and hit a wall, but the target realised what had happened and he and the guy he was wrestling froze. Phone lobber looked worried. He knew his boss well.

But Samson wasn't angry, for he smiled at Emma as he retook his seat in the booth. Or maybe it was for show. He then gestured to another man, who came over. 'Find a pub called Evans Gate,' Samson told him. 'That kid calling himself Jekyll has hold of the governor's daughter. Bring her back here. And bring my phone back.'

Emma's shoulders relaxed. Minny was alive. But in the next moment, she dug her fingernails into the wood of the table. Joel hadn't been mentioned. She needed to know. 'My husband?'

They both ignored her. 'What about the other guy? Hyde?' the man asked his boss.

'He doesn't need a ride, or anything else ever again. Get going. Take a couple of other chaps.'

When the man was gone, she repeated the query.

'He might be alive,' Samson said, referring to Joel.

There was massive relief, but it was fragile. 'What does that mean?'

'It means I don't accept a thing until I have proof. A bit like you. I can tell you didn't believe they were dead. Now you know your kid is fine, at least.'

He poured himself more gin, and one for her. She put her eyes on the glass and there they stayed for a long time, as she mulled over her next move. For minute after minute, she remained in that position, blotting out everything, and tried to think of a plan.

Earlier, back at the prison, manipulation and chicanery had come oh-so easily to her, but now she was stumped. In the end, only one forward path presented itself. Simple, immediate, but likely useless. However, she had nothing else.

'Please don't kill me and my family,' she said.

No response. When she looked up, it was to find Samson with his head lolled back, mouth wide open. He was asleep. How she wished to smash her glass and drag a sharp edge across that throat.

Instead, she just sat there. Minny was coming. She could do nothing but wait.

EIGHTY-TWO

At one point Emma was jolted by a ringing phone. It was on the table before her. Given the cracked screen, it must be the device Samson lobbed at the wall. Someone had returned it without her noticing. The screen said UNKNOWN. It also displayed the time: 00.57.

She was tempted to grab the phone for surely the call was from the men sent to pick up Minny and Jek. They would be here within the hour. But she left it alone, fearful of Samson's wrath. Instead, just to give her hands something to do, she wet a portion of her suit jacket with gin and cleansed her nose and upper lip of doodles.

The phone soon stopped ringing. Around her, the partying had slowed. People were tired and drunk and now lounged about, some even asleep on tables or sofas or the floor. Most of the noise came from a man playing a golf-themed pinball machine.

She zoned out again and was next stirred by movement at the door behind the bar. In walked the man tasked with fetching Minny, followed by two others. But not Minny or Jekyll. He came quickly to Samson's side and shook him awake. Samson grunted, blinked rapidly, and reached for his drink. He clumsily knocked it over instead, but only a jot remained to trickle across the table.

'I tried to ring you,' the man said. 'They weren't there. Couldn't find them.'

Samson took a few moments to get his wits, as Emma almost lost hers. Minny hadn't been at the pub? Then where was she?

Samson swore. He grabbed his empty glass and launched it away. It bounced off a table, narrowly missing the head of a sleeping woman hunched over the wood, and landed between the open legs of a man out for the count on a sofa. 'Get someone to check if they've been arrested or something. We might have to skip out of this place. Fuck. Get everyone up.'

Samson stood and paced, rubbing his sleepy face, while his crony walked about the room and kicked and shook and nudged people.

'Where's my daughter?' Emma said.

'Shut your hole,' Samson said. He joined his friend in knocking alert the inebriated and unconscious.

Just then a phone rang. The guy playing pinball climbed over the bar and lifted a landline receiver from next to the till. Seconds later, he yelled to Samson. 'It's that Jekyll dude.'

'Put it on speaker,' Samson called back. Then he said, 'Tom? Where are you?'

'Someone was hanging around the pub and we couldn't get close,' said a tinny voice to the entire room. 'I've got the girl with me. But I came to you.'

'What's that mean? Where are you?'

'Outside. On the golf course.'

Here, some of Samson's people rushed to the windows and double doors, trying to peek through small gaps in the metal shutters. 'How did you know where we were?' Samson asked.

'One of your men told Hyde a while back.'

Samson looked around, as if likely to identify the gossiper by a raised hand. 'And why are you out there?'

'I brought your present. I've got her tied up on the fairway of hole two. Bring a club and some balls. I reckon we could have some fun with her. Bring as many people as you like. There's fun for all.'

Jekyll hung up. Samson laughed and addressed the room: 'That cheeky little runt. He thinks he's getting a payday. But he called my plan crap to my face. Shall I teach him a lesson in manners?'

The room erupted with votes of yay. Samson rushed to a glass display case by a wall, inside of which was a single golf club. The iron was with a picture of a famous golfer so had probably once been owned by him. Samson put his foot through the glass and grabbed the putter.

He then pointed at a sales display behind the bar and demanded balls and tees. Someone put down a box full of each. Samson yelled a name and a fat man in a suit stood up. They both headed for the doors that led out back.

'Can we come?' someone said.

'No, stay here,' was the boss's response.

The fat man turned a key that started to raise the exterior shutter. Emma saw a gun on a holster at his hip.

She was a maelstrom of emotions. On the one hand, Minny was here, close, alive and well. On the other, it was clear that she was about to be used for target practice. But Emma was determined that her daughter wasn't about to suffer alone. She needed to do something, and quick.

Like poking his unforgiving soul. 'Hey, Samson,' she yelled, 'why do you think that being sexually abused by your parents as a kid gives you the right to bully weaker people?'

His reaction was instant. He literally ran for her in a straight line, barging aside a table and booting away a wooden chair. She cowed as he stopped at the table and raised the club.

But then he thought better of caving in her head right there and then. 'You're now part of the game, you whore. I'm going to finally shut that damn foul gob of yours by whacking a ball down your throat.'

He grabbed her wrist and hauled her to her feet, then towards the doors.

There were three four-seater golf carts in a canopy-covered bay out back. Samson dragged Emma towards them. The vehicles had keys slotted in the ignitions. His fat comrade took up the entire front bench, so the gangster sat in the back with Emma. She hated having her leg pressed up against his, but he just about sat in the middle.

As the cart exited a patch of concrete and drove past the teeing ground for the first hole, she looked ahead and saw two human figures in the distance. They were barely visible in the darkness, but she knew Minny would be one of them.

But seeing her daughter did not slow rising panic. Her plan to force Samson to bring her along had worked, but now she had only minutes left to devise a method of saving Minny and herself. The shrinking distance was like a countdown.

Then there was Joel. Was he dead? With luck, Jek had lied about his death to cover an escape. Maybe Joel had gotten to the police, and vans of armed officers were, somehow, descending on this place right now.

'Silent all of a sudden?' Samson said. 'Regretting your words?'

'Why am I here? Why did you bring me when you escaped? What is all this about? Why didn't you just leave and be done with this?'

'You're on the news,' he replied. '*We*, I mean. It's a big story. Escaped convict and missing governor. And her missing family. There's blood in your kitchen and now that's being tied to a burned out cop car and three dead bodies in it. You're popular now, girl.'

Three dead police officers? Emma had to thump her stomach to dampen rising bile. The headache that had been resident since she'd been taken hostage in a cell now hit a higher gear. It was a terrible thought, but she prayed that the blood Samson referred to belonged to those faceless law enforcement personnel. Instead of her husband, whose condition was still shrouded in mystery.

'The big news corporations have to be politically correct,' Samson continued. 'But not people on social media. They're spouting all manner of theories.'

She understood what he meant. Doubtless the fact that she was unaccounted for and had helped him escape would drive keyboard warriors to wonder if they were in cahoots.

He saw this realisation on her face. 'That's right. And that's why you're here, former governor. No one will hear your story. No one will find you or your family. But they will be given some evidence to support their ideas. That you and me set this thing up. Maybe a sighting of you in Spain. Something to make the world think you were paid well and you're living in luxury as one of my employees. Until they find your body out there. Maybe a heroin overdose, just to add salt to the wounds.'

Emma refused to look at him, but he insisted and grabbed her face, turning it so their eyes could meet. He said, 'Disgraced former Governor Catalano will not be pitied as someone who was blackmailed and fought for her family. I hope you didn't get a knighthood, because they'll be rescinding that.'

EIGHTY-FOUR

A lot of shit had hit the fan because of the Catalanos and the pair of bozos he'd tasked with seizing Peach Cottage, so he'd learned to take nothing for granted. He expected something to go wrong with this latest plan.

So he grinned like a Cheshire cat when the golf cart was close enough for him to make out Minny Catalano's face. It truly was her, there with the idiot Tom. She sat on the grass with her back to a motorbike, hands secured to the front wheel behind her. A strip of the binding tape wound out from the vicinity of her butt. She was as pretty as the pictures promised.

He ordered his bodyguard to pull up the cart five metres away. As Samson got out, he kept a good grip on the governor, in case she fled to her daughter.

His man stood nearby, holding his gun down by his side, ready in case of a problem with either of the bitches. But Samson didn't feel the same buzz of worry. Finally, the gremlins were out of the system, and nobody could fuck things up for him now.

'We good?' Tom said.

Samson gave this serious consideration. The bank manager

and Hyde were already goners. The governor thought she was going to Spain, and while he liked the idea of dragging her name through the mud, it was ultimately fanciful. He couldn't possibly take her overseas, alive or dead. It would be tough enough spiriting away the close few comrades he'd picked to join him in his new life.

Originally he'd planned the governor's death to be at the hands of an inmate after his escape, although that, too, had changed when anger had made him bring her along. But he still had her in the crosshairs, didn't he?

And Tom? He had gone off-plan by killing cops, which could have ruined everything, and by not killing the dad and daughter when ordered. But no damage had been done. And, like the governor, here he was with no way out.

So, despite all the detours and setbacks, the end result was going to be the one envisioned and thoroughly researched many months ago. Before morning broke, all the key players would be dead.

It meant there was time for pause. He'd brought the golf club only to keep Tom at ease, and thus vulnerable, but now, standing here, he warmed to the idea of whacking balls at the two women. Plus, the pretty daughter was warm and breathing. Not all changes to the plan were bad. He wanted to fuck her after the game, when she was less able to fight back. Shame she wouldn't be so handsome at that point.

So, yes, for the next few minutes he and Tom were good, and there was no need for a lie. 'We're A-one-okay,' he said. 'Tie this one next to her daughter. Governor, don't say a word to your kid at any point or I'll have my man shoot her in the knees.'

Tom approached and grabbed the governor by the arm. He whisked her to the bike, dumped her roughly on her ass, and used a roll of tape to secure her hands behind her back. Samson noted that his warning about no talking was heeded, but mother and daughter stared at each other.

Samson jabbed a tee into the grass. Four metres to the targets. He dumped the box of balls on the ground and separated them into two piles of eight with a foot. He selected one and balanced it on the tee. Tom stood nearby, watching.

'Should have brought a driver,' the kid said. 'An iron might send the ball high.'

Another negative review of Samson's procedures. The kid didn't know when to keep his mouth shut. 'One point for the arms and legs. Two for the body. The head is five points. Ten if you burst an eye or smash out teeth. First to twenty-five points. And you fetch any balls that miss.'

Tom nodded. 'A knockout for a straight win, unless the other guy gets a knockout with his very next ball.'

'Done. Now watch the grand supremo.'

Samson prepared to swing, but Tom said, 'Would it be cheeky if I went first?'

It would, but Samson could give the bastard a little head start. It wasn't a game he could ultimately win anyway. He handed over the club. Tom got in position behind the ball and said, 'If I miss, you can keep my payment.'

'And double for you if you get the governor in the face.'

Samson could have offered a million pounds, for it wouldn't matter. There would be no money swapping hands. He stood alongside Tom, four feet removed for safety, facing the targets. Annoyingly, they'd put their heads down to avoid facial damage. 'Look up, you two, or I'll bust your knees. Give the man here a chance to double his cash. How selfish.'

Tom laughed and raised the club. 'I was just thinking about knees,' he said, and swung at the ball as hard as he could.

PART 5

EIGHTY-FIVE

Earlier, back in the field, Jek put away Hyde's phone following his call with Samson and approached Minny.

'My dad is dead,' she said. She had cried a lot, he could tell, but now she was getting herself together. How long had she sat here with her father's body?

'I know. I'm sorry. But Hyde is also dead. That probably doesn't make you feel better. But the threat is over.'

'But not from you. You told your boss you were bringing me to him.' She stood, still with her back to her father's corpse. 'So let's get this over with.'

He was puzzled that she seemed so resigned to it. Did she feel she had nothing to live for now one parent was dead and the other might be? 'I'm not going to hand you over to Samson, Minny. I want to help you save your mother.'

'Bullshit. You have a mission, remember? And nothing is more important than it. So let's go.'

Her willingness to become a prisoner again, and face doom, bewildered him. 'Hyde thought Samson was loyal to him. No. When he needed us, yes. But Samson is planning to flee to

307

Spain, and he's got people over there already. He can't take gang members with him. That's why he chose Hyde for an important job like this. Not because he was a somebody, but because he was *nobody*. Expendable. Just like me.'

'What are you saying? He doesn't care about you? But he's sending a car. I heard that. So why did you help him if you think he doesn't care?'

'He just said he wanted me to go to see a man called Jonas. I've heard of him. He disposes of bodies. I would have been killed and... fed to pigs, maybe. Or whatever he does.'

'You think Samson plans to kill you? So you reckon giving me to him as a present will save you?'

'No, I–'

'I think you're right,' she cut in. 'You'll be a hero if you hand me over. I'm ready. Let's go. I won't resist.'

'No. That line he said, *I'm going to send you on your way*. Sounds like the kind of double entendre a guy like him would use. The way I'll be sent is no direction anyone would want. I called his plan a pile of shit, Minny. This is a man who gets offended easily and doesn't forgive. *That's* why the car is coming.'

She shook her head, and her next words were almost pleading. 'No, he will forgive you. You'll get all the power and money you want. You have to go to him, and you have to take me with you.'

A sense of the surreal washed over him, aided by the dark and the silence and dead bodies all around. Now he understood what she really wanted, and why she hadn't run for help. 'I plan to save your mum, Minny, and I know you want to help. And you can. In fact, I *need* your help. So there's no need to try to trick me. Please understand that I'm not going to hand you to Samson. We need to work together.'

She turned away from him and knelt before her father. He waited while she cried again and talked him. She finished with, 'I'm sorry I have to leave you here, Dad,' kissed his cheek, and then stood and faced Jek. 'Let's go see the man who caused all this.'

EIGHTY-SIX

The pub that Jek had mentioned to Samson was called Evan's Gate. It sat at a tree-lined crossroads with fields surrounding it. Jek's bike was parked fifty metres away, hidden in undergrowth. He watched as a dark car turned off the road and into the car park, which was empty. The pub was closed for the night.

'Is that them?' Minny said. She sat behind him on the bike, her arms around his chest despite the fact that they were parked.

'Has to be.'

The car paused in the car park with all its lights off. Jek could see at least three figures inside. Seven minutes later, the headlights blazed on. Jek pulled out his phone and called a number. He asked for the police and gave the address of the farmhouse. He said that the front door was open.

'You'll find two dead in there. You may have already found a burning police car with two dead officers. There's a man in a field across the road from the farmhouse. That's your five innocent victims. Be careful with your sympathy when you find number six also in the field, with his head just about cut off. Because he's the one who did all the killing.'

He hung up. 'Thank you,' Minny said.

This was her chance. The cops would come and she would be saved. She could leap off the bike and run to safety. But she didn't move.

The car did, however. It slipped out of the car park and away. Jek eased the bike out of the trees and followed. He had attached a battery-powered torch – found in the farmhouse – to the handlebars to replace the headlight, but planned only to use it in populated areas so as not to draw police attention – the lack of a helmet for Minny he could do nothing about. Here, on a remote lane with nobody else around, he followed the car's taillights at a distance, black and unseen.

The car drove roughly thirty miles south, into Newcastle-upon-Tyne. In Gosforth, they took the Great North Road between a couple of housing estates and Jek figured they were at their destination. Samson would have a house in one of the estates, probably rented anonymously and occupied by a number of his men.

He was wrong. The car cruised past and took a right into the driveway of a golf course called Great Swings. He arrived as three men exited and walked towards the clubhouse, a double-storey white building in the shape of an L. There were four cars already out front. He also noted the phone number on the welcome sign.

'Does Samson own this place?' Minny said.

'He's commandeered it for the moment.'

Jek cruised by and circled a roundabout to make his way back. Before he reached the main entrance, however, he spotted signposts that mentioned a walking trail pointing to a path between trees. He stopped at the entrance. He pulled out his phone and held it within reach of his passenger. He also turned his wing mirror so he could see her face.

'We could call the police right now. We know where he is.'

Her eyes went back and forth between the phone and the clubhouse. She took her time making a decision. 'No. They could kill my mum before the police get inside.'

He put the phone away. Her choice told him a lot.

The trail didn't follow the perimeter of the golf course, so Jek exited at the first available break in the trees. They emerged onto the fairway on hole one, roughly fifty metres from the green to the left. This late, the course wasn't open and it was pitch black, and nobody was about. However, lights blazed in the clubhouse about three hundred metres away to the right.

'Here?' Minny said.

'No. Hole two.'

Jek turned the bike left and raced across the fairway, over the green, and past the teeing ground for hole two, which a sign said was a three-par. The fairway curved like a banana and the green was 190 metres away. When they reached it, he stopped the bike.

'It's peaceful out here,' Minny said. 'It feels wrong.'

Jek took out his phone and dropped it in the hole. 'When you and your mum are safe, run here to get this, then call the police.'

Minny nodded. Jek tuned the bike back the way they'd come. About halfway, roughly a hundred metres from the green, Jek stopped again. The perfect spot. He was at the curve of the fairway and from here could see the clubhouse in the distance. He laid the bike on the grass and sat by it. Minny joined him. As discussed earlier, she sat with her back to the front wheel and reached behind to lock all her fingers around the tyre.

He had a roll of tape from the farmhouse, off which he tore a strip three feet long. He stuck one end to her wrist and trailed the rest out to her side. From ahead, where Samson would stand, it would appear as if the tape bound her hands behind her back.

'Will this work?' she asked as he pulled out Hyde's phone.

'It was the only way to get him away from his people. Samson will probably arrive with just his main bodyguard. But we can see the clubhouse, so if a bunch of goons come out, then you just run for that phone and I'll come up with a plan B.'

He called the Great Swings phone number. Soon, he was on the phone to Samson. After the call, he hung up.

Minny grabbed his face, to turn it away from the clubhouse and towards hers. 'I've asked a bunch of times and this will be the last, because we are out of time. So make sure I get an answer. I know you're not here just to save my mother. And I know you didn't do all of this to help Samson. So what the hell is this mission of yours?'

EIGHTY-SEVEN

As Jek took his shot at the golf ball, his mighty downswing changed angle, moving from vertical to diagonal. At the same time, he took a step past the ball, towards Samson. The iron's head arced into the back of the man's knee, buckling it instantly.

Samson screamed in pain and collapsed awkwardly onto his other leg, then onto his back. Even before he hit the deck, before he fully knew what was happening, the iron was raised high again. Jek dragged it downwards with enough force to hurt his abdominal muscles. The clubhead hit Samson's kneecap with a loud cracking sound.

Samson's bodyguard had put away his gun and lit a cigarette. Seeing his boss dropped, he spat out the smoke and hauled his weapon. He yelled, 'Stop, get away, leave him.'

The fat man repeated the order, over and over, while Samson hollered for him to shoot. But amid all that yelling, both men heard Jek calmly say, 'Kill me and you're dead.'

The bodyguard threw his eyes around, obviously reading Jek's threat as indication that hidden enemies were present, or a trap was about to snap. Samson continued to scream for blood.

But the bodyguard was spooked, and he loosed no bullets as

Jek stepped astride Samson's chest and teed up to use the gangster's skull as a ball. He paused the clubhead against the man's ear.

'There's no ready-made coffin for a fat bastard like you,' Jek said to the gunman. 'It'll cost your mum extra to have one built, and she might have to pay for two plots in a graveyard. If she's rich, go ahead and shoot. Otherwise, you might have a month, tops, to lose about five stone.'

The goon soon determined that they were alone, and he sighted down his gun again. But he wasn't fully certain Jek was full of shit. 'What do you mean, a month?'

'Samson's going to kill you. You messed up, let him get injured. You're toast, pal. He won't let that slide, no matter if you save him now. Every time his knee plays up after today, he'll think of you and how you caused it. I'd say within a month his annoyance with you becomes too much to bear. And you know it. But maybe I'm wrong about one thing.'

'Yeah? What's that?'

'If he cuts off your arms and legs, you'll fit in a standard coffin just fine.'

Samson continued to bellow for bullets to fly, but the goon had relaxed his shoulders a little, and the gun barrel had lowered a couple of inches.

'He brought you and you alone here because with me dead, he needs someone to watch the governor there while he has his way with the girl. Turn around, go back to the clubhouse, and tell your people that Samson took her into the woods, and you never saw him again. That'll save you. Now off you pop.'

Samson fell silent, his head turned to one side so he could watch his employee. Even he knew that Jek had offered a powerful argument.

And off the guy popped.

Minny already knew the plan and Emma had figured

trickery was afoot when Jek only pretended to tape her hands behind her back. But instead of running, they had been frozen in place by shock and fear, watching Jek's interaction with the bodyguard like a pair of transfixed cinemagoers sans the popcorn.

Now that the worst seemed to be over, they got their heads on straight, their feet under them, and snatched each other in a long-awaited hug. But still they hung around.

'Get running,' Jek yelled at them. That sparked movement. The women locked hands. Oblivious to the plan, the governor bolted towards the rough alongside the fairway and had to be redirected by Minny. Daughter towed mother in the direction of the green, some ninety metres away, where the second hole had something awaiting collection.

Jek saw all of this only peripherally, for his eyes had not left Samson since he'd taken the man's golf club.

Samson stared right back at him, his expression full of pain and defiance. 'What do you want? More money? Have it.'

'I just want an apology,' he told the gangster. 'Not an admission, because I know everything. Nothing else will change a thing. So, just that apology. Don't even think about playing dumb.'

Samson paused. Thought hard. 'That's it? Say sorry? And you'll let me go?'

Jek smiled down at him. 'I promise to send you on your way.'

EIGHTY-EIGHT

Just minutes earlier, when Jek had been alone with Minny on the golf course, he said, 'I told you I had a girlfriend. That's because my girl, JoJo, didn't end our relationship. I promised her that I'd never leave her, and we'd only be apart when she decided it was to be. And she never did. Couldn't. She went missing.'

'My God. I'm sorry.'

'Officially, at least. That's what the police think. Idiots. No one has heard from her. No proof of life. Just vanished without trace. But I know better…'

He told her that he'd been noticed by Samson because of his association with Hyde, but also because of JoJo. One night at a pub, Samson had been throwing a party to celebrate a not-guilty verdict in his assault case. Hyde was invited and he dragged Jek and JoJo along, where they were introduced to the man of the hour.

'He offered me a job delivering drugs. I took it. I was very young and impressionable. But he didn't do that because he was loyal to Hyde, or to help me out. It was because he liked the look of JoJo…'

317

When Samson met JoJo, he shook her hand and kept hold of it far too long for Jek's liking. Seeing his young friend's disgust, Hyde pulled him aside under the pretence of getting a round of drinks. At the bar, he said, 'Chill, boy. Samson's a player. He likes the girls. JoJo's pretty and blokes will flirt. Calm down and remember who he is.'

'I'm supposed to just let him have her?'

'Nothing you can do. But she's your girl and if she loves you, she'll say no, won't she? He won't force her into anything.'

He watched Samson and JoJo as the barman pulled drinks. JoJo shook her head at something, and stepped back when Samson tried to stroke her hair. Samson then walked away. Jek relaxed.

The very next day, Hyde called Jek and said there was a job on for him. Jek followed directions to a kebab shop, where he was escorted to a room above. Samson and two other men were there, and a box wrapped in brown paper sat on a table. After Jek was given instructions on where and how to deliver the package, he turned to leave.

Samson said, 'How's that sweet girl of yours? Tell her there's a real man waiting for her when she's bored of you.'

Taking Hyde's advice, Jek laughed and did his best to ignore the dig. But he couldn't disregard the next issue that arose, when JoJo called him a couple of days later and said Samson had sent her a video of himself posing naked.

He wanted to confront the man, but was dissuaded by Hyde, who said, 'Write your will first.'

Two days later, Jek was with JoJo in her bedroom when someone knocked on the door. She peered out the window and said, 'Samson's here.'

Jek had a peek and, sure enough, the gangster's car was outside. Everybody knew that blue Mercedes. Samson was in the back and one of his goons stood on the pavement. JoJo opened the window. Now sitting on the bed, Jek listened as the goon told her Samson wanted her to come down, get in the car, and he'd show her a good time.

She refused, but the goon didn't like that answer. However, at that point a neighbour across the road came out with her four kids, which prompted Samson to knock on his window and wag a finger at his man. Thirty seconds later the car was gone.

'I wanted to have it out with Samson,' Jek now told Minny. He noticed movement at the clubhouse. A shutter started to rise, exposing a pair of glass double doors.

'Hyde talked me out of it,' he continued. 'But Samson didn't stop hounding her. He came to the shop where she worked. He stopped her in the street. He sent her phone messages and posted letters. She ignored them all. And I had to ignore them. He pestered her for weeks, Minny.'

From this distance he couldn't see the faces of the men who exited the clubhouse and entered a golf buggy, but he hoped it was Samson and his bodyguard. However, a female with them was surely Minny's mother.

'And then we come to the night in question...'

Around 10pm, JoJo texted Jek, asking him to come round because she was bored. When Jek rode his motorbike around the corner, onto her street, he sharply cut in behind a van, to hide. Outside her home, some fifty metres away, was a familiar blue Mercedes. There was a van parked in front of it, which pulled away just seconds later.

His plan: watch Samson but warn JoJo. However, before he could make that call, he saw something terrifying. Her front door opened and out stepped Samson and another man.

Jek gunned the bike, racing towards JoJo's house, hoping to confront Samson before he left. Samson saw him and paused by the door of his Mercedes. 'Tom. Your girl's not in. I came looking for you.'

Jek drew to a halt and leaped off the bike. He ignored Samson and rushed into the house. He checked all the rooms, but Samson was right. It was late evening and they had a meet planned… but JoJo wasn't here. Nothing about the house seemed out of place, but that only proved Samson and his people knew how to eradicate someone with skill.

When he returned outside to question Samson, the man was in the back seat of his car, window cracked three inches. Waiting. Between the two men stood Samson's beefy colleague, a clear forcefield. Jek knew the gang lord had done something to JoJo. She must have been in the van that had left. Samson had probably gone back into the house to look around and make sure all evidence of a struggle was gone. Jek knew it like he knew his own fears and desires.

But he couldn't accuse this man right here, right now. If he exposed his suspicions, he would condemn himself. Even if Samson didn't kill him where he stood, Jek would never again get this close to his enemy. So, all nice and innocent, he said, 'I hate it when she does that. She asked me to come round.'

'Women, eh?' Samson said. 'Anyway, I came to pay you a bonus for the last job. Very well done.' Then to the driver, 'Pay him.'

Samson's driver whipped out his wallet and handed across some paper money. It didn't look like a pre-arranged gesture. Samson had obviously just thought it up. Jek took the money and faked a smile. It wasn't easy. 'Wow. Thanks. Are there any more jobs?'

'We'll see. Give my love to your girl.'

And with that, the driver entered the car and away it went. Jek went into JoJo's flat, and sat and cried. He prayed she would walk in the door any moment.

'But she never did,' Jek now said to Minny. He watched the golf cart bouncing over the hole one fairway, now just a minute from reaching them. 'Week after week. No word from her. The police had nothing. I know she's dead.'

'Didn't the police know? I mean, didn't they investigate?'

'Sure they did, until they knew Samson was their man. But he and his kind are untouchable. Nobody saw nor heard a thing. Some dodgy coppers on his payroll would have probably loved to stitch me up for it, but then that would be admitting she was dead. Far better if everyone thinks she just left. So to this day, despite the rumours, she's still officially missing.'

He stood and told Minny to put her hands behind her back, and to look distraught. She put her fingers on the bike wheel to make it seem as if she was bound to the vehicle.

'This time he wasn't taking no for an answer. She rebuffed him, and he murdered her. I just missed their clean-up. After that, Minny, I wanted this bastard dead. But I didn't tell Hyde what I knew or felt, just in case he told someone else. I continued to work for Samson, hoping to get close enough to stab a knife in his throat. But he was never present again when I picked up a package. My plan was to work hard, get into his graces, and hope for a chance to be next to him. But then it was too late. A month after he killed JoJo, he got banged up for murder.'

'I'm sorry about all of it, Tom. But this... there's no way out of this. Please don't do it.'

'You should be happy about it.'

She looked puzzled. He continued. 'You were eager to help me, eager to get close to Samson.'

'To save my mother.'

'No. You could have called the police when we knew where Samson was. I knew you wouldn't. Your mother wasn't your sole driving force. You had another plan. You wanted to kill Samson yourself, for your father.'

She lowered her eyes, which told him he hadn't missed the

mark. 'I was angry. I see clearly now. It's not the right way, Tom. It's dangerous and wrong. We're not like that animal. He belongs in prison, where he should have stayed. Don't do this.'

'I've waited three years. I got on this bastard's team just so I could get close to him when he eventually escaped. And now I've got him. There he is, like a pizza delivery, coming right to me. It's perfect.'

'This can't end well for you–'

'Stop, Minny. If he lives through this, you won't. Or your mum. Eye for an eye. Your dad deserves justice. They all do. And Samson making a comfortable life in prison isn't it. Just make sure the pair of you run for the phone the moment I take him out.'

'Please. I don't want you to die. Too many have already.'

The golf cart was close now, on hole two's fairway and zipping across the final fifty metres to him. It was twenty seconds away. He could make out Samson's face and his big smile. And Minny's terrified mother next to him.

'I died the same night JoJo went missing, Minny. So did Samson. He just wasn't aware of it.'

EIGHTY-NINE

'Why have you stopped?'

The question from Minny was a good one. Emma had spent hour after hour, day after day, solving the giant Rubik's cube, and now she had it bested. One more turn and it was complete. But her hands would not make that move.

She got up and went to the back door, and walked a few steps into the rear garden. She stared at the pond, whose surface was coated with leaves. Collecting them with a net had always been something Joel liked to do.

Never again, though. Nothing would ever be as it once was.

The garden was her sacred place, where she used to sit and think about her future during the scant free moments she got. These days she wallowed in the past instead. She would sit in silence, replaying various scenes from that fateful event and its aftermath. She refused to suppress these thoughts and images. The more she submerged herself in all that badness, the less potent its power to depress and weaken. If the dull ache in her heart became too much, as it was now, she would head out here and allow the same old visions and memories and worries to wash over her.

Joel's employers had expressed sympathy and shock at the loss of one of their own in a trio of ways. They'd had a minute's silence at every branch to honour his sacrifice. A slogan he'd framed and put on the wall of his office – **Nobody's perfect, but let's get a step closer every day** – was now in plaque form at every branch. Finally, Joel's method of robbing the bank, albeit of only fake money and dye packs, had been used to strengthen the company's security procedures.

But Emma felt the bank might have had its hand forced by public opinion. People had labelled him a hero for giving up his life to save his family. Hundreds, many of them strangers, had turned up to his funeral last week. Emma continued to get letters from well-wishers. The sweetest ones she read aloud to him late at night. She wasn't religious and didn't believe that the dead could see and hear their living loved ones... but you never knew.

'Do you want to be a YouCuber or not?' Minny said with a smile. She put down her phone, which she had been using to record her mother solving the Rubik's cube. It had been her idea to film the entire process and post an edited version on YouTube.

Emma's predicament was a little different. She was facing a charge of malfeasance in public office, which could carry a life sentence. However, her solicitor had told her there was a chance she could avoid any kind of jail time even if she was convicted. If a trial even happened. She had acted without freedom, under duress, and had made significant moves to try to avoid helping Samson escape, albeit by criminal measures. The public and the media were sympathetic and that could sway a Crown Prosecution Service decision.

Not everybody was on her side. But her opponents faltered when tasked with giving alternative methods of dealing with the problems Emma had faced, especially regarding Pleasance, the inmate she had poisoned to save his life. Those opponents, when outlining what she could or should have done, often described scenarios more suited to a superhero movie.

Even Darren, her deputy governor, had nothing but praise for her, and indeed even felt guilty that she, instead of him, had been targeted. It all gave the police and the CPS food for thought.

Voices were there to be heard, though, and those against her were many and loud. Worthy of imprisonment or not, her actions had been unlawful and public trust had been harmed. HM Prison Service would probably terminate her contract. She didn't care about that. In fact, while the CPS and her bosses went back and forth about what to do, she had made her mind up already. She no longer wanted to work in law enforcement.

'Come do the last move, Mum. It's not a world record, but we'll get thousands of views for this. We've filmed so much already.'

And Minny? The one positive to emerge from the ruins of this mess was a rekindling of her relationship with her daughter. They were best friends now. The teenager was glad she'd have her mother home more often. Maybe that was in part because there was no father around, but Emma would take what she could. It was early days and she didn't yet know if she'd emerge at the other end mentally trashed.

'Just give me a moment, sweetie,' she said.

Other players were already certain of their fates. After Emma and Minny had escaped the golf course, they'd called in the police. When armed officers surrounded the clubhouse, criminals fled in all directions, and all were caught. One man who tried to fight his way free with a golf club was shot and killed.

One of Samson's arrested men had given up Adley, who had been snared in London after a car chase. Hyde's girlfriend, the jogger called Denise, had handed herself in after hiding out for three days. Police had also unearthed all seven of Samson's bent prison officers via Markham, the one who'd exposed himself by posting a mobile into a cell, for he was singing like a canary.

And Hyde? Dead. Officers had found his body on the golf course, Jekyll sitting beside him. Jekyll's real name was Tom Cupton, but Hyde had thrown caution to the wind and used his real surname because it fit their alter-egos. What the Catalanos couldn't tell detectives, Tom did. He was fully cooperating. Others had also talked and now the police knew everything.

Alongside kidnapping and robbery, Tom was facing six murder charges. Two police officers. An elderly couple. A man called Darren Dunkirk, son-in-law to the bank staff member who owned Peach Cottage. His was the third body found in a burned police car. Tom claimed no knowledge that that killing had even occurred, but accepted his culpability for every crime committed since he and Hyde had taken prisoners.

Murder number six was Samson's. He freely told police he'd killed the gangster because of his girlfriend. She was the nineteen-year-old Samson was rumoured to have murdered three years ago.

Minny condemned Hyde but had sympathy for Tom. She had talked about writing to him in prison. Emma still wasn't decided about whether or not that would be wrong. Nor did she know whether to hate him or not. He'd willingly gone along with the kidnap plan, yet had done so with the policy of trying to avoid letting people get hurt.

The owner of the golf club had ties to Samson and had allowed his place to be used by the fugitive for a few days. Not so the breakers yard, for his men had kidnapped the staff as they arrived to open up. A simple CLOSED sign placed out front had kept customers away for the entire day, allowing the team of bad guys to set in place the mechanics of Samson's rescue, including bringing in a modified Mercedes Atego truck and Toyota Hilux Rogue 4x4.

Samson, according to some, had planned his escape for over a year and had intentionally engineered a transfer to Cheviot. There were rumours, unsubstantiated, of a plant in HM Prison Service. Another claim, this one with more weight because it came from Adley, was that the kidnap plot had been brought forward by a couple of weeks when Samson learned of the governor's holiday at Peach Cottage. Originally, the attack was to take place at her own home.

The thought chilled Emma. There had been worries about Samson's men seeking revenge if they knew where she lived, but the police weren't convinced. A rock star wasn't dead. According to them, nobody missed Samson and other criminals had already begun sharing out his empire like sweets.

When Minny called again for her mother, Emma returned to the house and took her seat at the kitchen table. She tried to put aside her dark memories, at least until she next went to the garden. Minny resumed filming. Of all the people involved in the hellish events of that day, her daughter seemed to have coped with it the best, or at least was hiding it well.

She missed her father, of course, but otherwise seemed to have no lingering fears, didn't have nightmares, and could still laugh and joke and live life. Supposedly resolute former Governor Catalano was jealous.

'Do the last turn, Mum.'

This Rubik's cube was a new one. It hadn't ever been part of a crime scene, but it was a mirror image of the former, and thus a reminder of that day. Of the loss of Joel.

Emma put a hand on the cube, then swiped it off the table, to crash and shatter on the floor.

THE END

ALSO BY ALEX ROSE

The Boss

The Pact

ACKNOWLEDGEMENTS

Many people come together behind the scenes to make sure the mess I hand to my publisher is knocked into a shape worthy of giving to readers. The main players are Betsy, Fred, Clare, Tara, and Hannah, but thanks must go to every single one of the Bloodhound Books Team.

I didn't add an acknowledgements page to my first two books, so I'll rectify that right now.

THE BOSS – see above.

THE PACT – see above.

THE TRAP is a work of fiction, but that doesn't mean I could go wild with invention. I stuck to some basic rules, so nobody lives to be 300, Earth's gravity is still 9.807 m/s^2, and cars don't fly. But sometimes the world doesn't play ball where I need it to, so I took a few liberties with bank and prison procedures, policies and terminology. For His Majesty's guests planning to escape prison and bank employees intending to rob the workplace, I don't recommend trying anything detailed in this book.

A NOTE FROM THE PUBLISHER

Thank you for reading this book. If you enjoyed it please do consider leaving a review on Amazon to help others find it too.

We hate typos. All of our books have been rigorously edited and proofread, but sometimes mistakes do slip through. If you have spotted a typo, please do let us know and we can get it amended within hours.

info@bloodhoundbooks.com